Discover for yourself why readers can't get enough of the multiple award-winning publisher Ellora's Cave. Whether you prefer e-books or paperbacks, be sure to visit EC on the web at www.ellorascave.com for an erotic reading experience that will leave you breathless.

WWW.ELLORASCAVE.COM

LAWYERS IN LOVE: THE PROSECUTORS
An Ellora's Cave Publication, November 2004

Ellora's Cave Publishing, Inc.
PO Box 787
Hudson, OH 44236-0787

ISBN # 141995136X

Gettin' It On © Ann Jacobs 2003
ISBN MS Reader (LIT) ISBN # 1-84360-601-1

Eye of the Storm © Ann Jacobs 2003
ISBN MS Reader (LIT) ISBN # 1-84360-690-9

Other available formats (no ISBNs are assigned):
Adobe (PDF), Rocketbook (RB), Mobipocket (PRC) & HTML

Cover art by *Syneca*.

Warning:

The following material contains graphic sexual content meant for mature readers. *Lawyers In Love: The Prosecutors* has been rated E–rotic by a minimum of three independent reviewers.

Ellora's Cave Publishing offers three levels of Romantica™ reading entertainment: S (S-ensuous), E (E-rotic), and X (X-treme).

S-*ensuous* love scenes are explicit and leave nothing to the imagination.

E-*rotic* love scenes are explicit, leave nothing to the imagination, and are high in volume per the overall word count. In addition, some E-rated titles might contain fantasy material that some readers find objectionable, such as bondage, submission, same sex encounters, forced seductions, etc. E-rated titles are the most graphic titles we carry; it is common, for instance, for an author to use words such as "fucking", "cock", "pussy", etc., within their work of literature.

X-*treme* titles differ from E-rated titles only in plot premise and storyline execution. Unlike E-rated titles, stories designated with the letter X tend to contain controversial subject matter not for the faint of heart.

LAWYERS IN LOVE
THE PROSECUTORS

Gettin' It On

Eye of the Storm

By Ann Jacobs

GETTIN' IT ON

Prologue
Bone Gap, Texas, population 468

"Don't see much hope for her. Twenty-four years old and nary a man in sight."

"It's a shame, sure as shootin'."

An old cowboy shook his head, then swigged his beer. "Pretty little thing to have her heart broke like that, but you can't blame Buck for runnin' off with Daisy. A man needs his woman hot, like chili."

"Yeah. Who'd want to crawl in bed with his best buddy?"

Guffaws erupted, then stilled when one of the guys looked toward her and whispered something to his pals.

Apparently she was everybody's friend, nobody's lover.

Her fiancé's defection was sparking more comment than the spread her folks had put out to celebrate the June first wedding they'd intended to be two for the price of one.

Casey Thompson wished she could slither through the floorboards at the Bone Gap Grange. The best she could manage was a hasty retreat from the vicinity of the table with the punch bowls and the water trough where they'd iced down the beer.

Facing all these folks and pasting on a smile was tough. But Casey couldn't have ducked out on her only brother's wedding reception. Even if it was supposed to have been hers, too.

"It's a shame about Cassandra, but I can understand Buck changing his mind. He's bound to be happier with a woman like Daisy warming his bed." The high-pitched whine and the way she dragged out every syllable of "Cassandra" left no doubt in Casey's mind that her former sixth grade teacher had just pronounced her opinion of the whole damn mess.

11

Casey couldn't blame folks for talking. After all, there wasn't a whole lot in Bone Gap to talk about, and she couldn't begrudge the homefolks their gossip. The prospect of a double wedding had set the town a-buzzing, even before Buck had dumped her and eloped with Daisy Lee two weeks ago.

Since then they'd been speculating about where on earth that sweet tomboy Casey Thompson was ever going to find a husband among the few eligible guys who looked at her like another little sister, not a potential lover.

Not in Bone Gap, that was for sure!

Casey was so over being the stereotypical girl next door. As soon as this ordeal was over, she'd be out of here. The sweet little PE teacher and rancher's daughter who'd earned the whole town's pity was about to break away.

In a little more than a week, she'd have become sexy Casey, personal trainer to the bunch of muscular hunks she'd be working with at Russ Green's high-end gym overlooking the bay near downtown Tampa, Florida. Sweet little Casey, everybody's pal and nobody's lover, was about to disappear forever.

Casey couldn't wait to change her image. She and her future roommate, Lisa, had plans to get her a new wardrobe. One that would showcase the sexy, fun-loving woman Casey was determined to set free—and attract the attention of those hunks she'd ogled at the gym during her interview. Even the yummiest hunk of all, a guy Russ had introduced her to while he'd been working out.

Assistant State Attorney Craig McDermott.

Well, maybe she ought not to aim for a specimen as prime as the buff young lawyer. Still...

The man had a smile that could melt Antarctica.

Casey's fingers itched when she thought about running them over those killer pecs, feeling the rasp of his five o'clock shadow against her skin.

She'd trace the laugh lines that creased his lean, chiseled cheeks, and he'd look at her the way Buck had been salivating over Dixie the other day at the Dairy Queen.

Fat chance. She'd have to be Cinderella to change that much, that fast. And Lisa was no fairy godmother. She might as well stick to guys who weren't way out of her league.

Casey figured she'd end up settling for a semi-hunk who could look at her and get it up. At least that way she'd be sure of shedding her damnable virginity.

But hey, a girl was entitled to put a face on her fantasies.

Chapter One
Tampa, two months later

"No, thanks, Todd. I don't date my clients." Anyhow, Casey wasn't about to date a client who looked like her dad's prize boar and whose breath reeked of liver and onions.

Casey handed the porcine banker a printout detailing the workout routine she'd developed for him. "Show this to your doctor and get his approval. You'll need a medical release before you start working out."

Last thing the gym needed was a lawsuit from good ol' Todd's survivors.

"You won't change your mind? I know this great Italian place where the pasta's irresistible– "

"I can't. And you shouldn't."

His jowls quivered, but he managed a smile. "Okay. I'm off to have a physical and get my doctor to sign off so I can get started with the program. Maybe you'll change your mind?"

"We'll see."

With any kind of luck Casey would have had a dozen lovers before Todd sweated off the excess one hundred fifty pounds he toted around. With a lot of luck, she'd have reeled in the man of her dreams before that happened.

"Did Todd try to hit on you?" Lisa asked a few minutes later when she'd finished a consultation with another potential client.

Casey laughed. "Yeah."

"Well, now you know you do turn some guys on."

Lisa laughed, too.

But it wasn't funny. After six weeks working at Russ's Gym, Casey had gotten propositioned by every out-of-shape nerd who waddled in. But she was still batting zero at attracting a guy who attracted her.

It wasn't working. Not the new clothes, and not the downright provocative manner she'd borrowed from Lisa.

Men she ran into—except for Todd and some others with serious deficiencies in the hunk department—apparently still thought of her as the tomboy next door if they noticed her at all.

"Am I being too picky?"

Lisa glanced across the gym at Craig McDermott. "Maybe you're not being picky enough. Why not try coming on to a guy who turns *you* on? A hot guy who's used to women making the moves on him. A man can tell if you're seriously hot for him."

"You're saying I should go after *him*?"

"Sure, if he's the one that's got you creaming your panties. Me, I like my guys with a bit more meat on their bones."

Casey followed Lisa's gaze to the free weight area, where her boyfriend-of-the-month, Mike Garcia, was pumping iron. A beefy guy with muscles on his muscles, he'd made Casey wonder—until Lisa had revealed more details than Casey needed to know about what a stud the guy was—whether he'd gotten a lot of that bulk by using steroids. Dark, swarthy, and possessed of a killer smile, Mike was a hunk for sure. But he didn't appeal to Casey the way McDermott did.

"You're welcome to Mike," she said.

"Yeah. I know. And you're welcome to Mister Tall, Dark and Preppy. Go on over there and give him some pointers on his routine."

As if McDermott needed any tips about physical fitness. Most likely he could teach Casey a thing or two. Still…

"I dare you."

Damn it. Casey wouldn't back away from a dare. And Lisa knew it.

"You're on." Putting a gentle sway in her step, Casey licked her lips and sauntered across the gym.

Five minutes later she retraced her steps.

Lisa had been right about the chemistry. Every cell in her body tingled from the up-close-and-personal encounter. Her nipples had tightened into rigid little points that reflected back at her from the mirrors on the wall, and the crotch of her leotard was damp from the short but arousing encounter. "Turned on" was too mild an expression to describe the sensations coursing through her body.

She glanced Craig's way again, admiring the way his powerful thigh muscles bunched as he hefted a heavy barbell to his shoulders and resumed the set of squats she'd interrupted.

Too bad all that chemical reaction seemed to be on her part.

* * * * *

Craig had never been more tempted to toss aside his well-laid life plans and follow up with personal trainer Casey Thompson. The woman had put out an invitation so blatant not even a sexual neophyte could ignore.

Looks-wise, she was pure dynamite. If he didn't miss his guess, she'd burn up a guy's sheets. It didn't take a genius to read her hip-swinging walk or interpret the provocative comments she'd tossed his way at the gym last night.

He'd damn near grabbed her and dragged her to the padded mat when she raked her gaze down his body and ran her tongue across her bright red lips.

But Craig had an agenda. Success. Big-time success.

For that he needed to concentrate on his career and keep his deprived hormones on the back burner. After all, he shouldn't be missing what he'd never sampled.

Yeah, right. Just thinking about Casey had his cock rock hard and aching.

"You take this one. Trial's set to start next Wednesday."

Forcing his libido to let go of his brain, Craig flipped open the case file State Attorney Harper Wells dumped onto his desk.

State of Florida v. William Ranger. The case everybody in the office had been laughing about since Dwayne came back from the arraignment a few minutes ago and announced that Ranger was pleading not guilty by reason of temporary insanity.

Insanity his wife had allegedly brought on by kicking him out of their bed.

Craig skimmed the discoveries. Damn. Dwayne wasn't kidding. Billy Ranger or his lawyer had found a psychiatrist willing to swear the man had gone temporarily bonkers because he'd been sexually deprived.

Going without had made Ranger go on a binge of road rage and ram a woman's SUV on the beltline highway? No way could Ranger's attorney persuade a jury to swallow that argument. Not even if Tony Landry personally tried the case, Craig told himself when he recalled that a Winston Roe associate had handled the arraignment.

After all, Craig had been ready to burst his balls after ogling Casey at the gym last night, but he'd managed to take the problem in hand after getting home. Literally.

"Ranger's lawyer is claiming insanity because of what?" another assistant prosecutor asked when he walked in on the conversation.

Somebody filled in the late arrival, and he joined in the laughter.

"Anybody who buys that argument, I've got some land down in the 'glades I'll sell, dirt cheap. Craig will have no trouble getting a conviction." State Attorney Wells' booming voice reached the farthest corners of the room.

"It'll be a piece of cake." Craig wasn't sure he meant that, but he wasn't about to argue with his boss. Wells apparently thought he'd done a favor by assigning Craig to try the defendant the local press had dubbed the Road Rage Ranger.

The news of Ranger's no-sex insanity plea had just generated a chorus of guffaws.

"The defense has to be desperate if they're grasping a flimsy straw like that," one of the other prosecutors choked out between bursts of laughter.

"Craig will shoot that theory down. He's single, so he's got to know how it feels to have to spend a night alone every once in a while. Right, Craig?"

"Right, Andi." Craig forced a hearty chuckle. Good thing Andi Syzmanski, the very pregnant senior assistant to Wells, didn't know how many hundreds of nights he'd spent alone.

Twenty-seven times three hundred sixty-five of them, not counting the eight nights that had passed since his birthday. Or the however many extra days for leap years.

That came to…too damn many to count. Not to mention too damn many to own up to.

"Nobody goes nuts because their wife suddenly cuts them off," Dwayne said. "Doing without for three months before Stephanie had the twins didn't make me plow my car into the back of some woman's SUV on purpose."

"Hey, Dwayne, you don't count. Everybody knows you're undersexed." Craig jumped at the opportunity to shift attention toward his colleague.

Dwayne laughed again. "Up yours."

"Back to work. You'd think you were at Bennie's, not doing the people's business," Wells barked. He motioned toward Craig with a file he clutched in his meaty fist. "McDermott, come in my office."

Damn it, the last place Craig wanted to be was on Wells' carpet, and the last thing he wanted to hear was how easy this damn case should be for him to win. Wells wasn't a man to cross, though, so Craig did as he said.

"Damn detectives. Chief Delgado found out we're set to give his boys some competition this year and penciled in a

rookie cop for the triathlon. Swears the kid's unbeatable. Sneaky bastard only hired him because he knows we have you."

"Yeah," Craig answered noncommittally. He didn't mind obliging Wells and kicking ass in every one of the swimming events, but he wished his boss would forget about him doing the triathlon that was the high point of the annual competition between the state attorney's staff and the local detectives.

Unfortunately he didn't dare beg off, despite the lingering damage from a knee and hip injury he'd suffered in a car accident while in law school. He needed his pompous boss's support to push him along a fast track toward his ultimate career goal.

The state attorney looked at Craig as though he were a college coach sizing up the state of his athlete's conditioning. "You keeping yourself in shape, son?"

"Yes sir." He'd be okay. Craig told himself the chorus of doctors who had warned him to avoid impact activities like martial arts and running had only been covering their collective asses.

After all, running was only one third of the triathlon, and one of the other thirds — the long-distance swim — was an activity the same doctors had recommended as therapy. It wasn't as if he was going to do a ten-kilometer run every day. He was being damn careful not to disturb the surgeon's handiwork when he trained with weights.

Craig couldn't help appreciating the special attention he'd earned because Wells was looking at him to help secure a win in this competition.

"So what are you doing to get ready?" Wells asked.

"Working out every day at Russ Green's fitness center. I haven't been in such good shape since I was an undergrad."

Wells rubbed his palms together and shot Craig an oily grin. "This year I'm finally going to kick Delgado's ass," he said, as though he'd be the one out there sweating for the glory of his office.

Craig half-listened while his boss went on, gloating at the prospect of besting Rocky Delgado's detectives for the first time in the six years they'd been competing to raise money for a local children's shelter.

"Craig?" Wells scowled at the message he'd just fished off his desk. His deep voice resonated with apparent concern.

"Yes sir?" Craig doubted anything about the upcoming games had precipitated his boss's sudden change of mood.

"The woman Billy Ranger rear-ended is State Senator Frank Gomez's niece. Frank told me she spent a week in the hospital and is still hobbling around with a cane because of the broken ankle she got when Ranger whacked her."

"I noticed she's Gomez's niece." Somebody had written a terse comment to that effect on a sticky note and slapped it onto the folder that held the Ranger case file.

"Then you know it's doubly important to get a conviction. As important as it is for you to win your events at the games."

"I understand." If Craig hadn't fully appreciated the political ramifications attached to the Ranger case before, he did now.

Wells set the message down and laughed, his chins quivering. "You shouldn't have any trouble blowing Bill Ranger's idiotic defense right out of the courtroom." With that parting comment, he picked up the phone and waved Craig out of his office.

Damn it, why had Harper Wells gotten it in his head that he should be the one to prosecute this case? It wasn't as if Craig had asked to try every alleged sex-related crime committed in Hillsborough County short of aggravated rape and murder. And it wasn't his imagination, either. Everybody in the office commented on a regular basis about how he was becoming the number-one prosecutor of alleged sex criminals.

Not long ago, he'd asked why. The state attorney's reply rang in his ears. *You play well to women jurors. And defense lawyers*

tend to go for female juries when they're defending cases about men hurting women. Hell, boy, you've got to know women like your looks.

Craig doubted he had an extraordinary talent for persuading female jurors that alleged sex offenders were guilty as sin and deserved whatever punishment they got. Besides, being the state attorney's de facto poster boy for sex-related crimes embarrassed the hell out of him.

He had to admit his very politically savvy boss hadn't gotten to be the most successful state attorney in Tampa's recent history by reading people wrong. His own impressive conviction rate in the eleven months since he passed the bar attested to Wells' good judgment in assigning cases, he admitted grudgingly.

That conviction rate was beginning to gain Craig the attention of the big law firms he was determined to impress. And all his hard work would be for nothing if he couldn't convince a jury that Billy Ranger was guilty. That he couldn't have been driven out of his mind, temporarily or otherwise, because his wife had cut him off from pussy.

How could he make a jury believe him when he didn't know exactly what it was that Ranger had been missing?

He needed to find out, and he had less than a week to do it.

One thing for sure, he wasn't about to confess his ignorance and ask any of the clowns he worked with. They'd laugh him out of town if he admitted to being the world's last twenty-seven year old male virgin outside a monastery.

Hell, they'd laugh him clear back to Texas.

The answers he needed wouldn't pop up between the covers of any sex manuals, either, although Craig intended to go buy some to read. He'd try a bookstore out in the suburbs somewhere, nowhere near downtown or nearby Old Hyde Park. That way he'd be less likely to run into some bigmouthed coworker.

Damn it, he didn't need a stupid book. He needed firsthand experience. Fast.

And he needed a woman to help him get it. A girl who wouldn't balk at fucking just for fun, one it wouldn't take him months to sweet-talk into bed.

Once more, Casey's image flooded his mind.

He glanced at a clock mounted above the water cooler. Five o'clock. It was a given he wasn't going to get much accomplished on the case tonight.

Unless…

He packed up his briefcase and headed for the gym.

* * * * *

An hour later, Craig finished his last set of leg presses and adjusted the pins on the machine. On his way to the sauna, he wiped sweat off his brow.

Then Casey caught his eye.

How could she not? The sassy personal trainer's outfits got more outrageous every time he saw her.

The neon green second skin she had on today covered her from neck to toe, but it showed enough to give Craig a quick refresher course in female anatomy, along with a good start on a raging hard-on.

Fuzzy hot pink socks slouched below shapely calves he itched to check out, up close and personal. He imagined they'd be firm yet giving.

Much like Casey herself seemed to be.

He tried to clamp down on his libido without success. Thank God his workout shorts fit loose and baggy.

"Hey, Craig."

He hoped to hell his tongue wasn't hanging out. She looked good enough to eat. And she was headed his way, her dark-brown ponytail and trim hips swinging in unison.

He couldn't drag his gaze away from breasts that swayed just enough to call attention to nipples that poked impudently against that slippery looking thing she had on.

Her smile had to pack at least a thousand watts, if his body's reaction meant anything.

"Casey. How are you?"

"Fine. You're looking good."

He flexed a bicep and grinned. "Thanks to you and your boss."

"More like, thanks to good genes and clean living." She stepped closer.

Clean living was the last thing on Craig's mind. When Casey laid a soft palm on his sweaty forearm, the heat she generated shot through him like a prairie wildfire.

The flowery smell of her perfume mingled in his nostrils with the earthy odors of sweat and whatever pungent stuff Russ used to lubricate the Nautilus machines.

He wanted her.

Pure temptation stared Craig in the face. Temptation with twinkling dark eyes and a flirtatious smile—and a body that screamed "Take Me" in brilliant billboard letters.

His balls tightened and his cock got even harder when he imagined himself peeling her out of that neon green invitation to sin.

Why had he decided to have his sex solo until he found the ideal woman? The woman he'd mentally defined but hadn't found time to start looking for.

Casey destroyed his reason, made him strain his memory to recall—he paused to do another quick set of dumbbell flies—why the fuck had he decided gratuitous sex promised more trouble than satisfaction?

"You there?" Casey's tongue snaked out and wet her bow-shaped upper lip.

"Yeah."

Her pink tongue beckoned him to taste it, sample its hot slick promise. What delicious tortures he imagined her soft, wet mouth could wreak on his already aching balls!

What the hell had he been thinking when he'd vowed at the grand old age of sixteen not to let his cock rule his brain?

She grinned. "Penny for your thoughts."

Craig's mind didn't function when Casey was within arms' reach, reminding him of sweet, tart lime sherbet melting in his mouth on a sultry day. "You pretty much steal my thoughts away, pretty lady," he said, grateful his brain still worked well enough to formulate a halfway cohesive reply.

His cock had no problem expressing its needs. His tongue felt as though he'd swallowed cotton. His jaw wouldn't work. His gaze settled on her breasts that would spill from his hands, and on tight little nipples he imagined would taste so sweet when he drew them into his mouth.

He'd always been partial to lime sherbet.

"Cat got your tongue, there?" she asked, her dark eyes sparkling.

"Just thinking, pretty lady." *And getting hornier by the minute.*

"What about?" She raked him with an assessing gaze that settled on the hard-on that had grown past proportions that his loose shorts could conceal.

"Oooh," she said, her grin widening as if she liked knowing what she did to him.

As if she wanted to do some sexual research of her own.

He sure as hell wanted to do some with her. "Want to grab a late snack after you get off from work?"

"Sure." Casey's smile brightened even more, and her dark eyes twinkled with amusement– or was it promise?

Chapter Two

Casey would have pinched herself, but she didn't want to show up black and blue for Craig. Glancing at her watch once she got home, she saw she had less than half an hour to change for their date.

She didn't have time to worry or to drool. But she couldn't help it.

No sane woman could help drooling over Craig McDermott. He was the kind of hunk she'd dreamed about attracting when she spent her college years in Lubbock under the watchful eye of her great-aunt. The kind of prime male specimen she'd never even seen in Bone Gap, Texas, population 468.

Tall, dark, and gorgeous, with a body to die for and brilliant blue eyes that would melt the clothes off a nun, Craig was way out of the league of Cassandra Thompson, hick girl from the Texas sticks.

Casey didn't kid herself. She might flirt and wear sexy clothes, but inside she was still the naive rancher's daughter whose fiancé had dumped her. *When it came down to the wire, I couldn't picture crawling in bed with my best friend.* Buck's shamefaced confession still rang in Casey's ears.

But she'd put that behind her. Damn it, she'd become a new woman. She was going to indulge her senses and grab everything life offered. Including having hot, fantastic sex with Craig McDermott if her luck held out.

Maybe Casey had finally attracted a real live hunk who'd rid her of her inconvenient innocence. Anticipation zinged through her body, along with a shiver of trepidation. What if

Craig realized she wasn't at all the savvy woman she pretended to be?

She couldn't let him find out. No way was she going to spend her whole life getting rejected because she was too sweet, too innocent, too much like some guy's little sister.

"Going out?" Lisa stuck her head through Casey's bedroom door and grinned.

"Yeah." Good. At least she could still sound casual.

"Who's the lucky guy?"

"Craig McDermott."

Lisa joined Casey in her bedroom and plopped down on the window seat. "See. I told you that outfit ought to do the trick."

Casey took a breath, then faced the mirror and dared to glance at the chartreuse unitard her roommate had insisted she wear today. "Oh no," she muttered as she watched her cheeks turn beet-red at the sight of her nipples, hard as rock and jutting out like tiny erections against the skin-tight material.

"Sexy, isn't it? Didn't I tell you—"

"You told me. I just didn't realize it looked quite this tartish." Casey peeled off her second skin and started rummaging through a drawer. "I've got to hurry. He's picking me up in twenty minutes."

Lisa picked up the handful of lycra Casey had just shed and tossed it in the laundry basket. "Was the lawyer of every woman's dreams salivating when he saw you in this?"

"Not exactly. He did look...well, excited."

"Horny's more like it." Lisa met Casey's gaze and frowned. "Honey, are you sure you're ready—"

"I'm certain. If I don't do it now, I'll lose my nerve. Besides, this guy's gorgeous. Those eyes. That smile. Do you think he likes me?"

"Get real. There's not a straight, red-blooded man alive who wouldn't want to crawl in the sack with a woman who

looks like you do in workout togs." Lisa's brow wrinkled, and she shifted her gaze to the floor. "Just don't make seducing you too easy for him."

"I don't want to make it too hard, either."

"That's exactly what you do want. Keep his cock so hard he can't think straight." Lisa shot her a knowing grin.

"How?"

"Hot looks. Sexy innuendo. Lots of 'accidental' casual touching in erogenous places. That ought to do it for a start. Oh, and go for lots of tongue action when he kisses you goodnight."

"Accidental?"

"Think subtle. Lay your hand on his thigh while he's driving. Let your breasts brush against his chest when you're slow dancing. Get in close enough to rub against his cock. I can't believe you. Don't you know anything at all?"

Casey hoped it would be dark if, when, and where she got the nerve up to touch Craig's hard-muscled thigh. Otherwise he'd see her blush and realize she was nothing but a fraud.

"I know how to French-kiss," she told Lisa without making eye contact as she tugged on tight jeans and struggled with the zipper.

"That's something."

Not much, if Lisa's tone conveyed the sarcasm Casey thought it did.

Casey slipped a low-cut, belly-baring tank top over the lacy red bra Lisa had helped her pick out last weekend at the mall.

"Does this look okay?"

"It looks dynamite. But wait. I've got shoes that'll be a perfect match."

Lisa got up. When she came back, she had a spike-heeled red sandal twirling around on the index finger of each hand. "Here. Wear these instead of those cowboy boots you like so well. McDermott's plenty tall, and he strikes me as a guy who'd appreciate a pair of legs in high-heeled shoes."

"He's not going to see my legs," Casey said, but she sat on the edge of the bed and tugged off one boot. "Is he?"

"Not tonight unless he's one hell of a fast mover. But these shoes will make him think about how those legs will feel wrapped around his waist. Trust me."

Casey had relied on Lisa this far. She might as well trust her for the whole journey from simpering virgin to bona fide bad girl. Bending, she pried off her other boot and put on Lisa's heels.

Then she stood and looked in the full-length mirror. The lightweight silk knit crop-top clung to her breasts almost as lovingly as the unitard had a few minutes earlier. "Do I need something else on under this?"

"Absolutely not. You want to look hot."

When Casey glanced at her reflection again, she wasn't so sure. "I suppose I do."

"Then relax. You'll have McDermott panting after you like a rabid dog."

She wasn't at all sure she liked that analogy. "I think I'd rather have him panting like a faithful puppy."

"No you wouldn't."

"Why not?"

Lisa shook her head. "Too tame. You want rabid. Trust me."

Casey guessed she'd have to. Her own knowledge about men and sex left a lot to be desired.

"Casey?"

"Yes, I trust you. I don't know what I'd have done when I got here if you hadn't taken me under your wing."

"You'd have managed. Hey, girlfriend, you'd better hurry. That's your date knocking at our door."

* * * * *

What was he thinking about, taking Casey Thompson on a date?

Hell, Craig knew exactly what he was doing. Field work. Sort of a background investigation to help him figure the best way to prosecute the Road Rage Ranger.

So he was going to have to forfeit his virginity in order to do his job as an assistant district attorney. So what? He was up for the sacrifice. In more ways than one.

The door opened, and he caught a whiff of something that reminded him of the wisteria vines that bloomed in his grandma's garden every spring. An innocent smell, sweet and a little bit old-fashioned. A good-girl smell.

Then he caught an eyeful of Casey. Her silky fire-engine red top bared the upper curve of her breasts, then stopped several inches above her exposed belly button. It fit her like a glove. Hugged her the way he itched to do.

Seeing her in that top would give any grandma apoplexy.

Only a blind man could fail to have noticed her low-riding, skin-tight jeans or the spike-heeled red "fuck-me" sandals on her feet.

Craig didn't think good girls wore stiletto heels with their jeans.

He knew damn well that good boys didn't salivate over the idea of finding out whether a girl's silky top or her naked breasts would feel softer to their hands and tongues.

Craig definitely was salivating. Of course his good-boy days would soon come to a screeching halt, assuming he could talk Casey into bed.

"Hi, Craig."

"Hi." He hoped his tongue wasn't hanging out. He knew damn well his cock was trying to bust out of his jeans when he stared at Casey framed in the open doorway.

Anything for his career.

Who the hell was he kidding? The need to check out the logic of the Ranger's insanity defense was only an excuse to sample what Casey had been tempting him with for weeks.

Windblown dark brown hair curved against her cheeks and caressed the smooth tanned skin of her neck and shoulders.

"Are you hungry?" he asked as they made their way to his car.

He couldn't help ogling her. Those jeans might as well have been a lethal weapon, the way they hugged her supple curves.

When he unlocked the door and helped her in, the sensation of his fingertips on her bare elbow went through him like an electric shock.

That jolt got strong enough to make a man cry when her top slipped off one shoulder. The glimpse he got of cleavage framed against silky red material and the black leather of the bucket seat raised his temperature at least a hundred degrees.

"Are you?"

What was she talking about? "What?"

"Are you hungry?"

He had asked her that, hadn't he?

"Yeah." He was hungry all right. But not for food.

Maybe if they went someplace dark, he could manage not to drool over her as though she were a prime T-bone steak cooked rare.

"I know a neat little country-western place on the north end of town. I thought we'd go have some barbecue and work off the calories with a little dancing. Sound okay?"

"Sure."

That one sultry syllable conjured up some arousing images. The two of them on a crowded dance floor, him holding her as close as two people could get and still have on all their clothes.

Anticipation thrummed through his brain as he maneuvered into a parking spot.

Damn it, every minute he spent with Casey in the close confines of his two-seater BMW made the Ranger's defense seem more plausible.

* * * * *

Joe Ray's Best Texas-style Barbecue and Honky Tonk reminded Casey of roadhouses near Lubbock where she'd gone with Buck. She looked around, surprised that Craig seemed right at home here until she remembered him saying he was originally a Texan, too, during the fifteen-minute drive out here.

To get her mind off the sizzling sensation that flooded her when he put his hand on the bare strip of skin above her waist, she tried to concentrate on the beat of the country music and the smells wafting inside from the outdoor open pit.

The mouth-watering aroma of sizzling beef and Joe Ray's secret sauce should have distracted her, but all she could think about was how good she imagined Craig would taste when he kissed her.

When they sat down, she focused on the dancers. Each couple swayed slowly, their bodies brushing together on a dance floor not much bigger than a postage stamp. Somehow they all seemed to have found intimacy in the midst of the raucous crowd.

Buck had probably met Daisy Lee at a place not much different from this one.

When Casey looked at Craig across the scarred table, she realized she didn't care. In the smoky room, those brilliant blue eyes of his–startling against his darkly tanned cheeks and dark-brown hair–drew her to him like a magnet. He was a stranger, but she wanted to get personal with him.

Very personal.

Just looking at him, Casey got hot, tingling sensations between her legs and in her nipples. For the first time she understood the feeling — the heady rush of desire a husky-voiced singer was crooning about onstage.

She wanted him to hold her, warm her in all the places on her body where icy blasts from Joe Ray's high-efficiency air conditioning system had her skin puckering up with goose bumps. She could hardly wait to run her fingers through his expertly cut dark hair, rest her head against his chest, and listen to his heart beat while they swayed in time with a slow love song.

He held her hand, massaged her palm with his thumb.

Funny. Casey thought she'd noticed everything about Craig when she watched him work out at the gym, but she hadn't realized he had such large, strong hands. Sexy hands. She hadn't even considered that hands could be sexy.

But Craig's were. They were big, with long fingers dusted on the knuckles with impossibly soft, dark hair. Callused but clean, like the man himself who exuded rugged strength along with his city-lawyer polish.

She'd seen him grip hefty barbells with authority–but Casey sensed that he'd handle a woman gently. Muscles rippled in his forearms, reminding her that under the rolled-up sleeves of a charcoal-gray western-style shirt, more well-honed male flesh hid.

"Casey. You there?"

She met his gaze, felt his amusement. "I'm here."

"Well?"

"Well, what?"

"Do you want beef or chicken?"

He must have thought she'd lost her mind. So must the tired looking waitress standing beside their table, her pad and pencil in hand.

"Beef."

Casey hoped the woman hadn't been waiting for long.

He turned to the waitress. "Two sliced beef sandwiches. Sauce on the side. I'll have a draft beer. Casey?"

"Beer's fine."

"Make that two."

The way he spoke—low and resonant, not loud but deep and compelling—reminded Casey he made his living talking juries into putting criminals away. When he turned the full force of his gaze on her, she shivered. He'd have very little trouble persuading her to follow anywhere he led.

He even oozed sex appeal while he ate.

When Casey watched him bite into the spicy-hot sandwich, she noticed the alignment of his bright white teeth was imperfect enough to make him seem real. The flaw set off a face that otherwise seemed perfect, from those mesmerizing eyes that had haunted her recent dreams to a stubborn jaw and an aristocratic looking nose.

She'd always thought of blue as a cool color. But his eyes radiated heat. That heat threatened to consume her when he settled his gaze on her breasts.

How would she feel when he brushed his mouth across them? Her nipples tensed at the thought of him licking her there, nipping that sensitive flesh between his teeth.

Her cheeks burning, Casey dragged her gaze away and sipped her beer. The icy liquid did little to cool her off, nothing to dispel the arousing pictures from her mind.

"Want to dance?" he asked after he drained his mug.

Casey nodded and took his hand. The chemistry was there for him, too. She could tell by the heat in his eyes and the husky, almost hoarse tone of his voice.

Slowly they wound their way through the crowd to the center of the tiny dance floor. He set her hands on his shoulders, then wrapped his sinewy arms around her waist.

The song was slow, its lyrics about a guy who'd found a girl who wasn't at all what he'd dreamed of–and fallen in love. Casey rested her head on Craig's shoulder and let her imagination soar.

He wasn't the average guy she'd envisioned. The kind of everyday Joe who'd jump at what she had to offer. Just like the

singer wailed about his girl, Craig was more. Much more than she dreamed of. More as in movie star gorgeous, successful and self-assured.

He was accustomed, Casey was certain, to having women who knew just how to ring his bells.

The lights were dim. He held her close but not too tight and led her in the slow, sensual dance with utter self-assurance but without the slightest hint of force.

Yes, Craig was more than Casey had bargained for in every way.

She laid her cheek on the soft material of his shirt and rubbed the stubbly hairs on the back of his neck. The tang of his woodsy aftershave mingled with her own perfume and the aroma of barbecue that permeated Joe Ray's place.

The smells turned her on. The music turned her on. Most of all, Craig turned her on.

She snuggled closer, took pleasure in feeling his hot, hard muscles against her thighs—and in his obvious erection that throbbed against the sensitive flesh of her lower abdomen. She'd never felt this way with Buck, all tingly and hot and acutely conscious of every place where their bodies made contact.

Casey had mildly anticipated a wedding night with Buck. But she wanted Craig on a level that went far deeper. A primal level, female needing male. A level that didn't require a wedding band to make it right.

His hot, hard penis scorched her belly through their clothes, fed the flame inside her.

Silently she reiterated her determination to unleash the sexual, sensual side of herself. The part of her that strict parents, Buck, and Bone Gap, Texas had suppressed for so long.

"You've got to know what you do to me." Craig's whisper rumbled in Casey's ears.

She wiggled her hips and blew gently against the exposed skin above his collar. "Do I turn you on?"

"Yeah." He slid one hand down from her waist, cupped her buttocks and drew her even closer.

He was hard as stone. And hot, in spite of frequent wintry blasts from the overhead air conditioner vents.

Things were going too fast.

Casey panicked. She was in way over her head. Suddenly her muscles wouldn't obey her brain and quit their trembling.

"What's wrong?"

"Nothing."

Was Craig psychic?

Did he somehow know she was nothing but a fake?

Casey finally forced her body to relax, but only after tamping down the panic that threatened to consume her.

"Are you sure?" With his callused thumb, he rubbed the palm of her hand.

"I'm fine."

"What say we go somewhere a little more private?" he whispered when the song had finished.

Casey took a deep breath, reminded herself she wanted him more than she feared making a fool of herself. "Okay."

Chapter Three

When Casey laid a hand on his thigh and started to rub perilously close to his already throbbing cock, Craig almost pulled in at the chain motel at the exit from the interstate.

Hell. Sex came naturally, didn't it?

He was no idiot. He knew how it was done.

In theory.

But when he glanced over at Casey, he changed his mind. Tonight was not the night.

He liked her. A lot. And he wanted more than a one-night stand with him cast as the bumbling idiot, which was the likely way she'd see him if he went at this half cocked.

He'd probably burst a condom, trying to put it on.

If he had one on him, which he didn't. If he managed to get that far before she laughed him out of bed.

Of course he could just tell her he'd never slept with a woman before and hope she'd help him out. Sure he could. As if his pride would let him admit how precious little he'd been around to a living soul, let alone to a woman he liked as much as he liked Casey.

No, he had to do some research before he took the plunge. He'd better take her home and detour to a twenty-four-hour bookstore. It was painfully obvious that he needed to buy some how-to books and burn some midnight oil.

When her fingers brushed his balls through the heavy denim of his jeans, he couldn't suppress a moan. He did manage to keep from thrusting his hips forward to intensify the feeling. And he held the Z-3 on the road. Barely.

He caught her teasing hand and brought it to his lips. Trying hard to sound nonchalant, he said, "We've both got work tomorrow. Let's not start what we're not going to finish tonight, okay?"

"Okay."

He wasn't certain he liked the implication inherent in her quick agreement. The way her fingers curved to cradle his cheek, though, bolstered his ego and propped up his confidence.

"Hey, Casey, don't get me wrong. I want to check out this thing between us. How about meeting me tomorrow when you get off work?"

"I've got to work late. It's my turn to close up the gym. You can come do your workout late if you want to."

"Sounds good."

More than good. Erotic fantasies flooded his mind. Fantasies of him and Casey in the pool, naked. Warming their chilled flesh afterward in the sauna. The pulsing jets in the whirlpool tub would pound at their taut, straining muscles while he pounded into her.

Considering the possibilities had his cock rock hard and straining against his jeans. His thoughts had dissolved in a steamy fog.

"If you want, you could do your workout after everybody else has gone," she suggested.

"Oh, yeah." The workout he had in mind had nothing whatever to do with pumping iron or swimming laps. Casey had to know that. Or did she? There was something incongruously innocent about the smile she shot his way when they paused at the door to her apartment.

No. He had to be attributing his own damn inexperience to her. And that was ludicrous, considering the way she dressed and flirted–not to mention her body language and those not-so-subtle caresses that had him practically bursting his zipper.

But her little-girl smile made him cautious enough to settle for a quick, almost brotherly kiss before he turned and walked away.

* * * * *

A few minutes later Craig checked out the parking lot of a suburban chain bookstore. Relieved that he didn't recognize any of the cars, he pulled into a shadowed slot under the umbrella of a giant oak tree.

Inside, he took another surreptitious look around. Other than a couple of clerks and a handful of tattooed, multiple-pierced teenagers who looked as though they'd have made stereotypical defendants in a criminal trial but seemed seriously out of place at the upscale bookstore, the place seemed deserted.

He headed for the section marked "Relationships." *How To Please Your Lover. A Thousand Ways to Sexual Pleasure. Carnal Invitation.* He even saw a coffee-table edition of *The Kama Sutra.*

He perused shelf after overstuffed shelf, pausing to glance at some of the dust jackets. The art work varied from cutesy cartoon couples to hearts and flowers to stuff that was downright erotic. Obviously sex sold well. The question now was what to buy.

The choice was endless. Big books, little books. Books with pictures worth a thousand words, and books with authors whose names preceded letters that indicated they'd spent decades learning all about fucking in its seemingly endless variations.

Hell, it could conceivably take him longer to learn all about sex and seduction than it had to get through law school.

Craig selected one authoritative looking book that rivaled the telephone directory for sheer weight. Presumably it contained all the basics. Tucking the fifteen-hundred-plus-page manual under one arm, he grabbed a couple of the little books that had attracted him with their eye-catching cover art and titillating titles.

Then he headed for the cashier. Obviously he had a lot of homework to do.

* * * * *

Casey needed to do some learning of her own.

For a long time she stood in the open doorway of her apartment, staring first at Craig and then at the taillights of his BMW. She touched her fingers to her lower lip and tried not to tremble.

She wanted him. He wanted her, too. Even she could recognize the signs.

But she'd convinced herself Buck wanted her, too. At least she'd thought he did a few times, when he got hard and sweaty while they petted in the backseat of his four-by-four. He'd just never wanted her enough to take that final step.

She had to hold Craig's sexual interest long enough to get rid of her troublesome virginity. But she wasn't sure how to accomplish that.

When his taillights disappeared, she closed the door.

Her whole body still tingled from his touch, but fear of turning him off with her appalling lack of knowledge had her mouth dry and her breathing ragged. She'd even forgotten to put a lot of tongue into their goodnight kiss, the way Lisa had suggested.

"Have a good time?" Lisa asked when Casey set down her purse and sank onto a big pillow on the living room floor.

"Oh, yes." Who wouldn't have a good time, looking at and dancing with Craig McDermott?

"You going out again?"

"He's going to meet me at the gym tomorrow, at closing time."

Lisa whistled. "Fast work."

"What do you mean?"

"Picture you and him, all alone in the gym. The lights are turned down low. You've got your choice of saunas and steam rooms, hot tubs and swimming pools. Imagine all those gorgeous muscles of his, pumping away just for you. There's nothing between you but sweat and skin. Yummy, girlfriend."

Casey shuddered to think what their boss would say about his gym becoming the kind of seduction scene Lisa described. "Russ would—"

"He'll never know unless you tell him. Go for it."

Casey would, but... "I don't know how to do it," she blurted out when she found her voice.

"Sure you do. Just go with the flow. Experienced men like breaking in virgins. Or so I'm told."

"So you're told? Surely you were one, once."

Lisa shrugged. "I was fifteen and I've always thought he was a virgin, too, even though he never would admit it. That was a whole different scene than what I'm envisioning for you and McDermott."

"Sounds interesting."

"It wasn't. The whole thing took ten minutes, tops. Jake pulled off the road just past the crossroads near my parents' farm, and we did it on a blanket in the bed of his dad's smelly pickup truck.

"It's funny. The most vivid memory I have of that night isn't about losing my virginity. It's about us being scared shitless every time a car passed by that we'd get caught."

What Lisa recalled was a whole lot different from having sex in the pool or spa, or on the gym floor surrounded by all those mirrors.

Except for the possibility of someone coming along and catching them.

Unfortunately the finale of the scene Casey envisioned featured Craig walking away in disgust when he realized she

was a dud–a sexy shell with nothing inside but raw nerves and fading dreams.

He might even laugh at her hopeless ignorance. She couldn't stand it if he did that.

She grabbed her roommate's hand. "Help me. I'm not fifteen, I'm twenty-four years old. Naive won't cut it. I want to turn him on, not—"

"Not leave it all up to him?"

"Exactly. You've got to tell me what men like."

"Okay. But I still say all you need to do is what comes naturally. Come on."

Casey stood and followed Lisa into their tiny kitchen. "What are we doing in here?"

"We're getting these." Lisa opened the refrigerator and fished out two good-size cucumbers.

"Remember the old cliche, 'A picture is worth a thousand words?' If you're determined to fool him, this ought to do the trick. Listen up. I'm going to show you how to really get him going."

"Huh?"

She pressed the smaller cucumber into Casey's hand. "These, girlfriend, are make-believe cocks."

"Are they this big and hard?"

"Some aren't, but I've seen bigger." Lisa stroked her cuke and grinned. "Bigger is better. Trust me."

Casey's belly burned where Craig's erection had burrowed in during their dance. She stared at the dark green vegetable in her hand and felt heat migrate to her cheeks as she made some mental calculations.

The real thing would dwarf the cuke unless she missed her guess. "Better let me practice with the big one," she told Lisa.

"Okay."

Her cheeks on fire, Casey clutched her cucumber and watched Lisa lick hers as if it were a cherry lollipop.

"What? Why're you doing that?"

Lisa reached the stem end of the cucumber and gave it a noisy slurp. "I never met a man yet who didn't like to have his equipment played with. You try it."

"Try licking the cucumber?"

"Squeeze it. Watch out, not too hard. Don't want to damage the merchandise. Now lick a little. Taste him but don't bite." Lisa paused and demonstrated her technique.

"Come on, you can do it. Pretend it's him. Swirl your tongue around. Now give him some suction. Love him with your mouth. And lap up the pre-cum that's bound to bead up in the slit at the very tip of his cockhead. He'll love it."

The thought of getting *this* up close and personal with Craig's hard cock scared Casey half to death. It also got her insides to tingling again, the way they'd quivered when he kissed her goodnight. Maybe she could after all…

She took a tentative swipe at the cucumber with her tongue. "Ouch. This thing has bumps."

"Don't worry. He doesn't. But wait."

Lisa set down her cuke and hurried out. When she came back a minute later, she set a box of condoms on the table.

"One of these ought to take care of the ouch. Besides, you may as well get some practice, putting them on. Smart women never let strange cocks into their pussies unless those cocks have on a condom."

She fished out a small square packet and tossed it Casey's way.

After several false starts and a good bit of teasing from Lisa, Casey got the condom rolled onto the cucumber. She stifled a giggle. "Maybe I ought to name it."

"Craig?"

"Not! How about Mr. Big?"

"Whatever floats your boat. I'm calling mine Mike."

Lisa smiled when she named her current boyfriend, then swirled her tongue along the length of her cucumber and pretended to lap the imaginary pre-cum she'd mentioned off the rounded tip.

"Okay, girlfriend, follow the leader," Lisa said when she came up for air.

Casey gave Mr. Big a tentative swipe with her tongue. He wasn't bumpy now.

"Feel better?"

"Uh-huh." Casey tried to ignore the damp slippery feel of the lubricated condom against her lips and tongue.

"Now, take him all the way in your mouth like this, and swallow."

Casey did. And following Lisa's example, she sucked and licked and practically swallowed her cucumber whole. When she imagined it was Craig she was loving this way, juices started flowing from her pussy.

Maybe she could do this after all.

Half an hour later, Lisa proclaimed Casey expert in the art of giving a man pleasure.

As she lay in bed later and stroked her swollen clit, she imagined taking Craig in her mouth…or her wet, empty vagina. Her cheeks burned with embarrassment when her stomach muscles clenched and more hot juices flowed onto her busy fingers. Closing her eyes, she let the feelings grow, expand, take her on a sensual journey.

The tingling feeling in her belly intensified, then diffused, leaving her with a gentle sort of twinge that didn't quite cut it. There had to be more to orgasms than this.

She had the feeling there would be, if he were there. He wasn't, though, and as much as the idea turned her on, she knew she'd never dredge up the nerve to kneel in front of Craig and

do to him what Lisa had taught her to do to that cuke-in-a-condom.

Well, maybe she could if it was dark. After all, the last thing she wanted was for Craig to realize she was as green as Mr. Big.

* * * * *

The next morning Craig stared out his kitchen window with scratchy eyes, fighting off an urge to unzip his pants and take his aching cock in hand.

There was nothing he could do to relieve the eyestrain, and he didn't have time to take care of the hard-on that wouldn't go away.

The smell of brewing coffee filled his nostrils as he stared at the array of how-to sex books that had kept him up all night.

The woman riding her lover on the cover of the volume in front of him looked a lot like Casey. Hell, every woman in the illustrations looked like her. And every man reminded Craig of himself.

His fingers itched to explore her supple body. He wanted to massage her feet and stroke her gently behind her knees the way the author of that little book had suggested.

Could he really turn her on that way?

With any luck, he'd find out tonight.

Funny. Mouths and boobs — hell, every guy over the age of twelve knew you kissed and groped boobs awhile before moving on to insert hard, hot cock into tight, wet cunt.

But he'd never considered until now the erotic pleasure he could give and receive by touching a woman's soft, smooth skin in other places. Now he itched to stroke Casey from head to toe, explore every inch of her delectable body.

The smell of wisteria blossoms would surround her, add a sweetness to the heat as he followed the path his hands blazed with his mouth.

He'd have her begging. And he'd give her all she wanted.

Sweat broke out on his forehead. His balls were ready to burst.

And he had to be in court in less than an hour.

* * * * *

By noon, Craig had decided he could easily become a sex fiend. For the first time since he'd begun working as a prosecutor, he'd damn near sympathized with a defendant.

Still aching with unrelieved lust, he'd felt for the guy he tried this morning for solicitation. He'd sympathized when the defense attorney begged the jury to understand how long his client had gone without a woman.

As he stood around outside the courtroom waiting for the verdict, Craig hoped to hell his empathy hadn't been evident to the jury.

"Hey Craig. Waiting for a verdict?"

State Attorney Wells' voice boomed out from down the hall. The man wore a self-satisfied grin, so Craig figured he must have scored a hit in the murder trial he was prosecuting.

"Yeah. Shouldn't be too long now. How's your case going?"

"Fine, fine. Done any research yet on the Ranger case?"

"Some." Craig wondered if the all-night perusal of the books on his kitchen table counted as research.

Wells cracked him on the shoulder. "Good. Don't you go crazy now. Can't have you losing sleep before the competition."

"I won't."

Any sleep he lost would hopefully be sacrificed in a sexy personal trainer's bed. Or a pool deck or hot tub.

His cock begin to stir. Again.

The bailiff caught Craig's eye. "Jury's coming in," he said.

Wells lifted his hefty briefcase and waved Craig away. "Go collect your conviction, son. I'm counting on you."

With any kind of luck, Craig wouldn't let his boss down. Attaining his own career goals depended in large part on keeping the egotistical Harper Wells satisfied for the next couple of years.

He sure as hell didn't intend to spend his whole career prosecuting two-bit lawbreakers like the poor horny jerk now quaking at his lawyer's side and listening to the guilty verdict that would raise Craig's conviction rate another notch.

No way.

Before three years were up, Craig intended to be choosing among lucrative partnership-track offers from several of the big criminal defense firms like the one where his opponent was now slaving away as an associate.

A killer conviction rate and plenty of press coverage in the next year or so would buy his ticket to success. Success he hoped would finally wipe the sad, defeated smile off his mother's face.

That sadness had haunted her since his older brother Alan's shotgun wedding had ended her dream of him becoming the doctor she'd once wanted to be. To Craig's disappointment, it hadn't gone away when he'd graduated from SMU, or even when he earned his law degree with honors.

Mom never had admitted how much Alan's quitting college had hurt her. But Craig knew. He never forgot how she'd looked, sitting on the porch the night of Alan's wedding and bawling like a baby when she thought no one was around to hear.

He'd been sixteen, more interested in sports and partying than school. A few months later, when he damn near ended up in jail because of a bonehead Halloween prank he and some friends had pulled, he'd realized his mom had excellent reason for having put all her hopes in Alan. After rebuilding the section of a rancher's fence that he'd run through with his buddy's truck, he'd sworn to turn his life around and make her proud.

And he had. But even now—eleven years, two degrees, and a law license later—Craig doubted his mom believed deep down

that he'd ever become a rousing success. He was fairly certain she worried that he'd revert to being the screw-up kid he used to be. And he couldn't say he blamed her.

"Congratulations, McDermott."

Craig grinned and shook his opponent's hand. "Thanks, Jim."

Jim Granger, who'd graduated from law school a year ahead of Craig, shrugged. "My guy was guilty. If he hadn't been, my boss would have tried the case himself. Speaking of Tony, he's going to argue the Road Ranger case. Heard you're the prosecutor. Trial's starting next week, right?"

"Yeah. Wednesday." Seven days away and counting.

Jim followed Craig out of the courtroom. "Tony's asked me to take the second chair. I'm looking forward to seeing a client sprung, even if it will be him instead of me getting the credit."

"You wish. Ranger's going to be doing hard time." Craig hoped he sounded more confident than he felt.

"You're not that good, McDermott. You just think you are. Remember, Landry never loses." With that, Jim strode down the hallway toward the door.

The hell of it was, Craig doubted he could persuade a jury no man went insane, temporarily or not, because he needed sex–no matter how active his former sex life may have been. Especially if he had to argue against Tony Landry, the head of the criminal division at Winston Roe.

He knew damn well he couldn't even argue with conviction unless he experienced in the next few days what he'd deliberately avoided for the past eleven years.

A few minutes later, Craig stepped inside the state attorney's offices and headed for his desk. He'd get that knowledge and see the Road Ranger sent away, or die trying. If the job required that he study precedents by day and sex by night, twenty-four seven, that would be okay, too.

Not to mention pleasurable. Sighing, he turned on his computer and accessed an online law library. Insanity was a

favorite defense, if the number of cases Craig found was indicative. Fortunately it didn't often work.

Not one of those cases involved a shrink claiming that temporary loss of reason had been triggered by a sudden dearth of sexual activity. A couple mentioned insanity defenses based on supposed sexual addictions.

Craig printed those abstracts, even though the connection seemed farfetched. He made a mental note to research the topic further and tried to look at the bright side. Chances were, since he hadn't located any precedents, Landry hadn't either, so he'd have an uphill battle, trying to set one in this case.

Sighing, Craig leaned back in his chair and rubbed his aching head. For a moment, he stared beyond a bank of grimy windows. The sun was already going down.

He glanced at his watch. Eight o'clock. He'd be meeting Casey at the gym in less than half an hour. Blood surged to his cock, taking his breath away. Lightheaded now, Craig figured there was no use trying to do more research. He shut the computer down and closed his eyes.

Funny. In one day, Casey had burrowed her way into a spot inside him that he'd been guarding for years. He had an uneasy feeling that once he got the sexy personal trainer in his bed, he'd want to keep her there. Her sweet old-fashioned scent still lingered in his head.

Might she be a good girl after all, beneath that frankly provocative exterior?

Not likely. A muscle in his upper thigh tensed at the spot where she'd laid her hand last night. She was definitely a party animal. And that was good, because the last thing he needed at the moment was a woman he'd have to woo for months before he could coax her into bed.

He stood, shrugged into his suit jacket, and picked up the gym bag where he kept his workout clothes. "See you tomorrow," he said to Andi Syzmanski as he passed her office door. "You working on a big case?"

The pretty, pregnant redhead looked up at him and laughed. "I wish. I'll be here all night, finding case citations for Wells to use at his murder trial. Unfortunately I'm not one of the jocks who's going to win our boss his bet with the chief of detectives next weekend. And with Gray working for Winston Roe, I'm automatically excluded from trying any cases they're defending."

"Sorry about that. I'm off to the gym. Gotta tone the body so I can help Wells get his win."

"Take care. Say hi to Gray if you see him there. He was planning to drop by Russ's and talk about a workout plan that he might be able to handle."

"I will. Don't work too late. I'm sure your husband's already worrying about you overdoing it before Junior there makes an appearance." Craig had once felt sorry for Gray Syzmanski because of his eye patch and the limp that had him using crutches most of the time. He'd pitied him, that is, only until he'd watched Gray trounce top assistant state attorney Sandra Giancone-Delgado's ass in a trial several months earlier, just before she'd resigned to be a full-time mom.

He figured Gray had a lot more to envy than to feel bad about. After all, he'd made himself a reputation as a trial criminal defense lawyer second to nobody but his boss, Tony Landry. And after working there less than a year, he'd been named a partner in Winston Roe. Add Andi and the baby they were expecting, and Craig figured Gray must be riding damn high.

Chapter Four

As Craig jogged the short distance from his office to the gym, his excitement grew. But so did the knot of apprehension in his belly.

He'd forgotten something. A condom.

No way would he have sex without one. He'd heard Alan whine too many times in the past eight years that it had only taken one lousy session of unprotected sex for him to get Lurleen pregnant and destroy his future.

Where the hell was the closest pharmacy?

Then Craig remembered. There was a bright red condom machine on the wall in the gym's locker room.

He'd need quarters. Digging into his pants pocket, he felt a handful of change.

Okay, he had that covered.

His face felt uncharacteristically warm when he walked into the locker room past a couple of guys who were heading out. He hoped to hell he wasn't blushing while he fed six quarters into the condom machine and waited for his purchase to spill out the chute.

The foil-wrapped package caught the light as it fell into his hand.

He must have gotten the last one, because a flashing message on the machine said, "Sold out."

A good omen. Craig took off his suit and hung it in his locker. Fate must have intended him to have sex tonight, or it wouldn't have saved him that last condom.

The last of the gym's other customers left as Craig pulled on his exercise gear. He reached for a pocket, looking for a spot to stash the rubber.

"Damn." The cutoff sweat pants didn't have any pockets, and neither did his T-shirt.

He fumbled for a minute, then stuck the little square under the elastic waistband of his pants.

Uh-oh. He imagined the thing dropping out onto the floor for Casey to see.

Talk about embarrassing. But it would be worse than embarrassing if he lost it, since there weren't any more in close proximity.

That would be downright tragic.

He tossed the condom into his gym bag and took the bag along when he went to do his workout.

* * * * *

Craig looked good enough to eat. His rippling muscles and tanned skin that glistened with sweat took Casey's breath away. And made her mouth go dry, anticipating…

Maybe her senses were heightened because everybody else had gone and she was alone with Craig in the mirrored exercise room. His images surrounded her from all directions.

Her nipples tingled and her cheeks burned as she watched his muscles bulge and contract. A strange urge to taste the glistening sweat that beaded on his forehead and around his neck nearly overcame her, but she managed to resist.

He took off his T-shirt and used it to wipe the sweat off his neck and shoulders. Then he set it on top of the gym bag he'd been hauling around from one station to the next.

What was in that bag that he didn't want to leave in his locker?

Oh, well. It didn't matter. She had better things to consider.

Such as the fact that he was now the next best thing to naked. And his body was to die for.

He didn't shave his chest the way a lot of serious bodybuilders did. She'd wondered about that, and she was glad he didn't. Her fingers itched to burrow into that dark, silky looking growth and caress the bronzed skin that glowed beneath it. She had to cool off or she'd make a fool of herself, but that wasn't easy. Everywhere she looked, his image scorched her gaze.

At least six-two, Craig looked more like a man who worked with his hands than one who made his living with his wits. Still, there was an elegance about his long, lean body. She doubted a stranger would look at him and realize he could press over two hundred pounds of iron above his head and make it look like a child's play.

No one would doubt his prowess in the pool, though. The man reminded her of a Thoroughbred race horse ready to win the Kentucky Derby.

Casey's heart pounded. Her nipples grew even tighter, and her pussy contracted and gushed out more moisture that dampened her leotard. She counted the moments while he finished his workout. When he came to her, she squelched a sudden attack of nerves.

He set his gym bag down and draped his T-shirt across his shoulders. "Want to join me for a swim?"

She shouldn't. Technically she was supposed to play lifeguard while clients swam. But Craig swam like a fish, and she told herself he wasn't a client now because the gym had officially closed. "Sure."

"Want to skinny-dip?"

What would Lisa say? Casey imagined her roommate would jump at the chance of ogling Craig in the altogether, but she couldn't go that far that fast. "What would my boss say?" she asked, half-kidding.

"Are you a lawyer, too?"

"No. Why?"

"Because you just answered a question with a question. Typical lawyer tactic."

His smile seemed oddly sweet. Almost shy. It wasn't at all in keeping with the brazen suggestion he'd voiced seconds earlier, or with the self-assured, almost cocky image he projected.

Somehow that sweetness made him seem even sexier. He must use that smile like a weapon, to disarm women and put them at ease. That thought made Casey all the more wary.

* * * * *

Watching her swim had him hard as stone.

He shouldn't have bothered suggesting they skinny-dip, because the expanse of well-toned female flesh her suit revealed only whetted his appetite. Teased him.

She must like neon. He narrowed his gaze on those strips of material that accentuated more than they hid. The color could only be described as neon purple, sexy and feminine all rolled into one. Like Casey.

Unlike most of the female swimmers he'd grown up around, she had boobs. Round, firm orbs he wanted to explore. Orbs that bobbed on the surface of the water as she rested on the pool ladder and held his gaze.

He wanted to stroke her all over, the way one of his books suggested. But he couldn't deny he had a special interest in those nipples that poked at the material of her suit. They reminded him of tiny erections.

If he didn't move he'd die, so he pushed off and started swimming again. At the far end of the pool he executed a flip turn, then punished his body for the next four laps with an all-out butterfly sprint. Every one of his muscles reminded him he hadn't trained for sprints since finishing his last swim season at SMU four years earlier.

His balls ached and his cock hurt like hell, constricted as they were by the racing suit that had fit just fine when Casey wasn't around. "I've had it," he told her. "What say we take a breather in the sauna?"

She smiled. "Okay."

Craig levered himself out of the pool and held out a hand. Then he grabbed the gym bag.

"What's in there?" Casey asked when he set it on the sauna floor.

Should he tell her? Yeah, probably. He wondered why she tied his tongue in knots when he had no trouble at all talking to a judge or jury. In any case he couldn't seem to join the two syllables now to form the word "condom."

"Nothing much," he mumbled, focusing his gaze on the pattern of wood slats that lined the sauna wall.

"You're blushing."

"No, I'm not. It's the heat in here."

He hated lying, but who but a twenty-seven year old male virgin would turn red at the thought of admitting his gym bag contained a lousy rubber? At least the sauna's scorching dry heat had deflated his erection some, which made his swimsuit fit better than it had before. He spread his legs, hoping to ease the pressure further.

"Can't take it?" she asked, her eyes twinkling.

"I can take the heat. Can you?"

"I think so."

Craig was certain now the flush that bloomed on Casey's face had come on too suddenly to have been caused by the hot, dry air.

Once again he got the impression she wasn't a bad girl after all, but a good one masquerading as the ultimate sex kitten.

And once again he discarded that idea as idiotic when she ran a hand up his leg, not stopping until her fingers were within

millimeters of his smashed-down cock and balls. Close enough that he felt their heat.

"Getting too warm?" he asked, settling his gaze on the purple scrap that barely hid her generous breasts.

"What?" Her cheeks turned brighter than her swimsuit. "Y-yes. I guess I am."

There was that hesitation that made her seem so damn innocent. He saw it again when her hands shook as she reached for the top of her suit.

When she peeled off the offending garment, he couldn't think at all. It was his turn to shake now that she'd revealed full, creamy breasts centered with rosy pebbled nipples.

God, she was gorgeous. The combination of her sweet smile and the brazen action was positively erotic.

Sugar and spice. A nursery rhyme he suddenly recalled claimed that was what little girls were made of. Big girls were, too, or so it seemed.

Craig's mouth went dry, drier even than the arid air they breathed.

His cock leapt back to attention so fast he thought it would split his swim suit. And it took superhuman effort for him to control his hands. They seemed determined to reach out and see if her breasts felt as velvety as they looked.

But the authors of his sex books had all said not to move too fast. And he was determined not to display his ignorance. "Let's hit the shower," he said while he could still control his mouth and fingers that itched to explore every inch of her tempting flesh.

* * * * *

At least in the sauna she'd had the scorching heat as an excuse for turning six shades of red. Casey hoped the cool water sluicing over her body was doing its job and fading her heated cheeks. She doubted it, though, especially now.

Craig's fingers slid inside his minuscule racing suit. His gaze on her bare breasts, he shoved the navy material down lightly furred, muscular thighs, past his well-defined calves. He stepped out of the suit and stood under the shower spray.

The man didn't exhibit an ounce of reserve. Of course he probably got naked in front of women all the time. She tried not to gawk, but his cock attracted her like a beacon.

She supposed she should strip down, too. After all, who took a shower in a swimsuit? But when she tried to force her hands to do the job, they refused her brain's command. Some hot number she was turning out to be!

Her cheeks burned. So much for the water cooling her off. *You've gotta get on with the program or he'll guess you're nothing but a fraud.*

For a long time Casey glued her gaze on a soap dish affixed to the shower wall at shoulder height. Taking a deep breath, she tried hard to fight down panic when she glanced his way.

He's naked. Buck naked. Of course he is, idiot. You saw him skinny out of that swim suit.

She should be getting naked, too.

Lisa would tell her just to peel off the bottom of her own suit and take a lascivious look at everything he'd bared.

Come on, Casey, do it.

She cursed herself for a coward.

"Are you going to leave the bottom of your bikini on?" He reached out and slid his hands under the waistband but made no effort to slide the material down.

"Oh, no." For some strange reason, Craig's amused comment helped to boost her courage. She reached blindly for the sides of her bikini bottom.

He grinned. "Let me."

"Okay."

He started to push the suit down but stopped just above her hipbones. "Are you okay with this?"

Was she? It was what she wanted. What she'd left Bone Gap determined to find. And from the first day she laid eyes on Craig, she'd wanted to find it with him. She drew in a deep breath, then looked him in the eye. "I'm sure. Go ahead, take it off."

She didn't sound particularly confident, even to her own ears. But Craig didn't seem to mind. His big hands felt warm against her hipbones when he pushed the fabric down. Her pussy gushed more hot slippery lubrication, and her skin burned at his touch when he slid the stretchy swim suit over her thighs.

When the suit finally pooled at her ankles, he lifted her feet, first one and then the other. Then he brought the material to his lips before tossing it aside. His eyes glowed when he met her gaze, reminding her that the hottest fires burned blue.

Then he lifted one of her feet again and stroked along its length. "You're beautiful," he said, his breath tickling her calf as he made his way up her body.

He sounded almost reverent. And a little shaky.

Get real, Casey told herself. The man was ego on the hoof. She had no business attributing her own nervousness to him. "So are you," she croaked when she finally got the nerve up to look at the pulsing column of hard, thick cock that put Mr. Big to shame.

He was huge. And his skin there looked velvety smooth, not spiny like the cuke. His balls looked tight, drawn up as they were behind the base of his cock. Heat radiated from Craig's entire body, but Casey was pretty sure his purple-veined cock with its plum-shaped head was the hottest spot of all.

He certainly wouldn't be refrigerator-chilled like Mr. Big when she took him in her mouth. She chuckled at the memory of her lesson Lisa had given her last night.

"What's funny?"

She didn't imagine he'd like being compared with a cucumber. "N–nothing at all."

He cupped her chin, tilted her head back until she met his gaze. "Hey, baby, you're making me nervous, looking at me like that."

She was making *him* nervous? He had her quaking from head to toe, but she'd be damned if she'd let him know. Inhaling deeply while she mustered up some courage, she shot him what she hoped was a sexy smile.

"I guess that's your problem." Deliberately, she slid her hand down his body and curled it around his penis. "I was just thinking how much I'd like to taste you here."

"Huh?"

"Don't tell me you wouldn't like it." Every man did, or anyway that's what Lisa had said.

He skimmed a hand across her breasts, made the nipples pucker. "I'd like it all right. It's just—"

"Too soon?"

"Yeah. No. I mean, you don't have to."

She gathered her courage and slid her hand all the way down his cock, giving a playful squeeze at its base. "What if I want to?"

"Be my guest." That came out as a rumbling whisper that punctuated the hard, steady pulsing of his flesh.

Warm water sluiced over them, drenching Casey's head as she slid to her knees. Craig's thigh muscles twitched when he widened his stance, as if to give her better access.

She could do this.

Really. He wasn't bumpy and he wasn't green, and his rigid erection pulsed with life.

She reached out with her tongue, sampled the silky, slightly salty drop of pre-cum that nestled at the tip of his cock head, then followed the path her hand had taken with her mouth. He was blazing hot and hard as stone.

As the shower spray pelted her from above, she retraced her path and took him in her mouth. Her tongue swirled, tasted,

sampled the textures and tastes of him. He grew hotter and harder and, impossibly it seemed, bigger.

"Oh, God." He sounded as if he were in pain.

Oh, God was right.

She'd never felt like this before, so out of herself and into what was happening to him and her and them. A delicious ache centered low in her belly and between her legs when she cupped his heavy sac like an offering in her hands.

"Stop that. Baby, I can't take any more."

She couldn't let him go. Not until that ache went away.

She took him deeper in her throat, swallowed.

He wrenched himself free. "The first time I want to be inside you," he said, sounding tortured.

She wanted him inside her, too, easing the throbbing ache between her legs. But she couldn't talk. All she could do was kneel there, soaking wet, feeling the shower spray pelting her with a thousand needles of sensation.

He drew her to her feet, pulled her close. "My turn now."

As though she were a precious work of art, he touched her, explored her, heated her. The ache between her legs intensified and more hot, slippery stuff dripped down her inner thighs. Why didn't he touch her there? She opened her legs, invited him in. But he took his time, teased her with butterfly-light touches and open-mouthed kisses.

He ravaged her mouth. Her earlobe. He buried his fingers in the wet strands of her hair and drew her head onto his shoulder. His silky chest hair chafed the tender tissue of her breasts.

He was driving her insane.

When he barely grazed her nipples with his thumbs, shards of sensation attacked her weeping pussy. He bent, nuzzling her pussy with his lips and tongue. He followed his mouth with gentle, arousing touches of his callused fingertips. His breathing grew ragged, almost as labored as her own.

What would he do next?

What should she do? She clutched his broad, hard shoulders, afraid she'd fall if she let go.

"Easy, baby. We've got all night."

They might have all night, but if he didn't get on with this seduction, she was going to die. No she wasn't. Nobody died from unrelieved virginity. If anybody ought to know that, she should.

But the empty ache between her legs told another story. It told her she *would* die if he didn't make his way there soon and fill her with his big, beautiful cock.

Then the sound of the burglar alarm rang in her ears. "Oh, no."

Craig lifted his head. "What was that?"

"The alarm. Somebody must have set it off."

"But it's not ringing now."

She thought she knew why. Russ must have come back. "Shhh," she whispered.

He shut off the water. "What the hell?"

"Russ. Sometimes he comes back to check things late at night. We can't let him find us."

"I hear footsteps."

Casey heard them, too. Heavy footsteps that sounded ominously close, as though Russ had figured out that somebody was in the showers and was coming in.

"Yo there, Casey. You in there?"

Craig nudged her. "Say something."

"Russ? It's me. I'm okay."

"Sure you don't need any help?"

The laugh that followed that pointed question reminded Casey how close she and Craig had just come to giving her boss one hell of a show. A show that would have cost her job. She'd have had to quit from embarrassment if Russ didn't fire her.

"I'm fine," she repeated.

"Well, kid, don't do anything I wouldn't."

Casey had never noticed before how Russ had an evil sounding laugh. But that laugh reverberated through the place as his footsteps grew faint and disappeared.

She turned back to Craig. "Where were we?"

"I'm afraid we're finished for now. Your boss's sudden appearance has sort of taken the wind out of my sails."

When he hugged her, she realized what he meant. In less than a minute he'd wilted like a week-old cucumber somebody had forgotten in the vegetable crisper.

Come to think of it, Casey's body had cooled off, too, though thankfully her reaction wasn't nearly as obvious as his.

"It's okay," she told him, trying to sound as though she almost had sex in the workplace every day.

Russ's unexpected presence had to be an evil omen—a sign that Casey was destined to remain a virgin until the end of time.

Chapter Five

But maybe she wasn't. Maybe there was hope for her yet. Casey felt Craig's body surge to attention when they hugged under the dim porch light at her front door.

"I've got to spend the next couple of days preparing a case. But I'm going to miss you." He paused, then took both her hands. "Spend the weekend with me. We can leave Friday afternoon and go down to Sanibel."

"I'd love to." With luck, no one would interrupt them there. Surely even a virgin could seduce a hunk sometime during seventy-two uninterrupted hours.

Casey couldn't wait. Her troublesome virginity was going to be history by Saturday, if not before.

* * * * *

When he got home, Craig stood in the shower, hard and aching. As he had hundreds of times before, he grasped his cock just below the head and pumped it with a slow, steady rhythm while needles of hot water pelted his body.

Shit. All he could do was remember the feel of Casey's hands. And the hot, wet heat of her mouth. And yearn. His hand didn't feel like Casey's.

He should have gotten over his embarrassment and fucked her after Russ had left. That would have taken care of the hard-on that had abated only temporarily when the gym owner had showed up and rained on his parade.

Now his balls were turning blue and it seemed his usual method of getting off wasn't going to work. He wanted to come.

Worse than ever before. Only thing was, he wanted to come with his cock buried in her mouth — or her steaming little cunt.

One thing for sure, he'd never see a locker room in the same light again.

Who'd have thought the smell of chlorine and sweat could be an aphrodisiac? Or that a guy could maintain a hard-on in a sauna? Certainly not him. But he was pretty damn sure he'd never step into a shower again and not get horny. He'd never feel the millions of needles pelting his body with sensation and not get hard.

And he'd never forget the hot, wet suction of Casey's mouth…

The pressure built in his balls, then spilled over to his cock. Craig closed his eyes and let go, imagining he was still in the locker room and it was Casey's tight cunt and not his fist ringing him while his seed spurted over and over.

As he soaped himself, Craig anticipated Friday night. The clean salty air coming off the Gulf of Mexico, whipping at Casey's hair. Waves crashing along the rocky shore outside while they pounded into each other on a bed inside the resort hotel where he'd just booked a room.

Damn it. He was hard again just thinking about fucking her. When they made love for real, there was no way he was going to be able to hold back. He'd come, the minute he stuck his cock inside her hot, wet body. And she'd realize he was nothing but a rank amateur. Worse, she'd think he was a selfish bastard interested only in his own pleasure. That humiliating thought did more than the cold water he rinsed with to reduce the aching in his balls.

But not enough.

The friction of the towel when he dried off revived his cock again. The hard-on hadn't wanted to go away since he'd decided that now was the time to break his self-imposed celibacy. And singled Casey out to be his first lover.

There might be something to Billy Ranger's claim. Lust definitely could fuel sexual obsession. And do crazy things to a man's cool, rational logic.

It was doing a number on Craig's brain.

He nibbled on the eraser end of the pencil he should have been using to work and made a futile effort to get Casey off his mind.

Right now he was worrying more about perfecting his technique between the sheets than honing his closing argument in the domestic violence case that would conclude in the morning. That was bad.

He forced himself to ignore his erection and start writing. When he finished summing up the reasons a wife-beater belonged behind bars, he'd treat himself to some more lessons on the techniques of seduction—skills he intended to make full use of on the weekend.

He hoped his preoccupation with sex wouldn't outlast the consummation.

* * * * *

Casey could barely wait. After she undressed, she touched her nipples the way Craig had done, imagining his hands moving lower, burning a path down her body.

She pictured him fitting his long, hard body over hers, probing, teasing…

Then she remembered. The minute he plunged inside her he'd know she was a fraud.

Oh, no. What could she do?

The terry robe she wrapped around her naked body abraded her nipples. As she moved toward the kitchen, it brushed her belly and thighs.

Her fingers felt like jelly. They quivered, too, she noticed when she was trying to fish the last dill pickle out of a jar to go with a cheese sandwich sizzling in the electric skillet.

Lisa joined Casey in the kitchen. "What's cooking?" she asked.

"A grilled cheese sandwich. Want one?"

Lisa shook her head. "We ate out."

Casey heard the front door close with a soft whoosh. "Mike's not spending the night?"

"He's got a meeting in Orlando first thing in the morning." Lisa hugged herself, and her smile hinted at the satisfaction she'd apparently just received.

As if the moans and groans Casey had heard when she passed by her roommate's bedroom door hadn't already told her what had been going on.

Unlike Craig, Mike obviously hadn't left without taking care of business. Casey's hands started shaking again.

The jar slipped from her grip and crashed into the sink.

"Oh, well. I didn't want that last pickle after all," she said, her gaze fixed on the shattered glass.

"I take it tonight didn't go as you planned," Lisa commented as she rescued the sandwich from the smoking skillet and put it on the plate Casey had set out. "Hey, girlfriend, tell me all about it."

Casey looked up from the sandwich she was tending. "Russ came in."

"Oh, God."

"Exactly."

Lisa slid a chair back from the table. "Sit. Talk to me."

Casey couldn't. It was too embarrassing. "I did what you said. But he made me stop."

"Russ?"

"No. That was before he got there. Craig stopped me. He said he liked it too much."

"What?"

"You know. What you taught me to do with the cucumber."

"Giving head. That's what you call it. Not to worry, though. Some guys don't like to come that way." Lisa plopped herself into the other chair and looked Casey in the eye.

"That's what he said."

"Then did he do it to you?"

"Do what?"

Lisa shook her head, as if she thought Casey had no brain. "Return the favor."

"Not exactly. I think he would have, but then the alarm went off and Russ started looking—he came within inches of walking in on us. It was awful."

"Casey, exactly what did Craig do?"

"Well, we were in the shower. He made me stop doing the cucumber thing. Then he started stroking and touching and kissing me. Everywhere but…"

"Everywhere but where you wanted him to?"

Casey's cheeks burned. "Yeah."

"I'd say you've found yourself one dynamite lover."

"What do you mean?"

"Sounds as though Craig's a guy who knows how to get you hot as a chili pepper. And that he wants to make sure you're burning up for him before he moves along to the main course."

"Oh."

A to-die-for man with plenty of knowledge. Experience. Knowledge and experience Casey didn't have but wanted to acquire. Feelings of inadequacy bubbled up inside her again and threatened to spill out of her eyes as tears.

She forced a tepid sounding laugh. "I'm so, so sure he's going to want to teach a rank beginner."

Lisa patted her hand. "Don't worry. He will."

"We're going to Sanibel for the weekend."

"Dynamite."

Suddenly Casey wished she'd said no. She should have tried to string Craig along a little longer, enjoyed him more before jumping in for the climax—and losing him, which she was afraid would happen when he learned the truth.

She shook her head. "Not so dynamite. I may chicken out."

"Why would you do that?"

"I was thinking one-night stand, maybe somewhere like the gym where we wouldn't even sleep together afterward. But a whole weekend? I don't know anything. Nothing. Nada."

Panic welled up in Casey's gut. She felt as though she might puke.

"What don't you know?" Lisa asked.

"For starters, what do I wear and when? Do I go get a bunch of sexy black lace lingerie or sashay around that hotel room naked? Do I strip down the minute we get there or wait and see what he has in mind? Will I need stuff for the beach or will we spend the whole weekend in bed?"

When Casey paused to catch a breath, she found she couldn't hold back tears any longer. They tickled her cheeks as they streamed from her eyes.

This was going to be a disaster. She was going to lose Craig, and she'd just figured out that the man meant a lot more to her than a super-appealing means of losing her virginity.

She reached out and grabbed Lisa's hand. "W-what do I say and do? God, I'm such an idiot. And, damn it, I like him a lot."

"Sure you like him. You wouldn't be hot to seduce him if you didn't. Come on, get a hold on. You've got two days. Time enough to spruce up your bedroom wardrobe and more. Much more."

Two days. God, she was so not ready.

Casey knew that in her head. But her body disagreed. Craig had set nerves to tingling and throbbing in body parts she hadn't realized had nerves. She had to give it a shot and hope everything would turn out for the best.

"Okay, what do I buy?" she asked.

"Some naughty undies. And spring for the works at Tony's House of Passion."

"The works?"

"Facial, massage, hair, nails, makeup. A Brazilian bikini wax." Lisa clapped her hands. "I know, you should get a tattoo."

"Ouch!" The very idea of somebody poking needles into her cooled Casey off faster than an icy shower.

"You're right. You don't want to be sore when you're gettin' it on for the first time. But Tony could give you a temporary one. Maybe a little rose on your hip."

Somehow Craig didn't strike Casey as a man who was into body art. But she could be wrong. The small red heart tattooed on Lisa's shoulder attracted a lot of lascivious looks from clients at the gym. More even than the eight jeweled studs that marched around the edge of one of her ears.

"I don't know," Casey murmured.

"Then don't do it. McDermott's probably too buttoned-down to appreciate one anyhow. Besides, he's already seen you. He'd notice if you suddenly got yourself tattooed or pierced."

Casey smiled. "I always wanted to pierce my belly button."

"Do that later. When you've got some private time to heal."

Lisa fingered the gold ring in her navel through the thin silk of her robe. "I got this done when I swore off sex for Lent, my senior year in high school. It took almost that much time for the pain to go away. To tell the truth, the thing doesn't do much except give some guys a visual turn-on."

Okay. She wasn't getting a tattoo and she wasn't getting pierced. Casey still had a way to go in the next two days. The other preparations Lisa had mentioned sounded more pleasurable than the prospect of having needles poked in and through her.

"Will you go with me?" she asked.

"Sure. I'll call Tony's and set up the appointments. We'll take off from work and do it tomorrow afternoon."

* * * * *

The next afternoon Craig sandwiched a workout in between the end of the domestic violence trial and some night court arraignments that Wells had tossed his way.

Casey wasn't at the gym, and that disappointed him. The woman was getting under his skin. In more ways than one. He understood missing the hot surge of lust that hit him every time he looked her way. That, he'd take care of this weekend. He wasn't so certain he'd ever get his fill of her bright smile or the flirty way she looked at him. How the hell could he make love with her and not complicate things?

Damn it, he'd die if anyone found out he'd never... He was ready for firsthand sex education but not for a life partner. He liked Casey too much. Obviously, if she'd taken the afternoon off to get ready for a big date as Russ had told him when he asked, she must like him, too.

He couldn't think about that now. He had things he needed to do. And he didn't have a lot of time.

The bright red condom machine caught his eye. It still said "Sold Out." He'd have to stop by a store and buy one. Make that several. Fresh ones. He chuckled, recalling one author's comment that like milk cartons at the neighborhood convenience store, condoms had expiration dates. The warning that as birth control they were ninety percent effective at best wasn't quite so funny.

Oh well, Casey was probably on the Pill.

Recalling an interesting chapter in one of his books, he decided he should take along some toys. Toys that were a far cry from beach balls and surfboards.

Craig shook the water out of his hair, then toweled it dry. If he hurried, he'd have time before he had to be in night court to

check out that new triple-x rated store across the street from the gym.

Moments later he hesitated outside the shop called Erotic Invitation, staring at the well-endowed mannequins in the window. Then he fought off a wave of embarrassment and stepped inside.

No way was he going to let Casey know he was a novice.

* * * * *

Tony's House of Passion should have been called Tony's House of Torture.

Casey squelched a squeal and gritted her teeth.

She could hardly believe this sadist named Luisa was humming.

Humming, mind you. Humming some sweet old-fashioned lullaby that Casey remembered from her childhood. The woman was obviously enjoying the pain she was inflicting on Casey's tender flesh.

For the past four hours Casey had been kneaded and pummeled, steamed and iced down, plucked and scissored and body-wrapped, all for the sole purpose of beautifying herself for Craig.

Obviously Tony's knew their business, because they'd saved the worst for last.

Having to get naked and spread her legs for this sadistic Brazilian Amazon should have served as warning of what was coming. But it hadn't. The pubic trim had only hurt her pride. And the warm wax actually felt soothing going on.

She hadn't been prepared for the agony that followed when Luisa started slapping pieces of cloth onto Casey's mons and labia and ripping the wax away.

"Just a few more pulls, *senhorita*. Then I use the tweezers." Louise snatched another strip away.

"Please hurry. Ohhh." It felt as to Casey if Luisa had torn her skin right off. If she lived through all this, having sex with Craig had better blow her mind.

"Want some more champagne?" Lisa asked.

Casey held out her glass, then gulped the tingly liquid. Maybe if she drank enough, it wouldn't hurt so much.

That was wishful thinking. The champagne didn't help. Tony's probably didn't have enough of it around to dull this kind of pain.

Luisa snatched off another strip of hardened wax from between her legs.

Casey howled again.

Some sex goddess she was. She sounded like one of her daddy's calves that had gotten caught up in a barbed wire fence.

It didn't help when Lisa laughed.

"How can you be finished already?" Casey asked when she caught her breath.

"Waxing takes longer the first time. I just needed a touch-up."

Casey took heart at the hint that this process apparently got easier with repetition. Lisa didn't seem to mind the monthly visits she made here.

"It hurts like hell," she said after Luisa had yanked away another of the strips.

Not to mention that her legs were aching from being spread apart and manipulated into positions that would do a contortionist proud.

"Trust me. Craig will like the results. So will you. Your pussy'll feel smooth as a baby's."

Casey hoped so. She didn't imagine that getting tattooed could hurt any more than having most of her body hair ripped out by the roots.

Luisa tapped Casey on the hipbone. "The worst is done. You relax. I trim you nice little heart."

A few minutes later Casey checked out Luisa's handiwork in a three-way mirror in Tony's dressing rooms.

Except for a very tiny patch of short curls shaped like a heart and centered on her pubic mound, she was indeed as smooth as a baby.

She shook her head. "Well, I can definitely wear my new thong bikini now. No wonder it hurt!"

Luisa dusted her hands off on her white lab coat. "Your man, he will love it," she gushed. "So soft. So smooth. So sexy."

Casey wasn't sure she liked the bare-ass look, but she was afraid to hurt her torturer's feelings. If she did, the woman might take another look and find a hair or two that she'd missed.

"Look, now you can wear this." Lisa held up a black lace G-string, then dropped it into Casey's hand.

Casey slipped it on. The scrap of lace covered up her heart-shaped patch of hair but not a whole lot more.

She reminded herself of one of the strippers she'd seen in X-rated movies on late-night cable TV. Only the garter belt and fancy stockings were missing.

"I couldn't–"

"Sure you could. Try this, too."

Suddenly a see-through black garter belt hung from Casey's boneless fingers. "You're sure?"

"Mike loves mine."

"What about stockings?"

Lisa handed over a package of off-black thigh-highs with seams up the back. "I've got fishnets, but I think these will be better for you. They go with this."

Casey gasped when her roommate held up a scoop-necked black minidress that looked as if it might fit a four-year-old.

"I'd never squeeze into that."

"Yes you will. It stretches." Lisa demonstrated.

It stretched all right. It also sprung back with a vengeance as soon as Lisa let it go.

The dress just might cover the bare essentials. But Casey doubted it.

"Maybe I ought to concentrate on stuff to wear in the bedroom. I don't think I could go out in public in that."

"The purpose of this *is* to lure him into the bedroom, girlfriend. Wear it in the car on the way to Sanibel if you want to get him really, really hot." Lisa laughed again, as though she thought Casey's reticence was downright funny.

"Craig will think I'm a hooker."

"No he won't. Role-playing's fun. Pretend you're a stripper. Strip for him when you get to your room, and then make him strip for you. I think I'll get Mike that hot cop outfit we saw in the other room."

A few minutes later, Casey left Tony's House of Passion with her new Brazilian bikini wax, a barely-there thong bikini, a fistful of see-through barely-there undies, and one black spandex washcloth masquerading as a dress.

Not to mention the matching short black satin robes she'd picked up for herself and Craig.

After all, they'd have to take a break from sex every now and then.

Wouldn't they?

She'd resisted Lisa's suggestion that she take along a black leather riding crop they'd looked at.

Come to think of it, though, the idea of bending over while Craig used the crop on her bare backside had her wet and twitching between her legs. Maybe she should have bought it.

After all, she was determined to become a bad, bad girl.

Maybe later…

Chapter Six

Erotic Invitation lived up to its name, and more. Craig gave a cursory look at the other customers in the sex toy store. Good. Nobody he knew was here.

He gave the men's sexual aids a cursory glance but saw no need for the tubes and vacuum devices that promised erections to any guy who hadn't been declared dead. He had the opposite kind of problem and a definitive plan for solving it, for which he was grateful. Those things looked like medieval torture devices.

So did the cock rings — but he recalled that one of his books had mentioned they came in handy to prevent coming too soon. Craig took another surreptitious look around before stepping up to the display, again finding no one he recognized. Quickly he dropped the least wicked looking of the rings — one that resembled an overly thick, rounded rubber band — into a shopping basket the clerk had handed him when he came through the door.

That handled, he moved on. The quantity of choices rivaled that at Toys 'R' Us, though no kid should lay eyes on the toys in here.

There were strap-on cocks. Vibrators. Dildos. Anal stimulators and oversize make-believe tongues that wiggled when you turned them on. Some looked disturbingly real, like parts neatly dismembered from their owners' bodies. Suddenly Craig felt compelled to protect his own gonads.

The dildos came in all colors, shapes, and sizes. There were even double ones, one of which was nearly three feet long. Some boasted add-ons he couldn't imagine a reasonable purpose for, but he figured Casey might like a vibrator. The guy who wrote one of his books had mentioned that lots of women did. He'd

enjoy watching what it did to her rosy, sensitive nipples to be stimulated that way.

After checking out the inventory, he settled on a flesh-colored plastic vibrator with a generic shape. It reminded him of a slender flashlight. He took another furtive look around and found the coast still was clear, so he grabbed the vibrator and dropped it into his basket.

He looked for condoms next. Erotic Invitation had a wide selection of them. The choices boggled his mind. French ticklers. Banana bangers. Multicolored and tiger-striped rubbers in small, medium, large, and colossal sizes. Ones with ribs and bumps and all sorts of painful looking protrusions.

What the store's buyer apparently had forgotten to order were plain garden variety safe-for-sex rubbers like the one his encyclopedia of sex recommended. He doubted any of these condoms had been designed with safe sex being the primary goal, so he made a mental note to stop by the all-night pharmacy near his apartment on his way home and buy a box of the plain vanilla kind.

Vanilla?

A display on the end-cap drew Craig's attention. It advertised vanilla condoms, along with a selection of other flavors. According to the hype, the things were edible. Maybe he'd buy some just for fun.

Casey might like the taste of them. She certainly had seemed to enjoy tasting him. His cock twitched, as if it wanted him to know it liked her intimate attention.

Chuckling at the irony of it, he picked up a pack of cherry-flavored ones. Hopefully she wouldn't get the significance.

Beyond the condom aisle, a display of edible oils caught his eye. He figured since he was a sucker for chocolate, he'd like licking it off her nipples—and her pussy, too. Wincing at the price, he picked up a small bottle. There must have been some good reason for the stuff to cost ten times as much as chocolate

syrup from the grocery store, although he couldn't figure out why by reading the ingredients listed on the label.

Oh, well. It wasn't as if he was going to make chocolate milk. He dumped the bottle into the basket.

Maybe he'd get a video. The store had thousands of tapes and DVDs. Labels on end caps proclaimed one row straight sex, the next gay and lesbian.

Another row promised films of threesomes and orgies, but since he recalled a comment in one of his books that most women didn't get turned on by porn flicks, he decided to pass on getting one. He did, however, stop to check out the books and magazines, and picked up one of the tamer ones that advertised an article about phone sex on its cover.

The imaginatively displayed leather and chains against the back wall didn't turn him on. And the selection of torture devices next to them actually made him cringe. Using any of the things on display could get the user sent up for ten to twenty if his or her partner complained.

"You into S&M?"

"No." Craig swung around toward the sound of a gravelly voice.

The man was wearing more chains than the store had hanging on the wall, and he had more scars on his face than Al Capone.

Craig had seen him before—at the courthouse being arraigned, he thought.

What had the charge been?

Drugs? Assault?

He didn't recall, but from the way the guy was ogling him like a starving dog eyeing a tasty treat, he guessed the crime might have had something to do with sex. Gay sex involving some of the wicked looking devices that gave him chills just looking at them.

Craig had a sudden urge to run. He was used to dealing with weirdos in court, where there were always plenty of cops to keep things under control. Unfortunately he didn't see any cops in Erotic Invitation. He imagined the store owner liked it that way.

Craig's would-be dungeon master reached out a black-gloved hand and patted him on the butt. "Don't get pissed, honey. I just asked."

Panic set in, fast. "I've got to go."

Craig grabbed a small leather whip from the display as he strode away. Not that the puny thing would do much to beat off the S&M freak.

Fortunately the clerk was speedy. And Craig's wannabe S&M partner didn't follow him to night court.

Afterward at the pharmacy near his apartment, Craig bought several boxes of condoms.

* * * * *

Practice makes perfect.

Anyhow, that's what Craig's mom used to say when she tried to get him to do his homework.

He stripped, laid some condoms on his kitchen table, and sat down to work up a hard-on and try them on for size. The thought of guys unzipping their pants and trying them on in the store, the way people tried on shoes, made Craig laugh. If he stayed with the DA's office long enough, he'd most likely prosecute some pervert for doing just that.

With any kind of luck, ogling the illustrations in the magazine he'd bought would get him in the mood. God knew he didn't need much help. Thinking about tomorrow night with Casey had his cock hard and aching before he even found the centerfold.

He unwrapped the condom he'd bought in the machine — and watched it split when he tried to roll it on. Good thing Russ

had interrupted them the other night. Otherwise he could have gone from virginity to expectant fatherhood in a matter of a few seconds.

That possibility didn't horrify Craig as much as he'd imagined it would. Still, he figured he'd better check out some of the supposedly foolproof rubbers he'd just bought. The things really did come in different sizes. It took him three tries to find ones that fit.

Okay. Maybe he'd call Casey and experiment with phone sex. God knew he was primed to come. No surprise to that. His cock had been more or less hard for the better part of three days and nights.

The condom got tighter as he got harder, so he took it off. Then he turned on the speaker phone and dialed Casey's number.

"Hello."

His balls tightened at the honeyed sound of her voice. "Hello yourself."

"I thought you said you'd be curled up with some dry old law book tonight after you got out of court."

"I was reading, but I couldn't get you off my mind."

"I've been thinking about you, too. Where are you?" she asked.

"Sitting at the table, looking at a book." She didn't need to know the book was a porn magazine, or that it was opened to a page with pictures of a naked woman with big boobs, sucking some guy's cock while he ate her pussy.

She also didn't need to know the woman reminded him a lot of her.

"I'm in bed," she told him.

He wished to hell he were right there with her. "Want me to come join you?"

"If you do, I'll make you come," she said, and he could almost see her sexy smile.

"I'm counting on it. This time tomorrow. Why don't you make yourself come for me now?"

"On the phone? That wouldn't be any fun."

He lowered his voice almost to a whisper. "I bet we could make it fun."

"I'm not sure I know what to do."

Her nervous laugh made him wonder again if he'd pegged her wrong. She sounded breathless. Almost virginal. But turned on. Definitely turned on.

Craig had to quit attributing his own insecurities to Casey. "Let's improvise," he told her, certain she wouldn't appreciate the dialogue the porn stars had spouted to each other in the little phone scene he'd just read. It hadn't done a lot for him, to tell the truth.

Sliding the magazine aside, he opened one of his books and started flipping pages.

He knew he'd seen a chapter on verbal seduction somewhere. He skimmed the topic headings. "What do you have on?" he asked when the silence started getting to him.

"Sweats. How about you?"

"I'm naked. Why don't you take off your clothes?"

More silence. Then the rustling noise hinted that she was doing what he suggested. His balls ached, and his palms grew damp.

"Okay. I'm naked too," she said. "What now?"

"Touch your face. Stroke your cheek the way I'd do if I were there. Let your hand slide through your hair, softly, like you do to me when you're dragging my lips down to yours for a kiss."

"Imagine I'm touching you, too. Your shoulders. Now I'm rubbing my thumbs across your nipples. Does that feel good?" Casey's voice poured over him like honey, soft and sweet and incredibly arousing.

Craig lowered his voice almost to a whisper. "Run your fingers over your breasts. Feel how soft they are. Lick your lips. Pretend you're licking me. Imagine how hard my cock is now. It's throbbing. Wanting you."

That was no lie. Craig followed his own advice and encircled the base of his cock with his thumb and forefinger.

"I'm going to put on a condom. Pretend it's a cherry-flavored one. Imagine eating a cherry lollipop. Licking and sucking until the flavor's all gone. Until all that's left is me. Me hot and hard for your wet, tight pussy."

He opened a little foil pack and rolled a non-flavored rubber into place. It went on easier this time.

Her breathy groan made him wonder if his words had nudged her close to the edge. Painfully hard himself, he wanted to echo her needy sound. But he didn't. Instead he lowered his voice to little more than a hoarse whisper. "I'll lick you, too. Your pretty pink nipples. Your belly. I'll nip at the sensitive spots on the insides of your thighs and behind your knees, and lap up the slick juice from your pussy. I'll taste you all over."

When he paused and listened to her ragged breathing, he got a rush from the effects of his sex talk. "Think about hot wet velvet. That's how my tongue will feel in your mouth. On your pretty breasts. Your fingers and toes and pussy and everywhere in between."

Casey gave out a little moan, then caught her breath. "I love feeling your hands on me, too," she told him.

"There's not a place on your beautiful body I'm not gonna make love to. You know, you smell like the purple flowers on my grandma's backyard arbor every spring. I like the contrast. Incredibly sexy woman and sweet old-fashioned smell."

"You like old-fashioned?"

Craig liked Casey. Everything about her. But he wasn't about to come across like a wet-behind-the-ears schoolboy. After all, the article said phone sex should be explicit. "I like you hot, wet, and wanting me as much as I want you. Are you?"

"Uh-huh. And I like you hard. Are you hard now?"

"Hard isn't the word." He was about to burst out of the condom.

"Craig?"

"Yeah, baby?"

"Tell me how we'll make love."

Lightning quick came to mind, especially when he recalled what she'd done to him with her mouth and tongue. "Maybe I'll tie you up and have my wicked way with you. Does that turn you on?"

"Could you be a little more…uh, specific?"

"I'll taste every inch of your luscious body. Make you come and come and come before I slip my cock inside you and take us both to heaven." In his dreams. More likely, he'd push inside her and explode faster than a speeding bullet. Casey's ragged breathing punctuated the silence. So did his when he used his own hand on his cock the way she'd used hers last night.

Maybe if he came now, he'd be able to hold out longer tomorrow. Craig tried to hold back the primal sound that came out a few seconds later when he let himself go. But he couldn't.

"Hey, are you okay?" Casey asked, her voice a little shaky.

"I'm fine," he croaked between waves of pleasure far more intense than he'd felt when he gave himself hand jobs without Casey on the phone and on his mind.

Then it hit him. She sounded as though she didn't realize he'd just climaxed. But she had to know. She was the one with all the sex savvy.

"Just thinking about you made me come. I bet I can make you come, too. Are you hot?"

"On fire."

He pulled off the condom and tossed it in the trash before going on. "Touch yourself."

"Where?" She sounded as though she didn't know. As though she were still a virgin.

Craig figured he'd play along, let her pretend she really didn't have a clue. "Spread your legs, the way you're going to spread them for me. Use one finger and slide it along your pussy. Feel how wet you are. Then find your clit—that little nub of nerves above your vagina—and concentrate on it."

"Ooh. I'm wet and slick down there. And I think I've found it. What now?" she asked.

Imagining Casey fingering herself was getting Craig hard again. "Rub round and round in a circle. Feel your clit getting hard. And wetter. Are you getting wetter, baby?"

Her heavy breathing hinted she was getting close. "Sopping," she hissed, and then she moaned again.

"Okay. Pinch your nipples with your other hand. Tug at them. Pretend it's me licking and nipping at them while I'm pumping my cock into your pretty little pussy. I'm ready, too, you know. It hasn't been ten minutes since I came and you've got me ready to come again."

"Oh, yesss," she hissed. "Come for me. And make me come. Oooh, it feels so good."

"Rub your clit a little harder. Feel good?"

Chapter Seven

"Oh, yes. Yessss. Craig, I'm coming. It feels so-oo..." Her voice trailed off as waves of sensation kept coming one after the other. "Thank you," she told him when the tremors finally slowed to a gentle purring deep in her belly.

"Go to sleep now. Dream about me. I'll pick you up tomorrow at five-thirty."

Craig's soft chuckle brought Casey back from a world devoid of everything but the tempest that had just claimed her. A storm like nothing she'd experienced before. Sensations churned inside her, then slowed to a languid rolling simmer. Fiery heat gave way to a soft, warm afterglow.

She'd just had her first climax with Craig.

And he'd done it for her from a distance with that deep, mesmerizing voice and some sexy suggestions. To be more accurate, he'd made her do it to herself.

She couldn't wait to come again. With Craig, next time in the flesh instead of on the phone. Only with him. Next time they'd do it all. Tomorrow night she was going to make love with a man so skilled at sex that he'd made her come just by talking to her. On the phone, yet.

He'd seduced her completely with his voice. No visuals. No smells or tastes or touches. Just erotic suggestions made in the sexiest ways Casey could imagine.

She could hardly wait for him to make love to her for real.

* * * * *

He'd talked her into coming, on the phone. Seduced her with words.

And that terrified him.

Craig should have expected it. After all, he made his living persuading juries that defendants needed to be in jail. He had a knack for talking. Everybody said so, from Wells down to the reporters and court groupies who showed up whenever he took a case to trial.

He'd talked a good seduction. Too good, he thought when he imagined the main event scheduled for tomorrow night. Casey would be expecting fireworks, and he was afraid he was going to be a dud.

After all, she'd almost certainly been with men who knew their way around a woman a hell of a lot better than he did, even after all the reading he'd done.

Talking couldn't hold a candle to action. And reading couldn't substitute for experience.

Damn it, he should have picked a virgin to seduce. Preferably one who'd never been on a date before. An innocent who didn't have the moxie to realize he didn't know one end of a woman from the other.

Well, he wasn't quite that ignorant. Still he should have hit on a woman who was clueless.

But he wanted Casey. She'd burrowed her way under his skin. And not just because he was hot to fuck her. He was afraid he'd gone and fallen in love. No way would he tell her, though. Not when he knew she might laugh him out of bed after they made love.

The light from across the courtyard cast light through his kitchen window. For a long time he sat and stared at it. Then he glanced at the stack of books on the table and mentally consigned his brother to hell.

If Alan had waited a couple more months before knocking Lurleen up, Craig wouldn't be a twenty-seven-year-old virgin, scared shitless of messing up his first sexual experience. He'd have sampled sex with his high school girlfriend–probably

plural girlfriends. He'd have been oblivious to the risks involved.

Of course he probably would have kept on the fast track toward self-destruction in other ways if it hadn't been for his brother's fate. He'd most likely have found himself in courtrooms several times by now, only as a defendant instead of a prosecuting attorney.

On balance, he guessed he should thank his brother. If he were a criminal and not a lawyer, Casey wouldn't give him the time of day. Still, nothing had scared him this much since the day a year ago when he had to stand in front of a jury and deliver his first opening argument.

Then he'd had to persuade twelve men and women to convict a repeat wife abuser the defense claimed had acted in self-defense. Losing that case could have meant being relegated to arraignments and legal research for the next six months or so. Winning had set him on the fast track toward achieving his own professional goals.

Craig would approach this weekend the same way he had that trial—he'd give it his best shot. Surely a guy who could make a woman come over the phone could have sex with her in person without turning it into a complete disaster.

And if he believed that, he figured he might as well make an offer for that piece of prime Everglades real estate that half the lawyers in his office were always trying to sell each other.

* * * * *

Early the next morning Craig shoved his insecurities aside, went to work, and started putting together his case for Ranger's prosecution.

"Want to work out together on the bikes this weekend?"

Craig looked up at Dwayne Cramer, the other triathlon participant for the state attorney's team at the upcoming games. "I can't." The last thing he wanted to think about now was that

damn triathlon and what participating in it was likely to do to his bum leg.

"Can't?" Dwayne sounded incredulous. "The race is only a week away."

"I know. But I'm spending the weekend down on Sanibel." Besides, there was no way Craig was going to climb on a bike or subject his body to the impact of an all-out run before he had to.

"Planning to do some open water swimming?"

More like he had a closed-door disaster on the docket. Unfortunately Craig couldn't talk himself out of embarking upon the debacle that was practically certain to happen. But Dwayne didn't need to know that.

"I'm planning to get in a swim or two. But I'm taking my girlfriend," Craig mentioned in case his colleague took it in his head to pack up his family and tag along.

"Girlfriend, huh? I just bet you're gonna hit the surf. Didn't your coaches in college tell you too much sex before a race saps a guy's strength?"

"Probably." They might have said that if Craig had ever asked. "But I'll take my chances."

Dwayne grinned. "Want some company?"

"No." An audience with a big mouth was the last thing Craig needed.

"Sounds serious."

"Could be."

"Have fun." Dwayne glanced down at Craig's notes and snickered.

"Better not get addicted to a woman the way Ranger says he did. You wouldn't want to go bonkers and start ramming cars on the Interstate when the lady gets smart and dumps you."

"Don't you have work you need to do?"

"Yeah. As I said, have fun."

"I will." Craig wished. He also wished to hell he could get his cock off his mind long enough to prepare for Ranger's trial.

Too bad that sex—or the lack thereof—was the cornerstone of the accused's defense.

* * * * *

Four more hours. Casey mopped sweat off her brow at the end of the lunch-hour aerobics class she taught and leaned heavily against the front desk at the gym. It was a good thing she didn't have anything scheduled for today that required serious thought, because Craig had been on her mind ever since he made her come last night. She conjured up a smile and a friendly wave for Todd when he waddled out of the locker room.

"So who's the lucky guy?" Todd slapped the medical release Casey had requested onto the counter at the gym.

"What guy?" As if she could get Craig off her mind even for a second.

"The one you said yes to after you told me no." He smiled, but his jowls quivered more than usual.

"What makes you think I said yes to anyone?" Surely she wasn't that transparent.

"I came by yesterday and heard you asking Russ for some time off. And you're marked off the schedule earlier than usual today. It makes sense that you'd have someplace to go and somebody to do it with."

Casey shrugged.

"Earth to Casey."

"Sorry, Todd."

"I just said to have fun. Whoever you're doing it with." Todd backed away from the desk and headed for the sauna.

Casey stared at the medical release he'd given her, then filed it away and tried to banish this weekend from her mind.

Eating lasagna with Todd wouldn't have left her with her brain fried and her libido in shaky control. But she had something much, much more appetizing on her menu for tonight.

She could hardly wait.

* * * * *

Control. That's what he needed. Self-control. Unfortunately it had flown out the window the first time Casey had touched his thigh. And he hadn't managed to get it back.

Craig checked his duffel bag again. Swim suit. Check. Shorts and T-shirts. Check.

He tossed in a pair of casual slacks. They might come in handy if she wanted to go somewhere halfway dressy to eat.

Oops. Better not forget the shaving kit. According to the experts, five o'clock shadow might be sexy to look at, but women didn't much like the feel of it against their silky skin. Craig unzipped the kit and stashed a box of condoms inside. He stuffed another box of them into the plain brown paper bag that held his sex toys.

Fat chance he'd dredge up the guts to try any of them. Still, the idea of teasing Casey with that vibrator got him hard. So hard his cock throbbed. But he didn't have time to take the edge off. He had to pick her up in fifteen minutes.

It was going to be a long, long two hours until they got to Sanibel.

* * * * *

Long, but not long enough. Casey didn't know whether she wanted to fall into Craig's arms or run as fast as she could in the opposite direction. He looked so good, so confident, so downright sexy as he filled the gas tank at the entrance to the Interstate. A shiver ran down her spine despite the ninety-degree day.

Ann Jacobs

88

"Want the top down?" he asked.

"Sure." She dug in her bag and found a headband while he pulled back the convertible top and let the late afternoon sun bear down on them.

At least she wouldn't feel as though she had to carry on a conversation—she'd be free to look at him and fantasize. And ignore the fear that he might laugh her right out of bed.

He slid under the wheel and pushed his dark aviator glasses onto his forehead, giving her a glimpse of those gorgeous clear-blue eyes. "You okay?" he asked, as if he'd read her mind.

"Oh, yeah. I'm ready."

He pulled the shades over his eyes and gunned the engine, then put the car in gear. A warm breeze grew stronger as they sped along I-75 toward Fort Myers.

Urban sprawl soon gave way to flatlands populated mostly by cattle and citrus trees. An occasional long-legged crane fished for its supper in the canals that led out to the Gulf.

The flatness of the land reminded Casey of the high plateaus of northwest Texas where she'd grown up. But it was different. Tropical and lush. Elemental and focused.

Like the way Craig made her feel. She'd taken off on a sensual journey that had only one destination.

When she laid her hand on his khaki-clad thigh, his muscles contracted. The way he had that first night, he caught her hand. But this time he didn't push it away.

He circled the back of her hand with one finger. Sensation spread up, then down.

Casey's cheeks grew hot despite the wind on her face. Muscles in her lower abdomen clenched, then mellowed to a liquid sort of glow.

He shuddered as if in pain. In slow motion he dragged her hand up. Her fingertips grazed taut, male flesh. His swollen cock felt rock-hard beneath her fingers when he squeezed them

closed around the throbbing shaft. The teeth of his zipper dug into her palm.

Being hard like that had to hurt him.

You can do him in the car. Get him primed for later.

Lisa's words echoed in Casey's ear. She found his zipper tab.

Swearing, he grasped the wheel with both hands.

Her confidence soared.

His knuckles whitened, and he held onto the steering wheel as though he was barely in control. He kept both eyes glued to the road as they sped down the nearly deserted highway.

"Casey, damn it, stop or I'll…"

"What, Craig?" She liked testing his control.

She dragged his zipper down, found the placket in his boxer shorts. Freed his cock and balls. When she ran a finger along the throbbing vein that ran the length of his rigid shaft, he shuddered.

Her pussy wept hot, slick honey, making her wish she could climb onto his lap and fill the aching emptiness that had suddenly become unbearable.

She thought he said something when she massaged the base of his cock with a slow, steady rhythm, but the words blew away on an arid wind faintly tinged with salt from the Gulf.

Casey couldn't resist tasting him. She bent, took him between her lips. The glistening drop of silky fluid at the tip tasted salty on her tongue.

She wanted more. She wanted it all. All of him filling the empty place between her legs. The void in her heart. She took more of him in her mouth. He bucked against her.

Then an air horn shattered the silence.

Chapter Eight

Casey's head collided with the steering wheel. Craig struggled to hold the car on the road. The way she shoved him back inside his boxers and tugged his zipper up felt more like desperation than seduction.

What a way to go from the brink of ecstasy to acute embarrassment in the time it took a passing semi driver to honk his horn! He'd lost his fucking mind. So, apparently, had Casey.

Damn it, he should have let her hand stay where it was, not urged it upward. He sure as hell should have put on the brakes before she'd started doing things to his cock that could have taken him to heaven — or just as easily landed them both in some rural county lockup.

At least one of them should damn well have remembered they were in a low-slung convertible with the top down — and thought about the show they'd be giving passing truckers.

Not to mention any Florida State Troopers who might be driving along the road in SUVs.

But her mouth had felt so good on him. Good enough to squelch the doubts that had assailed him ever since he realized he didn't have a snowball's chance of fooling her into thinking he was as savvy in bed as she. And too good for him to feel more than relief that it had been a semi driver and not a cop who'd passed by and gotten an eyeful.

Hell, he could hardly wait to get them to that resort hotel where he'd booked their room so he could beg her to continue. No matter what the end result might be.

Craig glanced at Casey and smiled. Then he noticed tears streaming from her eyes.

He pulled off the Interstate onto a two-lane state road and pulled over onto the shoulder.

"What's wrong?"

"God, Craig, I'm sorry."

He brushed the tears off her cheeks. "Sorry? I'm not. Well, I'm only sorry we had to stop. What you were doing to me—it just about blew my mind."

She only sobbed harder.

"Come on, baby. No harm was done."

"You must think I'm—"

He covered her mouth with one hand, then took off his dark glasses and looked into her eyes. "I think you're the sexiest woman I've ever known. And I can hardly wait to get you all to myself, with no bosses or truck drivers to horn in on our fun."

"You're not angry?" She blinked, then rubbed the back of her head.

"A little, but with myself. It never struck me what a vicarious thrill we might give to anybody passing by in a truck or SUV. But then, you had my mind pretty well occupied with other things."

Casey shot him the come-on smile that had drawn him to her in the first place.

"You've kept my mind occupied with *other things* since before you asked me out. But still...."

"Still what?" he asked.

"Couldn't we have gotten arrested for...for indecent exposure or something?"

That was the least serious of several misdemeanors Craig could think of that might have earned them a week or so in jail. Casey didn't need to know that, though.

"The driver who honked isn't likely to report us. Even if he did, no one would come after us. It would be our word against his. We already got our punishment—the embarrassment we felt when he honked that air horn." He rubbed the swollen spot on

the back of her head. "And this bump where the steering wheel got you."

As he stroked her, he wondered if the impact had done any real damage. "Are you okay?"

"Uh-huh." She plucked his sunglasses from his hand and set them on the console. "The sun's starting to go down. I want to see your gorgeous eyes."

"Then let's get back on the road. I've got plans that involve a beach view, a king-size bed, and long uninterrupted hours of getting to know you from head to toe."

* * * * *

"Here we are." After they crossed the toll bridge and drove onto the island, Craig slowed the car and turned onto a drive lined with palm trees and lush with tropical greenery.

Casey choked back a very un-savvy exclamation when she saw a gorgeous dusky pink hotel set at the tip of a sandy beach. Self-conscious, she smiled and took in the sights as they drove into the resort compound.

"Look, a tennis court. Maybe we can play a few games before—"

"The love we're gonna make doesn't involve a net and racquets." He took a hand off the wheel long enough to caress her bare thigh. "Come on, let's get checked in and…"

She tried for a nonchalant look as she preceded him into a lobby filled with art deco furniture and lush greenery.

At the registration desk she returned the clerk's welcoming smile, hoping her expression masked doubts that lurked dangerously just beneath her skin. Apparently Craig had no second thoughts. He laughed at something the clerk said as he signed the credit card slip with a bold black slash of his pen.

Of course he probably did weekends like this all the time.

Casey tried to tamp down the sudden jealousy that surfaced when she imagined him with other lovers.

"Have fun, you two," the clerk said as he handed Craig two plastic key cards. "You're in Room 169. It's on the ground floor overlooking the Gulf. Do you need a bellman to help with your bags?"

"No thanks. I can handle them."

Craig handed Casey one of the cards.

Did her hand shake when she took the card? She hoped not.

She followed him down a long hallway. Paintings along the way sent subtly sexual messages with their vivid swirling colors and blurred phallic symbols.

A message she got well enough without visual stimuli.

Craig opened the door to the room and set their luggage down. Casey sniffed the air. It smelled of sea salt and vanilla and something darkly sensual. Something elusive.

Musk?

She sought out the source of the strangely sensual scent. There it was. On the dresser.

Silver spangles embedded in two fat white candles caught her eye. Their red-orange flames flickered in the breeze.

She noticed Craig flipping through an advertisement for local restaurants. The room's sensual invitation didn't seem to have fazed him.

Casey tried not to care, but it was hard, watching him concern himself with food when all she could think about was getting naked and getting it on.

"What say we go get something to eat?" he asked.

"Okay." She wasn't about to argue. Part of her wanted him now, but a scared little voice inside her said to grab what amounted to a brief reprieve.

"There's a seafood place a half-mile or so down the beach. We can walk." He grabbed her hand and practically tugged her out of their room.

Strange behavior for a guy who'd had sex foremost on his mind moments earlier.

He seemed no more anxious than she was to stick around in the luxurious room that faced the Gulf and boasted a sunken whirlpool tub for two and a big round bed with a mirrored canopy. She even thought she'd seen him blush when he'd checked out titles of the DVDs in a tower beside the giant TV.

Were they erotica or porn or just plain R-rated movies with suggestive titles? She didn't know. But she was grateful she wasn't going to find out right away.

* * * * *

Dusk settled in as they made their way down the pale sandy beach. A neon crab sign and a giant pink neon flamingo flashed in the distance. Casey noticed a huge replica of a Budweiser can perched atop the building with the flamingo logo.

The summer sun formed a fiery ball in the western sky, its glow transforming the puffy white clouds to shades of rose and pink, lavender and gray. The same waves that bathed shores all along the Gulf sloshed gently against the sand. For the moment she let herself pretend she and Craig were the only people in a vast world of land and sea. A romantic world where raw sexual need cloaked itself in the tender emotion called love.

She squeezed his hand.

He squeezed back.

The unease that had gripped her when they crossed the threshold into their hotel room was dissipating. It seemed she and Craig had no need for conversation now. That their minds were perfectly attuned. Focused on this minute, this place, each other. It was almost as if they were in love, not merely almost lovers.

When he looked at the weathered wooden restaurant with its neon crab in a neon trap, then at her, she smiled and nodded. The delicious aroma of clean sea air and spicy seafood gumbo filled her nostrils when they stepped inside.

Seated at a rough-hewn table overlooking the Gulf, they looked over a menu someone had written by hand on a wobbly chalkboard. A waiter spread newspapers on the table, then set down some appetizers. Blue crabs, apparently the restaurant's featured dish, dominated the tray that also held a basket of fresh raw vegetables, several dips, and two small plates.

With his single hoop earring and scraggly beard, the waiter reminded Casey of the pirates who, legend said, used to do their dastardly deeds along the Texas and Louisiana coastlines. "Enjoy," the waiter said after scribbling their order on a dog-eared pad.

Casey wanted to do just that. If only she could tamp down the worry that had her stomach churning.

"Try this." Craig dipped a cucumber spear and lifted it to her lips.

At least it wasn't the whole cuke. But that didn't stop her from conjuring up Mr. Big in her mind–or remembering what she'd been doing to Craig an hour earlier in his car. Her cheeks burned, and she practically choked on the savory appetizer.

At that moment Craig skewered a cherry tomato, dunked it into the creamy dip, and popped it in his mouth.

Her skin sizzled. She had to be as red as the pile of crab shells on the tray. She dared a surreptitious glance Craig's way. Damn it, he apparently was anticipating nothing more at this moment than the beer-battered shrimp and home fries he'd ordered — that, and making short work of the rest of the appetizers. All she could think of was what they'd done before and what else they'd be doing later. Again she hoped he wouldn't blame her for her deception after they'd made love.

She latched onto the beer the waiter poured from a foam-topped pitcher as if it were a lifeline. Maybe it was. The icy amber brew slid down her parched throat, helped to cool her overheated body.

It seemed to have the opposite effect on Craig. His gorgeous blue eyes darkened almost to the color of a midnight

sky when his gaze settled on her cleavage. Cleavage she'd never before revealed so much of outside her bedroom.

A light gust of wind off the Gulf ruffled his dark hair but he didn't seem to notice. He seemed mesmerized. Vulnerable. Maybe he wasn't as collected as he seemed, because when the waiter set a plate of shrimp and fries in the center of their table, he hardly took notice.

That made Casey smile. How could his mouth not be watering at the sight and smell of the crunchy treats? Hers was. She picked up a jumbo shrimp by its tail, dipped it in cocktail sauce, and held it to his lips.

"Eat. You'll need your strength."

"Damn right I will." He grinned, then took the whole shrimp in his mouth, leaving Casey holding the severed tail. He never took his gaze off her when he reached for another of the deep-fried morsels and held it to her lips. "You'll need your energy, too. Eat."

She hadn't realized before now that eating could be a sensual feast. It was, though. When they'd shared the last shrimp, she watched Craig lick his lips. His tongue snaked out, caught a bit of foam, retreated. Then he did it again, slowly finding the last of the white foam as he looked at her.

Was he imagining licking her that way? Casey recalled his husky promise to taste every inch of her body. Suddenly she couldn't wait for him to do it. The wanting was suddenly much stronger than her fear.

She laid her hand high up on his thigh and met his gaze. "Let's go back to our room."

* * * * *

They took off their shoes and walked down the rickety stairs of the restaurant into the velvet darkness. A sliver of a golden moon barely penetrated the vast black sky.

The wind had picked up since they'd gone into the Crab Shack. Much like the urgency had built up inside her.

A sea bird squawked in the distance. Craig laced his fingers through hers, the way Casey recalled dates doing when she was a kid. His touch held no hint of the tentativeness or hesitation she remembered sensing from would-be teenage lovers, but then he was no kid on a desperate quest for grown-up sex.

A sudden gust of wind came off the water and whipped at her hair. Her bare legs grew goose bumps. She trembled from the cold, but her hand was warm and securely enfolded with Craig's.

He stopped. Turned. As though he felt the chill that had engulfed her, he cupped her face with both of his hands. He ran a thumb over her lips. "You're cold, baby. But you won't be cold for long." He lowered his head and took her mouth.

Softly. Tenderly. Then harder.

She opened to him, unable to resist his unspoken desire for more. He swept his tongue inside, still cupping her face with both hands.

The rising tide sent waves crashing against the shore. Mellow instrumental music wafted through the air from a nearby club, its tropical drumbeat mingling with the sounds of the sea. They were two, yet one, alone in a world where nature reigned, alive and primal on the beach where it merged with man-made temptation.

Craig deepened the kiss. He devoured her mouth. His tongue thrust deep, hard, in an erotic, exotic rhythm not unlike the sounds around them. Waves breaking over sand. Sea birds calling. Music beckoning patrons to the clubs along this finger of Sanibel Island sandwiched between the Gulf and the historic city of Fort Myers.

The cacophony of sounds would always remind her of Craig. A mix of exotic, erotic, and country-western twang. The mix was singularly sensual.

Casey wasn't cold anymore. She wrapped her arms around Craig and drew him closer. Seeking bare skin, she slid her hands under his soft knit shirt. He shuddered, but his skin was warm

when Casey stroked him. The rock-hard muscles above his waistband rippled against her fingers.

He broke the kiss and moved his hands down from her face. Her bare skin tingled everywhere he touched her–her neck, the upper curve of her breasts, her back. Though the darkness obscured his expression, she imagined his heated gaze following his hands.

The muscles in his back tightened beneath her fingers when he cupped the curve of her buttocks and pulled her hard against him.

He wanted her as much as she wanted him. Casey exulted in the knowledge, in the feel of his cock, huge and rigid behind the zipper of his khaki shorts. They weren't just having sexual foreplay. They were making love. At least she was.

She rested her cheek against his chest and listened to his heart pound against her ear. Should she share her feelings, let him know how dear he'd become to her after a few short days?

Suddenly he tore himself away and grabbed her hand. "Let's go inside now. You've got me crazy for you."

Chapter Nine

Crazy for you.

She might not have much experience, but Craig's comment sounded like a statement of raw sexual need, not undying devotion. Banishing her disappointment, she held her own feelings deep inside, certain he wouldn't want to hear them.

In their room a few minutes later, Casey gathered her sexy things and retreated to the bathroom. With luck she'd manage to gather up the nerve to go to him without too long a delay.

* * * * *

Craig stripped down, then stashed his sex toys and a box of condoms in a slide-open compartment built into the headboard on the big round bed.

He stood in the patio doorway, his gaze fixed on a faraway light that penetrated the almost moonless darkness.

Why was Casey taking so long?

He glanced at the wide expanse of hot-pink sheets and ivory blankets he'd turned back moments earlier. Maybe he should turn on some sexy music on the stereo, then crawl in bed to wait for her.

No. If he lay down, he'd be staring up at that mirror inside the canopy. Looking straight at his own doubt and vulnerability.

By the time Casey joined him, his face would be as red as the shells on the crab they'd had before dinner.

He mentally reviewed what he'd learned in his studies this week.

Slow. Easy.

His balls ached and his cock swelled to full erection. Slow and easy, he imagined, would be easier said than done.

Talk sex talk but nothing too explicit. Dirty language turns some women off.

Four-letter words wouldn't bother Casey, unless he missed his guess. Still, he'd watch his mouth. He'd never been much for using locker room language anyhow.

Be gentle the first time you make love. Even if it's not her first time.

Good luck there. Already he was close to losing it, and they hadn't even made it into bed.

"Craig?"

His mouth went dry at the sight of her, barefoot and apparently naked beneath a short robe. The thing looked like a man's shirt except that it was made out of something shiny, slippery looking, and blacker than the sky outside. Her legs seemed to go on forever.

He'd soon know how it felt to have them wrapped around his waist.

That thought sent blood rushing to his groin and left him dizzy with anticipation.

She unbuttoned the robe. But she wasn't naked underneath. His mouth went dry at the sight of taut, female flesh veiled in something black. Something so sheer he could make out the indentation of her belly button in the dim light provided by flickering candles and the fluorescent glow that flooded the room through the open bathroom door.

Her puckered nipples poked impudently against the fabric, beckoning his hands and mouth. But he couldn't drag his gaze from the tiny heart-shaped patch of lace that drew his attention to the apex of her thighs.

"Like the robe? I got you one, too." She tossed an identical garment his way. "You don't have to put it on if you don't want to."

Craig had the feeling he was about to embarrass himself. She only thought he didn't need to cover up. Her gaze scorched him as he shrugged into the robe.

Cool and satiny, the fabric should have felt like a caress. Instead it made his skin prickle everywhere it made contact. His fingers were beyond tackling the buttons, so he didn't even try.

His balls tightened when the edges of the robe brushed against them.

He had to think of something else or...he'd concentrate on her.

Her dark-brown hair, freed from its ponytail, cascaded down her back. Looking at it made him want to sink his fingers into the soft mass of curls. The candlelight cast golden shadows across her shoulders and breasts. His mouth watered with anticipation.

The first time, the man should be the aggressor.

He took one step toward Casey. Then he remembered another author's succinct advice.

Let her make the first move.

Casey stood her ground, a look that hinted at confusion on her pretty face.

Hell, he must be attributing his own insecurities to her again.

Which of the so-called experts who'd written those books had his head on straight? Why hadn't he just picked out just one book and stuck with it? Craig gave himself a mental kick in the ass.

Then his animal instincts took over and overrode his brain. He closed the distance between them and drew Casey into his arms.

She wasn't scared anymore, now that he held her. His hard male heat drove the chill from skin that still felt damp from the shower. She curled her toes into the plush carpet that cradled her bare feet.

She tried to tamp down the nerves that had kept her cowering in the bathroom long after she should have slipped into her new nightie and come out to entice her soon-to-be lover.

Ambivalent. That was the word for the thoughts that had gripped her. Wanting, yet reluctant to take the step she feared would reveal her deception. Needing, yet afraid she would drive him away. Not afraid of him, though. Never afraid of him.

Those thoughts faded in the wake of new, arousing sensations. His heartbeat, strong and steady against her breast. The sound of the tide and a cool breeze wafting through the door to the patio.

The faint taste of sea salt on her tongue when she nuzzled the tender spot where his shoulder met his neck.

This was what she'd wanted. Why she'd left Bone Gap and changed the way she dressed and talked. Why she'd enlisted Lisa's aid to remake herself into the kind of woman a man like Craig would want to sleep with.

Now he was about to make one of her fantasies come alive.

Casey banished the worries about those other dreams of happily ever after–dreams Buck had trampled along with her illusion that he'd desired her this way, too.

Craig's big hands molded her buttocks, lifted her. When his steely length seared her belly, molten liquid spread through her veins and pooled between her legs. Primal need chased away the remnants of her fear.

Then he kissed her. His lips urged hers apart, and his tongue mated with hers. He tasted like he smelled—clean, slightly salty, uniquely male.

He set her down, broke the kiss and nuzzled her neck before stepping back a little. "Let's go to bed," he said, holding out his hand.

Should she take off the nightie or leave it on? What would Lisa do? Easy. She'd strip naked and think nothing of it. Casey tried for a seductive smile as she slid her robe off her shoulders. The material tickled her feet when it puddled there. Craig's lips

curved in a smile. His gaze was pure blue flame, flame that fueled her ridiculous fear.

She was an idiot. She knew it. He'd seen her naked before. God knew she was all but naked now. So why were her hands refusing to grasp the nearly transparent material and tug it over her head?

"May I?" He skimmed his hands over her hips, under the nightie she still hadn't found the courage to shed. His smooth, hot palms and callused fingers slid higher, bringing the fabric with them as they caressed the indentation at her waist, the lower curve of her breasts.

She thought she felt his hands shake when he brought the nightgown over her head and let it go, to float slowly on the breeze until it settled on the floor a few feet away.

"God, you're beautiful." Craig sounded tortured as he scooped her up and deposited her on the big, round bed. He looked tormented when he lay beside her and started to pluck at her nipples.

His erection bored into her thigh. She thought about touching him the way he was touching her, then remembered what Lisa had told her.

Not unlike their brains, men's sensations are mostly in their cocks. Play with them there and you can't go wrong. But how? She reached down and brushed his thigh.

When he moaned and shifted onto his back, she slid a hand across his belly. Her fingers barely brushed the tip of his cock, even when she stretched as far as she could.

She liked his touch, anywhere. The solution was obvious. She'd have to move so she could touch him where he liked it best.

Trying not to think about the view she'd be providing him, she gathered her courage, sat upright, surveyed the scene, straddled his broad chest, and sucked the swollen head of his cock between her lips. With both hands she cradled his velvety scrotum.

All of a sudden Craig was staring at delicious looking silky female flesh bisected by nothing but the skinny piece of black elastic that anchored that intriguing little black lace heart to the center of her velvet-smooth mound.

Her outer lips were baby-soft and slick with moisture. Fuck. She was already wet, and he sure as hell was ready. Looking at her this way was enough to drive a man insane. Especially when he was enduring the exquisite sort of torture Casey apparently liked inflicting on him so much.

His brain was like mush, his cock hard as a stone. His balls were about to explode.

He wished he knew better how to treat her to some similar torture.

Brushing the elastic aside, he traced the damp cleft where it had been with his finger. When he found her clit and circled it, she rewarded him with a moan that vibrated around his aching cock.

He lifted his head and licked along the path his finger had just made. With his tongue, he explored the impossibly tight channel he'd soon fill with himself. She tasted delicious. The chocolate stuff he bought couldn't hold a candle to her own sweet honey.

She took his cock all the way down her throat and swallowed.

Shit. If she kept that up, he was going to come. But if she quit, he'd die.

Unless… "Come here."

"M-mmm?"

Her muted question vibrated through his cock to his muddled brain.

"Now." He had to hurry or the main event would be over before it began. He snatched off her ridiculous little G-string as he hauled her off him. Then he reached blindly for a condom and damn near slid off the big round bed.

"Are you okay?" she asked.

"Yeah." Some smooth lover he was turning out to be.

He sat up, then dived for the headboard and his stash of protection. He came up with one that was wrapped in silver foil.

It triggered a memory of the chocolate candy coins his mom used to put in his Christmas stocking. Very briefly. His whole being focused on another sort of treat. A treat he couldn't wait to sample. Not trusting his hands not to shake, he handed her the condom. "Put it on me," he croaked.

"Okay. Lie back."

Why the hell did she have to sound so calm, as if she did this every day? Eyes closed, he held his breath and tried to memorize the smell of sweet flowers and candle wax and musky bodies he'd always associate with Casey and making love.

He wanted her talented hands on him again. Now. Then terror struck. What if he couldn't do this? What if it wasn't as easy as Dr. So-and-So had made it sound in that how-to book?

He told himself now wasn't the time to panic. Or to hesitate. He was nuts. Every cell in his body was screaming that it was ready. He couldn't freakin' stop now. He didn't want to stop.

How hard could it be? For thousands of years men and women had been having sex. It stood to reason that not all of them had been experts. And every man had been a virgin once.

Small solace that was now.

Maybe she'd climb on top. Take charge. Maybe she wouldn't realize how green he really was. Craig could only hope. He prayed she'd hurry up with that damn condom.

Casey wished she could stop shaking. And that the crimped foil would quit resisting her efforts to peel it away. Why hadn't Lisa warned her that not all condoms came in easy-to-rip-off plastic wrappers? Finally. She had it open.

It was cold and wet and slippery and—finally—in her hand. She tried to hurry and pick off the bits of foil that still clung to the lubricated latex, but her fingers wouldn't cooperate.

Eyeing her target, she raised up on her knees. Craig was shaking, too. Small surprise considering how long she'd taken to peel off the stubborn foil. But he was also magnificent.

Remembering Lisa's instructions, she took her time rolling the slippery condom down the impressive length of his shaft, smoothing each tiny wrinkle until he stilled her hand.

"Climb aboard," he said, a sexy grin on his lips.

Her jaw dropped so far she felt it pop.

His sheathed sex stood at attention against his flat, muscular abdomen. Was it her imagination or had he somehow gotten even bigger?

"Hurry." He sounded pained.

Her mind churned. What did he want? *Idiot. He wants you to get on top.*

She could almost hear Lisa telling her to go for it. But no way could she… She didn't have the vaguest notion what to do. He'd know for sure if she tried to take the lead.

"You come here." She flopped onto her back, squeezed her eyes shut, and prayed he wouldn't take off running. *Not a sexy move, Casey.*

But Craig didn't run for cover. His hot, hard cock seared her belly, and the pressure from his upper body momentarily stole her breath. When he propped himself up on one elbow, she took in much-needed air. Slightly salty air heavy with moisture and the smells of him and her and sex.

"I'm here, honey. Now what do you want me to do?" He looked at her, his sapphire gaze intent.

Easy question. "Make love to me."

"My pleasure." His free hand traced a path along her hipbone. He retraced that path once, twice, three times. Heat built beneath his touch.

The gentle friction aroused her more. Almost as much as his rigid cock throbbing against her mound. But the touch of his hands wasn't nearly as terrifying.

"Casey?"

"Yes?"

She had no reason to be afraid. None. This was what she wanted. Who she wanted.

He raised his torso, nudged at her thigh. "Let me in."

"Oh." Damn, he shouldn't have had to ask.

When she spread her legs, she inadvertently kneed his washboard abs. Not a smooth move. At this rate she'd never be able to fool him. "Sorry."

"It's okay."

But he didn't sound okay. He sounded as though somebody was torturing him.

She shifted, opened wider to give him room. His sheathed cock grazed her mound and teased the sensitized tissue around her vagina. He flexed his hips, then pushed a little way inside her.

God, he felt huge. She clutched his shoulders.

Easy, Casey. You can take him. Women have been doing this for thousands of years.

Craig felt her fingers dig into his shoulders, even harder than her cunt was contracting around his cock. She was tight. Incredibly tight. This felt so good it hurt.

He gritted his teeth. No way could he go slow. But he had to try.

When he pushed in another inch, the muscles in her stomach tensed up. He had to be doing something wrong, but damned if he knew what. The book hadn't mentioned that this might hurt her if she wasn't a virgin, and no way could that be.

Unless, he remembered reading, he was unusually big.

He didn't think his cock was *that* big. He'd noticed a few guys in locker rooms with more impressive equipment than his. Still, she acted as if he was hurting her.

He stopped the slow forward motion of his hips and murmured her name. Every cell in his body screamed out at the loss of that delicious friction.

"Don't stop."

She didn't sound as if she meant that, but he was too far gone not to take her at her word. Maybe he should just get it in and over with. Over with being the operative words. He was about to burst.

He pushed.

She tensed up more. But she wrapped her legs around his waist when he started to pull back.

He took that to mean she wanted more, so he drove back in, harder this time. Something gave way, and she cried out. Suddenly he was buried to the hilt in her tight, hot cunt. Her wet flesh throbbed around him. And he had to move.

When he did, she moaned again. It wasn't a happy sort of sound.

Gritting his teeth, he held very still.

She let out a little whimper.

Maybe he was squashing her. He raised his upper body and propped himself up on his elbows. "Better?"

"It's okay."

When she looked up at him and cupped his cheeks between her palms, he noticed tears glistening in her eyes. "You're sure?"

"Yes."

She's sure she wants this over with fast.

Craig was about to oblige her. He felt it coming. If she'd let him touch her again he'd make their next time better. Now he had to—

Thrust hard. Deep. Once. Twice. Three times. He exploded, and then the room turned black.

Wet satiny skin surrounded him. He held a soft, warm woman in his arms. Craig wallowed in mindless sensation. What he'd just experienced was nothing like a solitary do-it-yourself job. It was mind-boggling — incomparable.

Right now Ranger's proposed defense didn't seem outlandish after all. Not while he lay here in the dark, his lover in his arms.

He could easily become addicted.

Chapter Ten

She wasn't a virgin any more.

Craig's chest hair tickled Casey's nipples, drawing her attention from the dull ache between her legs. She skimmed her hand down the sweaty skin along his backbone. Their lovemaking hadn't made her hear bells and see fireworks inside her head. Trust her to have been born with a hymen tougher than boot leather. She should have figured, considering her past luck.

Losing it had hurt. Until right before the end, when a sort of urgency had overwhelmed the pain and made her reach out to experience the stars she sensed lay just beyond her reach.

Did he know he'd been her first? Would he want to try again, or would her obvious deception make him turn away? "Craig?"

He shifted, aligned their bodies even closer. And snored.

Obviously he didn't want another go, at least not now.

His heart beat strong and slow, a soothing reminder of his presence. The sweat on his shoulder lent its own salty taste and smell to the air that wafted through the screened patio doors from a calm sea breeze.

Cast in the pale light from the fragrant candles, his face looked impossibly young. Content. He had eyelashes any woman would kill for. And a strong, solid nose and rugged jaw that shouted predatory male. His sculpted lips looked as delicious as they tasted. As sensual as they felt against the sensitive skin around her pussy.

Casey wanted more of Craig. Much more.

While he slept she explored him with her eyes, traced the path of well-developed muscles beneath satiny tanned skin dusted with soft, dark hair. Then she noticed the faded surgical scar on his outer thigh.

As if he sensed her attention, he moved again. Smiled. And sighed. Then he snored again. It wasn't an unpleasant sound, more like a throaty purr that increased slightly in volume when she rested a hand against his upper thigh.

He sounded downright content.

* * * * *

Could Casey possibly want more?

Through a sated fog, Craig felt her hands on him. Hands, not fists pounding at his flesh in retribution for the way he'd gone at her, the way he'd figured they might. Gentle, soothing hands were quickly bringing his wrung-out cock to life.

Some lover he'd been. He'd violated every rule he'd read about seduction.

He'd lost it. Lost himself in her incredible tight heat, surrendered his mind to sensation. He'd wallowed in the tastes and smells and sounds of sex. In his fuzzy brain he still saw shadowed visions of her face, her mouth, her incredible body cradling his.

He'd surrendered the rational man he was to a ravening beast interested only in his own gratification. And fallen asleep as soon as he'd shot his load. Now his cock was stirring again, apparently anticipating a repeat performance. Hell, he wouldn't blame Casey if she never spoke to him again, let alone–

"You awake?" she asked.

She didn't sound angry. "Uh-huh." He opened one eye. She didn't look pissed, either.

She looked sort of dreamy. Sweet and young and incredibly innocent. Not at all like the brazen Casey who'd practically gotten him off while they were driving down the Interstate.

"I'm sorry."

She was sorry? Yeah, he imagined she was. Sorry she'd ever laid eyes on him. "I'm sorry, too. We'll get it right next time."

"Okay."

Her smile confirmed it. Miraculously, she was okay with his less than studly performance. She was apparently ready to give him another shot at getting it right. Craig couldn't believe his luck, but he wasn't about to complain.

"Are you ready?" she asked, giving him the once-over and grinning, the way the Casey he thought he knew might have done.

"Any time, baby."

Her gaze settled on his cock. "Is that reusable?"

Hell. He'd forgotten about the condom. "No."

He really had lost his mind. Shooting for a sheepish smile, he got up and headed for the bathroom. "Be right back."

Craig dropped the used condom, watched it drift into the trash can. What were those red streaks? All the rubbers he'd bought were flesh-colored.

What the hell?

He picked it up and looked closer. That was blood. He glanced down at himself. It wasn't his.

Casey's? It had to be. But how? Could she have been a virgin?

His cock twitched.

No way.

But she acted as though she thought his definitely less-than-textbook performance had been okay.

Maybe… Craig told himself to get real. No virgin would do the things she'd done to him with her hands and mouth. Which meant he had to have been too rough.

He dropped the condom back in the trash. "Come here."

"Why?"

He had to see how badly he'd hurt her, but he couldn't say that. Craig mentally churned through possible excuses to look her over under the bright fluorescent light. "Let's take a shower," he said, pleased with that solution to his dilemma.

"Together?" Still naked, she stood in the bathroom doorway, a sexy smile on her face.

"Yeah. Is that okay with you?"

"Oh, yes." She raked a hot gaze down his body, lingering on his cock that was growing bigger and harder as she looked at him and he ogled her.

Her full breasts jiggled as she stepped into the oversize shower stall. He reached for them, then stopped. First things first. Needles of icy water stung his flesh and drew goose bumps along the delicious length of Casey's body. Craig adjusted the temperature and gentled the spray. He grasped her hips, knelt. Warm water cascaded over the back of his head as he moved his hands lower, urging her thighs apart.

"Craig?"

"I want to taste you again." When he nuzzled the little heart-shaped patch of short dark curls on her mound, his balls tightened with anticipation. He parted her satiny outer lips and blew gently. Her inner thighs quivered. If he'd hurt her, it didn't show.

With his tongue, he soothed her. Then he drew her clit between his teeth and exerted pressure. Gently, the way the book had said to do. She slid her legs farther apart, moaned. This time it was a sound he thought indicated pleasure.

Though his cock was practically screaming for attention, he ignored its plea. He closed his eyes and concentrated on the smells and tastes and textures of Casey. On making love to her.

Her fingers dug into his scalp, urging him on.

He wanted her to come. He sensed that she wanted that, too. The way he'd coached her to do to herself on the phone, he circled her clit with one finger while he ran his tongue around the entrance to her cunt.

She was so wet. So hot and slick. So incredibly tight. Maybe his cock was too big for her after all. How had she taken him in?

He stabbed at her with his tongue, slipping it inside when her muscles relaxed enough to let him in. She tasted of woman and sex and… A faint metallic smell filled his nostrils when he pulled away. The smell of blood.

Damn it, she'd been a virgin, too.

"Don't stop," she whimpered when he stopped playing with her clit.

God knew he didn't want to. But if he continued, he'd lose control. Hurt her again. He shut off the shower, handed her one bath sheet, and wrapped the other around himself.

"Casey, come on in the bedroom. We need to talk."

* * * * *

Craig indicated that she should sit in one of the barrel chairs by the patio doors, then sank onto the other one. The one that was farthest away from that big round bed where they'd done the deed.

He looked Casey in the eye. "You were a virgin."

He felt cheated. She could tell from his accusatory tone. She couldn't blame him. After all, she was a fraud and he'd caught her at her game.

But she wasn't about to give up. She'd brazen it out, pretend she'd done nothing wrong. Defiant, she looked him in the eye. "Yes. I was. Did I ever tell you I wasn't?"

"Not in so many words. But you sure as hell didn't act like any virgin."

"What do you mean?"

"The gym. The car. Remember?"

She hoped her hot cheeks weren't turning red. "You liked it."

"Sure I did. But I never considered that a virgin might be so into giving head. Where did you learn that?"

She wouldn't let him guilt her out. And she wouldn't let her humiliation show. Chin held high, she met his gaze. "I practiced with a cucumber."

Then Casey glanced at Craig's lap the way she imagined Lisa would have done. "You're a lot more fun to nibble on," she said, licking her lips.

He laughed. "I'm glad." But then his expression sobered and he riddled her with a steely gaze. "Now tell me why you didn't feel the need to let me know this was going to be your first time."

He didn't look or sound glad at all. "Weren't you a virgin once?" she asked, no longer able to brazen this out.

"What?" He hesitated, as though he had to concentrate to remember back that far. "Of course."

"Did you tell the woman it was your first time?"

"No."

No hesitation there, Casey noted. His obvious use of the double standard pissed her off. "Why didn't you tell her?" she asked.

"Guys want women to believe they've been around."

That made Casey madder. "Well then, maybe I felt that way, too. Why are you so angry?"

"Because losing my virginity didn't hurt me. But I hurt you. If I'd have known—"

"What? You'd have stayed a mile away?"

"No." He fixed his gaze on some point across the room and toyed with the knot he'd made in the bath sheet he had wrapped around his waist like a suit of armor.

"No? The way you're acting makes me think—"

"Casey, I wouldn't have stayed away from you. Not for long."

She wanted to believe him. But she wasn't sure. The man made his living persuading folks to his point of view, for God's sake.

"So why are we talking now?" She reached a hand out, touched his arm. "Why are we wrapped up in towels like mummies when we could be over on that bed, wrapped up in each other?"

His biceps muscle tensed beneath her fingers. "We shouldn't—"

"Yes, we should. I want to."

"Believe me, baby, so do I. But you need time—"

"Don't you dare try to tell me what I need. I need to come. And if you don't help me do it, I'll let out a scream folks can hear all the way back in Tampa."

He covered her hand, stroked the knuckles with his index finger. Gently. As if he were petrified that she'd shatter any minute. "Stay there," he said as he got up and strode over to the bed.

His tone didn't encourage disobedience. Casey watched him open the compartment where he'd gotten the condom hours earlier, retrieve a small bottle, and screw off the cap.

What was in it?

He knelt at her feet, peeled back her towel, pulled her to the edge of the chair, and gently pried her knees apart. The stuff he drizzled over her swollen pussy felt smooth and wet and soothing. It smelled a lot like the chocolate-covered cherries Dad always bought for Mom at Christmastime.

"Chocolate?"

"Uh-huh. Feel good?" He'd leaned in so close, his breathing set off vibrations against her inner thighs. "I love chocolate."

She squirmed with anticipation.

His fingers opened her up oh so gently, making room for his mouth to do its magic.

"Oh, yes," she murmured.

His velvety tongue bathed her satin slickness, sending wave after wave of sensation sliding through her.

"More. Oh, yesss." She gasped for breath.

He lifted his head, met her needy gaze. "Tell me what to do, baby."

"Don't stop."

He went back to his feast. A shock went through her when he drew her clit between his teeth and flailed it with his tongue. "Keep doing that. Please. And touch me. My–my breasts."

His groan reverberated against her hot, wet pussy, and what he was doing felt...incredible. She gasped as the most awesome glow she'd ever experienced started deep in her belly and radiated to every cell in her body. "Oh, God. That feels so good. Don't. Don't stop."

Oh, shit. This was what she'd been missing. The pleasant little tinges she'd felt the other night paled beside what was going on inside her now. "Yesss. God, I'm gonna die."

More shock waves radiated from her clit to her pussy to...all the way to the tips of her fingers and toes. And they didn't stop.

Neither did he. He lapped harder while he tugged away her towel and cupped one aching breast in each callused hand. He plucked her nipples gently, then harder. Tugged at them while he pleasured her with his mouth. The pressure let up, then built inside her again to an even more breathtaking level, even as she still shook from the force of her shattering climax.

She felt pressure, not pain. Never pain. Just the promise of ecstasy more intense than she'd dared to imagine. She took his dark head in her hands, pulled him closer as she strained toward another shattering release.

Seeing his large tanned hands on her breasts and watching him love her with his mouth were the most erotic sights she'd ever seen. Like a boulder on the edge of a steep cliff, Casey teetered on the brink. Then she tumbled again into blissful oblivion.

* * * * *

Sex could become addictive. So could waking up to a brilliant sun rising over the Gulf and finding his woman in his bed.

His woman? Craig gave his head a clearing shake. And stared at Casey.

Casey. A sassy-mouthed, super-sexy virgin with seductive skills she'd practiced on a cucumber? Unbelievable. But apparently it was true. He'd been her first.

An unexpected wave of male possessiveness came over him. He'd never considered himself a chauvinist, but he was glad he was her first lover. He wanted to be her only lover. And he wanted her to be his.

Not that he was ready to make a declaration of undying love. He didn't plan on admitting his own recent virginity, either, since she apparently hadn't guessed it for herself.

His morning hard-on throbbed against the juncture of her thighs. It wanted inside her hot, wet cunt, but he didn't want to disturb her rest. A lovemaking position one author had described where the lovers both lay on their sides like this nudged his libido, but he fought the surge of testosterone.

His brain was winning the fight until Casey shifted one leg, unconsciously making room for his cock between them. All he'd have to do was flex his hips and he'd be inside her. That would be enough. He wouldn't have to pound into her like a raging bull.

Right. And rivers didn't have to flow down mountainsides. Maybe after a few hundred times he'd be able to take sex slow and easy. But he didn't trust himself to be gentle now. She had to be sore, no matter how much she protested that she was okay. Right now she needed the sort of restrained sex he couldn't deliver. And she needed sleep.

Craig made himself get up and shower. The only hope he had of keeping his hands off her was to put some distance—and some clothes—between them. He'd take a long swim in the surf,

then have another go at preparing his opening statement in the Ranger case.

By then hopefully he would have put his fledgling sex life into perspective.

* * * * *

Ladies and gentlemen of the jury. My name is Craig McDermott, and I represent the Hillsborough County State Attorney's office.

Why the hell was he writing down the introduction he'd been reciting from memory in every opening statement of every case he'd ever tried? Craig lifted his pencil, nibbled at the eraser, and stared down at the yellow legal pad. A sudden breeze churned the pages, made him slam a fist onto the metal patio table to keep the pad from flying away.

"Damn it." He anchored the pad with one elbow.

Trying to write out here on the patio was insane. But he got a stranglehold on the pencil and gave it another shot.

We're here today to prove the defendant, William Ranger, willfully committed vehicular assault on … Who the hell was the woman whose car Ranger had rammed, anyway? And why wasn't he simply jotting down points he intended to make instead of trying to write the whole damn opening statement out verbatim?

Damn it, he didn't forget victims' names. And he didn't agonize over his presentations, either. At least he never had before. Not since his first mock court in law school.

Apparently having sex for the first time had short-circuited his brain. Craig stretched out his legs and wiggled his bare toes. His long open-water swim had taken the edge off his libido, but it hadn't done much toward getting his mind off Casey.

He glanced inside. She was still curled up around a pillow in the middle of that inviting bed, just as she'd been ten minutes ago. Maybe he should join her.

No. What he should do was get his ass in gear and finish outlining this opening statement. Staring out at the shoreline, he tried to gather his thoughts.

A pelican swooped down into the surf, came up with a small fish. Craig's stomach growled. He was hungry, too. He glanced at his watch. Ten-thirty. Time to order breakfast. It wasn't as if he were getting any work accomplished.

Chapter Eleven

Lulled from sleep a few minutes later by the aroma of bacon and orange juice, Casey opened her eyes and stretched.

"Hey, sleepyhead," Craig said.

"Hey, yourself. Have you been up for long?" She hated thinking she'd slept away a minute they could have spent together.

"A few hours. I went swimming. Want some breakfast?"

Casey wanted to feast on him, but she guessed she'd have to settle for real food—and the visual feast she got, looking at his dynamite upper torso across the small round table where somebody had laid out food and drink.

Catching a glance at herself in the mirror above the bed, she stifled a groan. This was not the way she'd pictured herself looking after a night of hot sex. She had the bed-head from hell. Her hair stuck out all over. The wrinkled sheet had left its imprint on her left cheek, and dark circles rimmed both her eyes.

Only her slightly swollen, reddened lips attested to the fun she'd had last night. The rest of her looked downright ragged out.

Where was her robe? She got up and stumbled around the perimeter of the bed but didn't see it.

"Looking for something?" Craig held out the robe. And grinned.

"Thanks."

Why couldn't she be half as calm and collected as he seemed to be?

Not to mention that it wasn't fair for him to look as put-together as if he'd had a full night's rest while she might have looked better if she'd just now survived a small war.

She put on the robe and fumbled with the buttons. "I–Does it always feel so awkward?"

"Huh?"

"The morning after. Waking up to face somebody you just had sex with."

He had the gall to grin. "Feels great to me. Come on. Breakfast is getting cold."

She needed to splash cold water on her face. Brush her hair. And–

"I'll be right back." She made a run for the bathroom.

* * * * *

"Are you sure you don't need to finish up that work you brought along?" Casey asked when they'd finished eating and were lazing around under a beach umbrella watching seagulls dive for fish caught up in an incoming tide.

"It will wait." Casey wouldn't. Every minute they spent together, Craig learned something new about her. It was as if she were two women.

Which one was real? Was she the bold, brash party girl with a taste for provocative clothes and an impressive talent for oral sex? Or the bashful former virgin who'd needed to cover herself from him this morning, the minute she crawled out of bed?

Could she be both? The possibility intrigued him. He wanted to get inside her head.

He foresaw no problem there. Everybody from his first-year law professors on had raved about his talent for examining witnesses. The same methods ought to work on a lover.

He shot her his standard disarming smile and launched the usual question he opened with when interviewing defendants. "Tell me about yourself."

The way she described Bone Gap, Texas and growing up on a ranch outside the small rural town, Craig got the picture of a woman whose values were rooted in small-town, even old-fashioned standards. Apparently she'd returned there after staying with an elderly aunt while getting her degree at Texas Tech. That picture didn't gibe with his first impression, or the one she'd built upon even after they crawled in bed last night.

"I'm an ordinary country girl." She smiled, but she didn't look him in the eye.

It didn't compute that the sheltered small-town virgin she described would blow his mind in bed. His cock twitched, as though it disagreed.

Her guarded expression reminded him of how witnesses sometimes looked when they were walking a fine line between spinning facts and outright lying. What was she holding back?

"Why did you leave?" he asked.

"Broken engagement. I decided life on the range wasn't for me. Didn't much like the idea of playing second fiddle to a cow. All of the above. Take your pick."

Craig slid his sunglasses off and met her gaze. "I grew up in a little town not far from Dallas. I doubt it was much bigger than Bone Gap."

"Really?"

Talking about his family always made him squirm, but he tossed out some snippets of his past as bait in the hope of catching crumbs he hoped would help him learn who Casey really was.

He mentioned that his dad had died young. She said hers always sheltered her too much.

Craig explained that his mother had taught school to support him and his brother after his father's death. Casey said her mom had stayed home, helped manage the ranch, and sewed frilly dresses she used to make Casey wear.

It didn't do his ego much good to admit his brother had been the academic genius while he was the dud. And that

admission earned nothing more from Casey than the fact that her brother hadn't been interested in doing anything but riding the range.

He was getting nowhere. He'd have to switch tactics. Talk about specifics that had motivated him. Emotional things he hardly ever thought about, much less put into words.

Overhead, a seagull squawked.

Craig cleared his throat. "If my brother hadn't goofed and had to drop out of college when I was sixteen, I'd never have become a lawyer. More likely, I'd have ended up in prison myself."

She smiled but offered no reply.

He talked about the wild kid he'd been and the brush with the law that had triggered his reform. When that didn't trigger more than an exclamation of admiration that he'd come to his senses, he confessed how he'd needed to make up to his mom for Alan's disappointing her.

"I started studying, and worked hard at sports, too, so I could get an athletic scholarship on the off chance that some college might let me in."

"Where'd you go?" she asked.

"University of Florida law school. Southern Methodist for my undergraduate degree, on a swimming scholarship. I worked like a dog to get the grades I knew I'd have to have in order to get into a good law school."

That apparently tweaked her interest. "I guessed you were a jock."

"Yeah. Still am, after a fashion. I'm competing in the benefit games next weekend."

"The cops versus lawyers thing? What events are you doing?"

"All of the swimming events. And the triathlon."

For a few minutes, they chatted about sports and fitness. Craig still knew virtually nothing about what made Casey tick.

He'd have to treat her as a hostile witness. "Why were you a virgin?"

She tried to dodge the abrupt question, but he held her gaze. "Casey?"

She looked trapped. "Nobody volunteered to provide me with any experience."

"I have a hard time believing that. Try again."

"Really. It's true."

"Come on. You expect me to believe there's a man alive who'd turn down the sort of invitations you gave me?"

Apparently she saw something that intrigued her at the edge of the watery horizon, because she kept staring out to sea.

"Well?"

"I– I never did anything like that before."

Words tumbled from her lips. Her broken engagement, the decision to change her image, her move to Tampa, even how her roommate had advised her on becoming the bad girl she wanted to be painted a picture of a very different Casey than the woman Craig had thought he knew.

"I'm sorry. I shouldn't have tried to fool you." Tears pooled in her eyes when she finally met his gaze.

He wanted to hold her. More, he longed to drag her back inside and show her he wasn't sorry at all. Sexy Casey Thompson turned on every wicked impulse that had ever crossed his mind. But Casey was also the sweet, innocent sort of woman he'd imagined one day becoming the mother of his kids.

Sugar and spice, rolled together into one dynamite package. He couldn't ask for more. Except that for the moment he'd forego the sugar. He wanted a lot more of her spice.

Standing, he held out his hand. "Let's go for a quick swim first."

"First?"

"Yeah. Gotta stay in shape for the fun we're gonna have later, right here in this room."

Her smile brightened as she stood and took his hand. "I'll race you."

"You'll be sorry. But you're on." With that, Craig took off for the surf.

* * * * *

Sand crunched between her toes. The surf swirled around her legs while the midday sun beat down from a cloudless sky. Every muscle in Casey's body protested the beating she'd put it through during the long surf swim.

"Wanna make it two out of three?" Craig asked.

"Not on your life." She took in a deep breath and prayed the burning in her lungs would go away.

Sensation sizzled through her brain, the heat of the day bringing sweat up on her brow. Mild heat, though, compared with the fires Craig kindled inside her. More than ever now, while mirrored goggles obscured his eyes, his not-quite-perfect smile captivated her. It reminded her of the wicked, wonderful things his mouth could do.

The bright light emphasized the beginnings of a dark shadow on his stubborn jaw. Droplets of water sparkled in the silky hair on his chest. His muscles rippled when he inhaled.

Damn it, he wasn't even winded. Of course he'd gotten an extra five minutes' rest while she slogged through the surf to finish the race she'd been so foolish as to suggest.

A wave broke across her legs, splashed soothing lukewarm sea water against the barely-there bottom of her new thong bikini.

If he wanted to take her now, all he'd have to do was peel down his suit and shove aside that teensy strip of material wedged between her cleanly waxed labia.

The beach was virtually deserted.

She toyed with the lace on his loose-fitting swim shorts, letting her fingers brush against his hardening cock. "Want to make love out here?" she asked.

"In front of God and everybody?" He sounded shocked.

"If we got down on our knees, no one could see much."

He drew her into his arms, nudged her belly with his erection. "You're an exhibitionist, aren't you?"

"I take it you're not?"

"I'm cautious. Occupational hazard. Don't much like the thought of spending part of our weekend in a jail cell."

"Chicken." She came closer and rubbed up against him the way a friendly kitten might.

Water caught on a sudden wind gust swirled around them, obscuring their lower bodies from the view of anybody onshore. Boldly, Casey cupped his balls through the wet material of his shorts.

Craig groaned, but he held her hand where it was. "Okay, I'm game."

Then he pulled her hand away. "Hold on a minute. I don't have any condoms on me, and I'd bet money you're not on the Pill."

She suppressed a gulp. "You'd be right."

"Wanna take a chance?" He slipped his hand between her legs, burrowed under the narrow thong, and tweaked her clit.

"N-no."

He pulled back his hand and scooped her up in his arms. Then he broke into a grin.

"Come on, if you're hot to get it on in the water, I've got an idea. How about trying out that big hot tub in our room?"

* * * * *

A few minutes ago he'd been willing to chance jail—not to mention a shotgun wedding. Craig adjusted the water

temperature and watched warm water pour into the big tub. He heard Casey moving around in the bedroom.

When he shoved his swim shorts to the floor and kicked them aside, he realized he was as hard as he'd been when they played with fire out in the surf. Apparently his cock wasn't giving up on getting satisfaction again—and soon.

Funny. The idea of making Casey pregnant hadn't dimmed his desire. If anything, it had made him want her more. Obviously she hadn't felt the same. She'd lost no time saying no when he asked if she was ready to take a chance.

Good thing one of them had sense. If and when he married, he wanted at least nine months to elapse between the wedding and the birth of his first child. Anything less would undermine the image of responsibility he wanted to convey and put the security he wanted for himself and his future family at risk.

"Craig?"

His cock twitched at the sound of Casey's voice. "Yeah, baby?"

"Is the tub almost ready?"

It wasn't, but he sure as hell was. "The water's about halfway up. Grab a handful of condoms out of that compartment in the headboard and come on in. We'll play around and see what comes up."

"Wow. You believe in coming prepared, don't you?" She sounded shocked.

Oh, God, he'd forgotten about the toys. Toys he'd decided not to experiment with, once he figured out how *not* savvy Casey was beneath that fuck-me veneer she always wore.

"I guess I do," he said, trying hard to recall just which goodies he'd stuffed in with the condoms.

"Want me to bring the crop?"

Casey's nervous giggle reinforced his image of her as a good girl. The kind he'd take home to Mom or introduce with pride to his colleagues.

The pump motor rumbled to life, and water burped through the jets. "Not unless you want to use it on me," he yelled over the dull roar.

When she paused in the doorway, whip in hand, he tried to keep his tongue inside his mouth. She was the next best thing to naked. Better, maybe, because those tiny pieces of cloth she called a swim suit directed his attention toward the delicious body parts they covered well enough to keep Casey from getting herself arrested. Barely.

Not well enough to hamper his memory or his imagination. She had the black leather crop in her hand.

He wouldn't mind making her his prisoner. Or becoming hers.

She wiggled the whip, setting its split-leather tails to dancing. "Lisa tried to talk me into buying one of these." Her dark eyes sparkled, and a grin lit up her face.

Apparently the idea of using it intrigued her. "Why didn't you?"

"I couldn't imagine wanting to hurt you. Why did you buy this one?"

He recalled the burly guy in leather and chains, his hasty last-minute purchase, and his even hastier exit from Erotic Invitation. "Protection," he said, not anxious to own up to the whole truth.

"From me?"

"No, baby. I can handle you. And I can't wait much longer to do it. Come here and I'll tell you about it."

She stepped closer, dragged the tails down his body.

"Stop that. It tickles." It also aroused the hell out of him. The supple leather swayed, made occasional feather-light contact with flesh that already was hard and aching.

She stopped and set the whip aside. "You like it, though. Admit it."

"Okay. I like it."

"Tell me now. Who'd you need protection from?" she asked. "If you won't tell me I'll have to assume you're afraid of me."

"A grungy guy dripping chains off his black leather vest and pants. From what he said, he apparently thought I'd like to join him for some S&M fun and games. I disagreed. Picking up the crop was a reflex action."

"Where'd you run into this weirdo?"

Craig shrugged. "In that store across from the gym. Erotic Invitation."

"Does that sort of stuff turn you on?"

"Porn? Not particularly. I went in there shopping for toys." He traced a line down her body, following shadows cast by the waning sun. "I thought we might have fun with some of them."

"Thought?"

"Yeah. Past tense. All I want to do with you is you."

"You want this, don't you?" She reached inside her cleavage and pulled out a foil-wrapped package.

"Uh-huh. Not quite yet, though. First I want to play."

She licked at his lower lip. "Sounds like fun."

"It will be." More fun than he'd have imagined before last night. "The water's ready, and one of us has on too many clothes."

Craig took the condom from Casey's hand and set it on the ledge beside the tub.

She stepped back and shot him a sexy smile. "Want to watch me strip?"

"Oh, yeah." He could easily get used to that kind of an erotic invitation.

Her motions as she took off her clothes were slow, sensuous.

Languid. That was the word he'd use to describe the way she lifted her hair off her shoulders, smiled, reached behind her

neck, and finally released the tie that held the tiny triangles of material over her boobs.

And downright sexy was how she looked a minute later when she bared those full, firm breasts tipped with deep pink nipples.

He wanted those hardened buds in his mouth. Between his fingertips. Brushing against his chest and driving him crazier than he was already. He wanted them now.

"You like this, don't you?" Her voice poured over him like honey.

"Yeah, baby. I like it a lot. Don't stop now."

He watched her slide her hands down over satiny flesh he'd explored last night–her warm, wet pussy he itched now to trace again with his hands and lips.

She hooked her thumbs into the thong bottom, slid it past her firm, smooth thighs and sleekly muscled calves to puddle around her ankles. The motion was a slow, sensual dance to the rhythm of the whooshing jets. A dance that was driving his cock insane.

Steam filled the room, veiling her nakedness but not his imagination. His mouth watered. He wanted to rub his cheek against that crazy little heart-shaped patch of curls, bury his face in the velvety smoothness of her pussy. Desire sizzled through every cell in his body.

He might manage slow some day. But today was not the day. His fingers nearly met when he clasped both hands around her slender waist and brought her into the churning water. Her breasts bobbed on the foamy surface, beckoning him to join her on the narrow ledge as he climbed in behind her. He found her foot with his own and tickled her toes. The last thing on his mind was teasing, but he attempted a grin.

"Hey, you're tickling me." Casey retaliated by splashing bubbles in his face.

Craig shook his head as he spit water from his mouth. Then he grabbed her and pulled her onto his lap. "Now you've asked for it," he growled.

She let out a little squeal, but she also wiggled her bottom around until he felt her cunt poised, hot and wet, tantalizingly close to the aching tip of his cock.

"I did, didn't I? From the feel of you, you're ready to give it to me." Burrowing her fingers through his chest hair, she found his nipples and rubbed playfully across the flat nubs. Hell, he'd never realized before how sensitive they were, or how sensation seemed to spread straight to his aching balls.

He fought for control when she grasped his cock in one hand, drawing him closer.

"Better grab that condom," he croaked, almost beyond speech. "Now."

"Impatient?"

"Damn it, Casey!"

He fumbled for the packet, cursed again. When he finally found it, he took it between his teeth and tore the foil away. Then he stood.

"Put it on me."

So slowly he thought he'd die, she took the condom and sheathed him. By the time she finished, his balls were ready to explode.

Then she pulled him down on the ledge, rose on her knees, and lowered herself onto him. Inch by inch she took him into her body until his cock was part of her.

Hot water churned around them. Her sweet old-fashioned scent filled his nostrils. Her hair tasted of salt-spray and felt like spun silk. With gentle hands she stroked his chest, and even that simple contact threatened to shove him over the edge.

He gritted his teeth and endured her slow, rocking motions that had him fighting to make this last. Damn it, he'd hold out or die trying. Casey deserved to come first this time.

He bent his head, took one hardened nipple in his mouth and flailed it with his tongue. Cupping both her breasts in his hands, he pinched the other nipple between his thumb and forefinger and was rewarded with her breathy little moan.

She spread her legs wider, took his full length inside. Her inner muscles contracted, milked him. Desperate to hold off the inevitable, he willed himself to hold back, to let her take her pleasure first.

"Oh, God. You feel so... Yesss. Craig, don't stop!"

His name came out of her throat over and over, between sexy little whimpers. Her nails dug into his shoulders. Her cunt clamped down on his cock like a vise, and it was all he could do to maintain control. "Let it happen, baby," he said between clenched lips as he twisted his hips, fucked her harder...deeper...

His balls rested in the slick, wet slit when he sank into her all the way. It felt so good, it hurt.

"Oh, yesss," she murmured, writhing on his cock as though she wanted to swallow it. Her grip on his shoulders tightened painfully, but he barely noticed.

He arched his back, withdrew halfway, then drove back deep inside her. "Come on, baby. Come for me."

Soon. Please let it be soon.

He'd die if he had to hold out much longer. Her thigh muscles quivered. She moaned, then screamed out his name. Her cunt clamped down on his cock.

He thrust once. Twice. One last time.

And then he let go, coming hard, spurting for what seemed like hours, even after her pussy had relaxed its hold on his spasming cock and she'd collapsed against him with a contented sigh.

Chapter Twelve

The sun lay low in the sky when Casey woke up the next morning in the big round bed, her face turned toward the open patio doors.

She vaguely recalled Craig lifting her from the hot tub, wrapping her in a towel, and carrying her in here–but the memory of them making love surrounded by the warm, swirling water would stay with her forever.

He'd made her implode. She'd actually seen stars. Now she knew why folks put such store in sex. In orgasms, anyhow.

She wanted to sample some more, but she didn't see Craig.

When she stretched, her muscles hurt some — but it was a good kind of hurt. A reminder she had a lover at last. Luckily, he hadn't seemed too upset when he realized she'd been a virgin.

That was good.

The fact that she was nine-tenths of the way in love with him was not so good.

Just because Buck had jumped every obstacle including their engagement to marry the first woman who'd tweaked his cock didn't mean Casey should expect a proposal from Craig anytime soon.

Make that ever.

After all, he was no laid-back cowboy from Bone Gap, Texas. He'd lived in Dallas before coming to Florida and settling in Tampa, and he was well on the way toward becoming a big-time, big city lawyer.

Yeah, Craig was a far cry from Buck, to whom a night at a Lubbock honky tonk had probably been the major highlight of his life. In more ways than one.

Casey stretched again, smiled. When she closed her eyes she felt his presence. Her skin tingled as if his touch were imprinted on every cell. The air she breathed still held his scent, and the taste of him lingered on her tongue.

But he was nowhere in the room. Or the bathroom.

"Craig?" she called as she pulled on her bikini.

"Out here."

Casey followed the sound of his voice and found him on the patio, stacks of paper anchored under seashells on the small umbrella table. A gentle breeze ruffled his hair.

She bent over, braced her hands on his shoulders, and strained to read whatever it was he'd written on that legal pad in a bold, slashing scrawl.

Claims sex addiction.

"Sex addiction? What does a lawyer need to know about mental illness?"

"The defendant claims he went temporarily insane because his wife cut him off." Craig turned, rubbed a gritty jaw against the back of her hand.

"So you've got to prove that's not true?"

"Yeah. Trouble is, when I'm with you I'm not sure he's that far off base."

"You don't mean that."

"Yeah, I do. You have no idea how much I wanted to stay in bed with you instead of putting this case together." He turned around and pulled her onto his lap. "Wanna go make love?"

She laughed and gestured toward his notes. "Exactly what is sex addiction?"

"According to the experts it's the way some people's sexual behavior becomes the major coping mechanism they use to handle stress."

"And what if they just use sex for fun?" She blew on his earlobe, then nibbled it.

His cock twitched visibly inside his shorts, letting her know it was interested. Sexually interested. "Apparently most people manage to keep their sex lives in perspective. For the sex addict, though, his sexual behavior is apparently something he can't stop for any length of time without suffering some sort of mental trauma. So say the shrinks."

"And this has what to do with your case?" Somehow sex addiction didn't sound like a subject that would often come up in court.

"Have you heard about the Road Rage Ranger?"

Who hadn't? The guy had plowed into some poor woman's SUV on I-275 a month or so ago. Intentionally, if the reporters had it right. "I've heard about him."

"He's the defendant I'm trying next week. He's claiming temporary insanity. Claims he rammed that woman because his wife refused to have sex with him."

"So is this Ranger guy a sex addict?"

"He may be. But I don't think so. I know If I were defending him, I wouldn't want to have to argue that sexual frustration drove my client legally insane–crazy enough to commit assault and battery on a stranger, whether he used a car or a gun."

"Insanity means a person doesn't know the difference between right and wrong, doesn't it?"

"Basically. The legal definition is fairly narrow. Defendants don't often get verdicts of not guilty by virtue of temporary insanity."

Casey brushed her lips across his cheek. "I take it you plan to get the man convicted."

"Yeah. It's a high-profile case. The victim's related to a state senator, which means there will be press coverage. Not that there wouldn't be reporters looking for a story because of the nature of the crime alone. It wouldn't be good for me if Ranger's lawyer gets him an acquittal."

She took that to mean Craig didn't need her distracting him. Standing, she told herself she could ignore being horny, and dismiss the cramping complaints from her pussy that apparently could care less about her lover meeting his professional obligations.

"Forget about your own sex life, then. Get busy. I'm off to bake on the beach awhile before it gets dark."

She hadn't gotten ten yards toward the water when Craig tackled her from behind. "Come back here. Preparing my case can wait. Right now I want to feed my Casey addiction."

* * * * *

If he were addicted, then she was, too. Addicted to feasting her eyes on his long, lean, very naked body...his gorgeous laughing eyes...his talented hands and mouth. Especially his tongue. And his big, hard, mouthwatering cock that made her pussy feel so good.

"Like what you see, baby?"

"What? Oh, yes." Casey's cheeks grew warm. She'd been ogling Craig, and from his amused tone she figured he knew it. "I like it a lot," she said, making herself look him in the eye as she tossed away the top to her swimsuit.

"I like you, too. Wanna have some fun?"

"Uh-huh." Meeting his challenge, she dropped her bikini bottom and stepped up close enough that she could reach out her hand and stroke his broad chest...or the hard male flesh that seemed to be growing bigger right before her eyes.

"Then lie down, close your eyes, and don't move a muscle. I'm going to make you feel good. Real good."

"Oooh." Eager for whatever it was Craig had in mind, Casey did as he told her. Deprived of sight, she found her other senses suddenly more acute. The feel of the satin sheets, cool and smooth where they brushed against her back, the salty but not unpleasant smell of the Gulf tickling her nostrils. Even the

sound of her breathing and his was amplified in the darkness. A creak and a rattle told her he was fishing in his bag of toys.

Though he didn't say a word, she knew from the faint sound of flesh brushing satin and a slight shift of the mattress that he'd just joined her on the bed. Reflexively she reached out to him, but he stilled her hands.

"I said, be still. Don't think, baby. Just feel. Trust me. You'll like what I'm about to do."

Though he hadn't restrained her physically, Casey made herself be still. If Craig said she'd like it, she trusted that she would. Trusted him. "Okay," she said, setting her hand down by her side.

She sensed him looking at her, felt the heat of his gaze. His breathing was slow and steady, like a well-trained marathon runner's. Warm and damp against her breasts...her belly...her mound.

"Cute," he murmured, nuzzling the heart-shaped patch of hair. "Did you do this for me?"

His breath set off tiny vibrations on her mound that quickly migrated to her pussy. "Mmm-hmmm," she said through lips she dared not open.

"I like it. A lot."

She felt his fingers ruffling the little heart, his breath moving down her leg. Heat radiated from her toes when he sucked them into his mouth one at the time, and that heat intensified in her pussy when he moved up, spread her legs apart, and nibbled the sensitive spots just above each knee.

The feel of her nipples hardening, of her own slick juices sliding from her pussy to ease his way, the rasp of his unshaven cheek against her labia had her wallowing in erotic sensations, wanting more.

A sharp buzzing noise invaded the silence, then softened. "What?" she asked.

"Be quiet. Enjoy." His breathing seemed more ragged now as he lowered his head between her legs.

Her clit twitched, anticipating the touch of his tongue. Then something cool and rigid buzzed against it. The sensation was...arousing. Too arousing. It made her jump nearly out of her skin.

"Sorry, baby." Craig's tone conveyed regret.

The buzzing slowed again. The touch of Craig's velvety tongue soothed her swollen flesh while he slid the vibrator into her sopping pussy inch by inch.

When it found and buzzed against a particular spot, she practically climbed out of her skin. Between that and the delicious things he was doing with his tongue, she thought she'd die of pleasure. "Oh Craig," she gasped as another wave of sensation coursed through her body.

"Found your G-spot, huh?" After that satisfied sounding comment he went back to sucking her clit.

Even the noise of the buzzing and suckling seemed to trigger more explosions deep in her belly. As yet another orgasm took her breath away, he pulled away, turned her onto her stomach, and stuffed something squishy under her hips.

His breath blew warm against her buttocks. Then, incredibly, he ran his finger around her puckered anus and even that excited her. "Someday you're going to want me here, too," he said. "But now I've got to get my cock inside your sweet, wet pussy or I'll die."

The hair on the outsides of his thighs tickled the inside of hers. The sound of foil tearing and the brush of his hands against her butt when he rolled a condom on made her pussy weep with wanting him to fill her. His ragged breathing filled her ears.

And he filled her to the hilt. No gentle probing, no tentative thrusts. His big, hot cock sank in her all the way, nudging her G-spot with every stroke. Casey had come and come and come before, didn't think she could come anymore, but he proved her wrong.

His spasming, spurting release triggered another climax that left her limp and panting. And, paradoxically, yearning for more.

* * * * *

Except for those few hours yesterday afternoon when he'd worked on his case against Ranger, Craig and Casey had spent nearly every waking moment on Sanibel Island making love. As he pulled up in front of her apartment Sunday afternoon, she wished the weekend didn't have to end. "Want to come up for a while?"

He turned off the engine, then reached over and squeezed her thigh. "Is your roommate home?"

His hand moved higher, and his fingers found her pussy through her flimsy silk panties. Since they'd made love, he touched her more intimately more often. She liked it a lot. Apparently he'd set aside his stuffy lawyer inhibitions or at least shoved them aside for the time being.

"Yes, she's here. I think her boyfriend is, too." Lisa's little red Toyota was in its usual parking spot, and Casey thought she recognized Mike's silver SUV across the street.

"Come on. I want to meet the woman who taught you how to—" he leaned close and whispered, "—suck cock with a cucumber."

He pulled a lever and the convertible top started to come up.

Good thing. Her cheeks were already burning. She didn't need to soak up dying rays from the setting sun. She'd get back at him, though. Make his big, delicious cock so hard he wouldn't be able to get out of the car.

"Want some now, big guy?" She slid his zipper down and cupped his balls through the skimpy dark-green briefs she'd watched him put on earlier. "I bet you do."

Predictably his flesh hardened. She licked her lips.

"Stop it," he said, but he flexed his hips as if he wanted more.

The tip of his cock popped out of his briefs, and she rubbed her thumb over the hot velvety skin, spreading the drop of lubrication that oozed from the dimpled slit.

Her mouth watered, so she bent and kissed him there.

Now he stopped her. He lifted her head, set aside her hand, and zipped up as fast as Casey imagined the firemen would when the alarm sounded at the station house down the street.

Before she could put her hands on him again, he grabbed them. "There's a time and a place—"

She silenced him with a kiss. "I know. It's...I just don't want this weekend to be over."

"It won't be unless you get us tossed in jail. You do have some private space up there, don't you?" He gestured toward the apartment building.

"My bedroom."

"Let me guess. Your roommate won't mind if we excuse ourselves and take a nap."

He got out, then leaned inside to get her bag.

Casey opened the passenger door and looked over at Craig. "She probably wouldn't. But I'd be embarrassed."

He laughed. "You? Did I trade the sexy lady who's blown my mind ever since I saw her for her shy little twin, somewhere on the way home?"

"No, but—"

"Want me to bring along the vibrator?"

He stuffed a handful of condoms into his pocket and reached back inside his duffel bag. "Casey?"

She could practically hear the hum, feel the gentle vibrations in her pussy. "M-mmm?"

"Remind you of something?" Grinning, he held the device up where she could see.

"Oh, yes." She gave his cock a gentle squeeze.

"Come on. Let's go play."

She wanted to. But— "I've never had sex with a man in my apartment."

"I know. Until day before yesterday you'd never had sex, period."

Her cheeks burned as she followed him up the sidewalk. Sooner or later, maybe she'd be able to take this all in stride. While she fumbled in her purse for keys, the door burst open and Mike stormed out. From the scowl on his face, she guessed Lisa must have slammed the revolving door on yet another lover.

"Is this not a good time?" Craig asked.

Casey shrugged. "Maybe. Maybe not. Let's see."

She poked her head into the living room, found Lisa staring out the window. "Lisa? You up to company?"

"Sure. I bet your weekend was better than mine." Her roommate's smile looked a bit anemic.

"I bet it was, too. Craig, come on in. You two know each other from the gym, don't you?"

Craig shot Lisa a smile. "Hey there. Thanks for giving Casey the lessons with the cuke."

"My pleasure."

"No, the pleasure was all mine. Believe me."

Lisa frowned. "I'm glad somebody had some fun. Excuse me. I need to go pout in private."

This didn't sound like the usual Lisa post boyfriend-of-the-month. Casey watched her roommate's back until she disappeared inside her room.

"Trouble?" Craig asked.

Casey nodded. "Lisa's the queen of casual relationships. Seems as though this one might not have been as superficial as she thought."

Casey imagined how she'd feel when Craig walked out that door for good. Worse than when Buck had left her practically at the altar.

"Casey?" Craig nuzzled her neck.

"What? Oh, my room's right next to hers."

"Worried that she'll hear you moan and whimper?"

She nodded. "Could we just say good-night out here?"

"Sure. I need to finish prepping the Ranger case anyhow. I'll miss you. Go console your roommate."

* * * * *

Sex wasn't addictive. He could do without. He was proving it right now. He didn't like it, though.

Wishing he were in bed with Casey and that her roommate's boyfriend had picked any other night to pick a fight, Craig sat at his kitchen table and stared at the outline of his opening statement for the Ranger trial. The pot of coffee he'd brewed when he got home was down to one last cup of sludge. And the sun was coming up outside.

All he could think about was Casey. The way her soft, full breasts filled his hands. The heady smells of old-fashioned wisteria and sexy modern woman that she'd imprinted on his brain. And remembering the tight, wet heat of her cunt gave him an instant hard-on.

Hell, maybe sex was addictive after all. If it weren't, he wouldn't be hard and aching after just—he glanced at his watch—twelve hours and thirty-five minutes of celibacy.

Still, he wasn't feeling homicidal. Or even violent. Just horny. And not for just any woman. He only wanted Casey.

He unplugged the pot and poured the last of the coffee. Its bitter taste nearly choked him. Maybe a shower would help. And breakfast somewhere, anywhere he didn't have to fix it. McDonald's, maybe.

As icy needles of water pummeled his body, it came to him. His weekend feast of fucking hadn't diluted his need for a whole lot more of it—at least not yet. But it had given a face and body to that need.

Craig needed Casey in his life as well as his bed. Not just now, but for the foreseeable future. If he weren't mistaken, he'd say he'd gone and fallen in love.

* * * * *

"I miss you, baby." His deep voice sent shivers down her spine and hot juices gushing from her pussy.

"I miss you, too." Casey's fingers tingled when she set the phone back in its cradle. Craig's brief call made her day.

"Your favorite hunk?" Lisa asked, glancing up from the paper when Casey came back to the table to eat her toast.

"Uh-huh. He's going to pick me up from work tonight. I may stay over at his place."

"I take it you're not a virgin anymore and that sex with the lawyer is good."

Lisa sounded…different. Brittle, as if her composure was about to crack.

"You're right. And sex with Craig is incredible. Lisa, what's wrong?"

"Nothing."

Unshed tears made Lisa's eyes look huge in her elfin face over nothing? Casey didn't buy it. "What happened with Mike?"

"I blew him off."

That didn't make sense, considering Lisa's obvious blue funk.

"Why, for God's sake, if doing it was going to make you miserable?"

"It would have hurt me worse if I'd waited until he dumped me."

"What makes you think Mike would have dumped you? He seemed crazy about you."

"They're all crazy about me. At first. But eventually they walk away. That's men. Every man from fifteen to ninety-five. Leaving women's in their blood."

Was this Lisa, who attracted men the way flowers attracted bees? Lisa, who picked and chose and then discarded guys a lot of women would die for? Casey had a hard time believing this woman was her super-savvy roommate.

"So you told him to hit the road?" she asked.

"More or less." Lisa stifled a sob. "He was getting to mean too much to me."

The way Craig was getting to mean too much to Casey?

No. In spite of her experience with Buck, Casey couldn't let herself believe that no relationship could last.

"If you really believe all men are bastards, somebody must have done a number on you." The words slipped from Casey's throat before she could call them back.

Lisa wiped the back of her hand across her reddened eyes, then met Casey's gaze. "Somebody did."

"When?" Certainly not in the three months Casey and Lisa had been sharing space.

"A long time ago. It doesn't matter."

Obviously it did, or Lisa wouldn't be sitting here mourning Mike. She wouldn't have sent him packing in the first place. Not if she cared about him.

"And if you believe that—"

"I don't want to talk about it."

But Casey needed to hear.

And she had a feeling Lisa needed to let loose whatever she was holding deep inside. "Come on, you can't toss out a juicy tidbit and jerk it back before I even get a bite. Spill it. All of it."

Lisa picked up her iced tea and took a long sip. "Guys can't be trusted. Period. They're fine for fun and games and absolutely essential for sexual satisfaction. That's all."

"When did you come to that conclusion?"

"When I was seventeen."

Casey guessed the iced tea must have sprouted some foreign object, the way Lisa was staring at it.

"What happened?" Casey asked when the silence started getting to her.

"Jake Wells—he was my first lover—swore from the time we were fourteen that we'd always be together. He said he loved me, every chance he got. But that didn't stop him from telling his daddy every guy in school had fucked me before he skipped town and left me three months pregnant."

"You had a baby?"

"She was stillborn. It was okay. Nobody wanted her anyway. Not my parents. Certainly not Jake.

"My wants didn't count. Anyhow, I figured soon enough that I was better off without a baby to raise on my own."

The sadness showed in Lisa's eyes, although her words sounded upbeat, almost callous. Casey reached across the table and held her hand.

"You've got to know not all men are like this Jake guy."

Lisa's laugh was hollow sounding. "You may be right, but I'm not willing to take a chance. Flavor-of-the-month's a safer bet. For me."

"Mike's history?"

Lisa nodded. "He had to go and say the words I least wanted to hear."

"That he loves you?"

"Yes."

Casey wondered if she'd cringe the way her roommate apparently had, if Craig should ever murmur those three words in her ear. She didn't think so.

But she might drag him off to Las Vegas for a quickie wedding if he ever proposed, instead of risking that he'd change his mind the way Buck had.

"So you'd rather let Mike go than risk getting hurt again now, however many years since Jake let you down?"

"I'd even rather do without sex."

That, Casey imagined, wouldn't remain a problem for long. Men flocked to Lisa like flies to hot dogs on the grill. Unless–

Unless Mike had already gotten under Lisa's skin before she sent him on his way. The way Craig was under Casey's skin now.

"If we don't get a move on, we'll both be late to work," Lisa said, sniffling as she grabbed her backpack in a very un-Lisa-like way.

Chapter Thirteen

Craig went through the motions, but thoughts of Casey kept intruding as he prepped witnesses for the Ranger trial.

Of all the people he'd rather not have as second chair, Dwayne Cramer was it. But the boss hadn't given him a chance to protest before he made the announcement a few minutes ago. If there was any consolation, it was that a second body at the prosecution's table would show the defense that the state attorney's office meant business.

He reminded himself that winning the case would keep him squarely on target toward his personal goals. Still, he clenched his fists under the table when the other lawyer joined him in the conference room. He had no delusion that Dwayne would keep his mouth shut while he prepared the psychologist who was to testify for the prosecution.

"How was your weekend?" Dwayne asked when he got situated at the table.

"Fine." He hoped his tone would discourage further conversation. Keeping Casey off his mind was hard enough without having Dwayne remind him of her.

"Get any work done?"

No such luck. He should have known Dwayne wouldn't take the hint. "Some."

Dwayne gestured toward his own left leg. "How's the training going?"

"Fine."

"No pain when you run?"

Dwayne didn't need to know he wasn't running or biking–that the damn triathlon itself would tax his patched up leg enough without him torturing it ahead of time.

"No," he said shortly.

Anybody else would have known his monosyllabic replies meant he wasn't interested in idle conversation. But not Dwayne. By the time the police department's psychologist arrived to be briefed on his testimony, Craig's mind was doing flip-flops between sex and murder.

Making love with Casey, murdering his colleague.

All the psychologist's talk about sex addiction skewed those thoughts toward Casey, so much that when the interview was over Craig could barely remember what the shrink had said. He'd taken notes, though, and presumably so had Dwayne.

"Piece of cake," Dwayne announced before the psychologist had cleared the door. "No jury will believe Ranger's a sex addict."

"Why not? Our own expert witness just said it's possible."

"Because Ranger didn't bash into his own wife, or crack her in the head. He ran his car into a total stranger."

Craig shook his head at Dwayne's lack of logic. "That makes him look more insane than if he'd taken out his frustration on the woman who caused it."

"Frustration, man. Not insanity. Trust me."

Problem was, Craig didn't. Dwayne, who had been with the state attorney's office twice as long as Craig, had won less than half as many convictions. "Let's hope our jurors feel that way," he said as he gathered his notes and prepared to leave.

Maybe a good, hard workout would clear his head.

* * * * *

It didn't.

Every time he glanced in one of the mirrors at the gym, Craig got a glimpse of Casey showing an adoring but apparently

feebleminded mass of whale blubber how to use the universal machine.

The hot pink thing she had on covered her head to ankles but concealed nothing.

How many other guys besides him and the beached whale had hard-ons from ogling her?

Everybody, he imagined.

Everyone, that is, who was heterosexual and not so narcissistic they had to gawk at themselves while they pumped iron. Inexplicably Craig wanted to put blinders on them all. Or dress Casey in one of those veils and robes like women in Saudi Arabia wore.

Yeah, that ought to do it.

He doubted Casey would agree. She liked sashaying around in her sexy workout togs and thong bikinis. She just plain liked looking sexy. Hell, he liked her looking sexy, too. But damn it, he was the only guy who was sleeping with her, the only one with a right to think lascivious thoughts about her.

Good thing she got off at seven. Maybe he could make it until then without dragging her somewhere private and getting his Casey fix. Making a superhuman effort to keep his eyes to himself, he finished his strength-building routine and headed for the pool.

Casey watched him leave, then turned her attention back to Todd.

"Take it easy," she told him. "You don't want to do too much the first day."

"I'm okay." Todd's protest came out on a gasp for breath as he suddenly let go of the handles on the machine and sent weights clattering down onto their stacks.

His jowls had turned an alarming shade of red, and sweat poured off his brow and through his tentlike T-shirt. The flab on his arms quivered like jelly.

While Casey had been feasting her eyes on Craig, Todd could have suffered a stroke. Guilt washed over her, but not enough to make her forget the rush she got, savoring the memory that for one magical weekend Craig McDermott had been her very own Playgirl playmate.

And it wasn't over yet. She'd be meeting him as soon as she finished up here.

"What's next, beautiful?" Todd wheezed.

Hopefully not a heart attack, she thought, returning Todd's anemic smile. "Come on over to the desk. I'll check your pulse and blood pressure."

"But I'll never get in shape—"

"You certainly won't if you kill yourself. Take it one day at a time."

Casey took Todd's vital signs and recorded them in his folder. Then she met his gaze. "It looks as if you've survived your first day with the weights. Go on now, hit the steam room."

"Could I talk you into dinner? A salad or something, maybe?" Todd's expression was pained, as though contemplating a meal that didn't contain several thousand cholesterol-laden calories tied his oversize stomach up in knots.

"I'd love to, but I have plans."

He frowned. Then his expression brightened. "Too bad. Maybe next time."

"Maybe." Casey felt shallow as she watched Todd lumber away. The banker seemed to be a perfectly decent guy even if he was as big around as he was tall. It wasn't his fault he didn't ring any bells for her.

Then she put guilt into perspective. It wasn't just Todd. Other guys who weren't grossly overweight or out of shape had asked her out, too, and she'd said no. Because none of them had attracted her the way Craig did. He drew her in a way she couldn't explain.

The attraction was stronger than her simply drooling over his to-die-for looks, less easily explained than by his athletic prowess and the ambition she had no doubt would take him wherever he wanted to go. She had plenty of reasons to have fallen in love with him. The question Casey asked herself as she got ready to meet Craig was what had he seen in her.

* * * * *

Not even sexual anticipation had managed to banish that question from Casey's mind. "Why did you ask me out?" she asked Craig once they finished eating a Chinese take-out dinner at his apartment.

He nuzzled her neck. "Guess."

His arms snaked around her, his large hands capturing her breasts and kneading them lightly through her shirt and bra.

"I mean, why did you do it last week, after spending months ignoring me every time you came to the gym to exercise?"

Instead of replying, he rolled her nipples with his thumbs and forefingers. Soon she was squirming and her pussy was gushing its juices down her thighs, but she had to know. "Why, Craig?"

"I needed to prove to myself that sex isn't addictive. For the Ranger case."

So he'd figured her for an easy lay. Well, she certainly had proven him right. Still, knowing it didn't set well. She pulled away, then turned and looked him in the eye. "You asked me out because you wanted sex?"

"No. I mean, not entirely. But you asked why I suddenly decided to ask you out when I hadn't before. I'd been busy. Concentrating on my job. Until this case came up, I had been avoiding distractions. Baby, you were definitely a distraction. Every time I came to the gym and looked at you, my cock got hard."

"So when you needed a quick fix of sex you hit on me?"

He had the decency to look abashed. "In a manner of speaking, I suppose I did."

"Why didn't you go see your regular girlfriend?"

"I don't have one. At least I didn't, until now."

"What about her?" Casey gestured toward a framed photo of Craig in a tuxedo, a sleek looking blonde at his side.

"That's Tara Enderlin. She's a colleague, not a girlfriend. As a matter of fact she's married to a detective lieutenant in the Tampa Police Department. He's the other guy in the picture."

When she looked closely Casey saw that the other man had his arm around the blonde.

"Oh."

Craig caught her chin in his hand, forced her to meet his gaze. "You don't have to worry about other women, baby. You're my only lover. The only lover I've ever had."

"Ever?" He couldn't have meant what she thought he just said.

Suddenly he seemed to have developed a keen interest in one of the takeout cartons on the table. "I couldn't refute Ranger's sex addiction insanity defense unless I knew firsthand what it was he'd gotten addicted to," he told her, his tone defensive.

"So you hit on me because you thought I'd be an easy lay." Fury got Casey hot, even quicker than their foreplay did.

"I hit on you because you'd turned me on since the first time I saw you. But, baby, you've got to admit you came on mighty strong."

The man had the audacity to grin. She itched to hit him. His ulterior motive didn't wash. Knowing he'd sought out the bad girl he'd thought she was because of his job was downright insulting.

"I'm out of here," she snapped, snatching up her things and heading for the door.

"Casey. Don't go."

Refusing to meet his gaze for fear of giving in, she clutched the doorknob like a lifeline. "We're through. Over. You've solved your professional problem, so you've got no need to come sniffing around me any longer."

"Wait. Please."

She paused, her hand still on the doorknob. She knew she ought to have walked out on the bum, but part of her wanted to stay. The masochistic part. Steeling her mind against him, she opened the door.

He took her bag from her hand and stepped between her and freedom. "Go sit down. We're not through yet."

"No." She wasn't going to give in easily.

Craig grasped her elbow and escorted her to one of the black leather and chrome sling chairs in front of a large-screen TV. "I said sit down."

If she didn't, would he back off? Casey didn't think so, considering the ferocity of his expression. Giving in for the moment, she sank onto the chair.

Craig hesitated. He did his best arguing standing up, but intimidating her was the last thing he wanted to do, so he took the other chair, then cleared his throat.

This was like arguing a case, he told himself, except that he was both the defendant and his lawyer. The outcome here meant a hell of a lot more than laying another stone on his pathway to success. That realization scared him shitless, but he tried to swallow his fear.

"Casey?"

"I'm listening. Say whatever it is you have to say," she mumbled through tightly clenched lips.

She was still pissed. Royally. He groped for words that would de-fuse her anger.

"I was attracted to you from the first time I laid eyes on you. Remember? You were taking a tour of the gym with Russ while I was working out."

"I remember." Her expression didn't soften, not one bit.

"If the timing hadn't been all wrong, I'd have asked you out when you first came to work." Craig thought he saw a flicker of interest in her eyes, but he couldn't be sure.

"I have goals. Things I want to do, and a timetable for getting them done. Then wasn't the time for me to get involved with a woman. Any woman. The time's not exactly right now, either, but it doesn't seem to matter.

"Casey, I want us to be lovers."

"Well, we were, so you got your wish. With amazing ease. You ought to be proud of yourself."

There was definitely a point to the tongue-in-cheek saying that a lawyer who defended himself had a fool for a client. Unfortunately he couldn't hire a colleague to get him off the hook now, the way he would if he ran afoul of the law instead of his lover.

Craig studied Casey. A small muscle twitch near her jaw and the rigid way she held her shoulders belied her look of passive disinterest. Her whitened knuckles called attention to the fact she'd clenched her fists—probably so she could restrain herself from strangling him.

"I am proud of myself," he said after a long pause. "Proud of picking the perfect woman to be my first and only lover. What man wouldn't be?"

"You really mean you hadn't had sex before we—?"

"Yeah."

That wasn't a fact he was particularly anxious to share. He'd kept it to himself for years. But if she wanted to rub it in, he'd let her. He was that desperate to get out of her doghouse.

"How'd you learn?"

"What?"

"How did you learn how to do it so well?" She hesitated, then added, "You asked me."

He couldn't resist pointing out that she was hardly a qualified judge as to how skillfully he made love. "As to how I found out what to do, I learned more or less the same way I learned the law. By reading. I went out and bought some sex manuals. They're in my bedroom if you'd like to see them."

The look she shot him hinted that she wouldn't be going anywhere near his bed any time soon. "You didn't ask your friends?" she asked.

"Hell, no. I'd have been laughed out of every locker room from high school until now if I had."

"Why?" She unclenched her fists, laced her fingers together.

"Why what?"

"Why hadn't you had sex before? Don't tell me you didn't have plenty of chances."

He wouldn't dodge the question or insult her by sprouting moralities, but he took care choosing his words. "Fear at first. Fear I'd get some girl pregnant and throw away my future, the way my brother had. Later, I guess it was partly habit and partly that I kept myself too busy to take advantage of the opportunities."

For a long time she sat there, her only movement that little twitch of a muscle near her jawbone.

Craig wanted to touch her, hold her. But he didn't dare, so he told her about his blueprint for success. He explained how he'd stayed on course so far, graduating near the top of his class from college and law school, passing the bar, and amassing an impressive record of convictions for the state attorney's office.

Warmed to his subject, Craig continued. "In a couple more years, I'll move over to the other side. Get a great job doing criminal defense with a big firm. Then I'll get serious about settling down, finding a wife who'll help me build my practice, and having a family.

"You see, baby, I kept away from women because I couldn't take a chance on fucking up and letting myself down."

"I see. What would happen now if one of those condoms you've got so many of should fail?" She spoke softly. Too softly.

He tried to take her hand, but she jerked it away. "It wouldn't be a serious problem now," he told her. "We'd get married. I'm beyond the point now where having a family would put my career in jeopardy. I wasn't when I was sixteen and had just stood up at my brother's shotgun wedding."

"You're sick. For years you avoided screwing women because of your ambition. Now you deliberately chose to have sex with me for basically the same reason."

"Baby, you've got it wrong. I made love with you because I wanted to. I still want you, more than I'd have thought possible."

"Well, want away. Seems to me you already got what you wanted. See you around." With that, Casey got up and walked out.

Craig could have gone after her, but he didn't know what else he could say. For once in his life, he was speechless.

Chapter Fourteen

She conceded that Craig had wanted her. At least he'd wanted her to warm his bed again on Monday night. Casey wanted him, too, so much she'd almost given in and stayed. In the end, though, her pride had won out over her hormones.

She and Lisa made a pathetic pair, red-eyed and as sad as they'd have been if someone they loved had died. For three days now, they'd holed up in their respective bedrooms, emerging only when they had to go to work.

Craig had called, and so had Mike. How many times Casey couldn't be sure, because the caller ID box was overflowing. She started to listen to messages, then changed her mind.

"Mike called, didn't he?" Lisa asked when she came out of her room.

"Fourteen times before the ID box filled up. Why don't you just give in and call him back?"

Lisa shrugged. "Why don't you call Craig?"

"Craig used me for sex. All Mike did wrong was tell you he loves you."

"Didn't you use Craig a little, too? Seems I remember you scheming to seduce the guy and lose your cherry, whatever it took."

Lisa walked over to the phone and checked out the numbers on the caller ID.

"Looks like Craig has called at least eleven times himself, unless you've got somebody else calling you from the DA's office."

Casey shook her head.

Maybe she had used Craig. A little. But she hadn't hit on *him* with the expressed purpose of getting a quick roll in the hay. Getting it on for research for his job, yet.

"Come on. If you'll call him, then I'll return Mike's call."

Lisa sounded like a pal Casey recalled from high school who'd liked nothing better than to use "If, then" propositions to get her friends in trouble.

Her girlfriend Tessa had never followed through on the "then" part of her promises. Casey had a feeling that Lisa might, though, considering how she'd moped ever since showing Mike the door.

She followed Lisa into the kitchen. "Would you give another chance to a guy who admitted he hit on you because he wanted an easy lay?"

When Lisa finished dumping coffee into the coffeemaker, she joined Casey at the table.

"I *am* an easy lay," she said reasonably. "And you did everything but advertise that you're one, too."

"I did not. I just wanted guys like Craig to notice me." Casey wondered when she spoke if she was lying.

"At the very least you wanted guys to think you knew your way around. Don't you remember asking me to help you look and act savvy?"

"Yes, but—"

"But nothing. You wanted McDermott to think you were hot to fuck him. Now when he admits that he thought exactly that, you punish him for it."

The gurgling sound of coffee brewing reminded Casey of the Gulf breaking onto the shore while she lay in Craig's arms. Maybe Lisa was right. Maybe she was punishing Craig. But she was punishing herself more. After all, she doubted he was suffering much.

He'd gotten the experience he was looking for, and now he probably was winding up another successful prosecution. The

Ranger trial, he'd told her, was to have begun yesterday morning.

Casey's punishment took the form of memories. The way his cock filled and stretched her pussy. The way her nipples felt when he tugged them gently with his teeth. The unique taste of him on her tongue and the hunger in his gorgeous blue eyes when he raked her naked body with his gaze. Those memories made her ache inside.

She'd die if she didn't quit thinking about him. Unfortunately, banishing him from her mind was impossible. She could, however, banish him from this conversation if she could shift the focus toward Lisa and Mike.

Casey looked Lisa in the eye. "You're a great one to talk about punishment. You're penalizing Mike for loving you. At least I had a real reason to walk out on Craig."

"Mike would hurt me eventually if I let him get to me." Suddenly Lisa got up, as if she were closing off her emotions. "Coffee's ready," she announced unnecessarily.

Casey noticed Lisa's hands shaking as she got mugs out of the cabinet. And when she splashed some coffee onto the countertop, she swore in a very un-Lisa-like way.

Then she sat and stared Casey down. "I've got it. You're in love with Craig. Otherwise you wouldn't care that he had you pegged an easy lay."

Casey blinked. "Where did that come from?"

Lisa looked more animated than she had since Sunday night. "You are. I knew it."

If Casey weren't, she probably wouldn't be so angry. If she didn't care for Craig so much, she could enjoy sleeping with him and practicing her skills as a lover while he pleasured her with what he'd learned from those books of his.

She could even have read some of those books and gotten a few ideas of her own. They could have learned the finer points of fucking together and had a great time doing it.

Casey's mind wandered to the selection of toys Craig had tucked in with his impressive stash of condoms. She'd love to have tasted that cherry-flavored condom.

Suddenly the idea of sucking a fruit-flavored cock struck her as hilarious, and she giggled.

"What's so funny?" Lisa asked.

"He had some cherry-flavored condoms."

"So? They come in all sorts of flavors."

"I just figured it out." Casey giggled again.

"Figured out what?"

"The cherry. He was a virgin, too."

Lisa's mouth dropped open, and she set her mug down with a bang. "You've got to be kidding."

"No. He told me when he was trying to explain why he'd decided to hit on me. Said he needed to get some sexual experience before he could argue against this client's defense."

"That doesn't make sense."

"This guy reporters call the Road Rage Ranger is claiming sexual deprivation made him purposely ram his car into a woman's SUV. The trial started yesterday."

"That still doesn't compute. And I can't believe a hunk like Craig McDermott was a virgin." Lisa laughed so hard, Casey thought she might burst into tears.

That made Casey mad. "Don't laugh at him."

What was she doing defending Craig?

"See, you are in love with him. Come on, give the guy a chance. Cut him some slack."

Casey wanted to, but her pride rebelled at the idea. "I don't know."

"Look at it this way. He explained why he hit on you when he did. The virgin bit has to be true—no guy would lie about something like that, any more than he'd tell you he couldn't get it up if that wasn't true."

"Yes, but—"

"But nothing. That has to be a good sign. It's not often you run into an honest lawyer, much less an honest lover. Call him."

"Are you going to call Mike?"

Lisa wouldn't meet Casey's gaze. "I want to, but I can't."

"Are you afraid?" Casey certainly was.

"I'm terrified. He could hurt me, worse than Jake ever did." Lisa shrugged. "If only he'd agree to keep things casual…"

Casual sex was all Craig would ever want from Casey. That knowledge hurt.

"That's why I won't see Craig again, either."

She and Lisa were a fine pair.

Casey laughed at the irony. Both of them were miserable, Lisa because she wanted nothing but casual sex from a guy who loved her.

Casey's problem was just the opposite. She didn't want to settle for casual sex from the man who'd stolen her heart.

* * * * *

The Ranger's conviction the following afternoon should have put Craig on top of the world, but it didn't. Neither did Tony Landry's invitation to make an appointment and come talk with him about a job at Winston Roe. All Craig could think about was that he'd fucked up with Casey.

He might as well have cut off an arm or leg. He didn't think it could have hurt worse than losing her. Everywhere he looked, he saw her. Felt her presence.

He saw her at his kitchen table where they'd shared Chinese take-out. Smelled the wisteria blossom scent that lingered near the chair where she'd sat four nights ago while he'd shoved both feet squarely in his mouth.

Apparently she hadn't calmed down since she stormed out that door. Craig surmised that from the fact that she hadn't

returned a single one of the calls he'd made since Monday night. Not to mention that she had managed to stay out of his sight at the gym, if she'd even been there when he'd come to work out.

Her absence hadn't kept him from seeing her in his mind, sassy and smiling and wearing one of those outrageous exercise outfits that drove him damn near insane.

He was horny. Worse, he missed being with Casey out of bed as much as he missed the sex. Maybe more.

On the way home tonight he'd left a handful of tickets with Russ for tomorrow's field games, but he had little hope that she'd show up.

His stash of sex books caught his eye. Maybe he should sue their authors. Or the publishers who undoubtedly had deeper pockets. The books pretty much covered the basic mechanics. He had to admit they even did a decent job of describing how to arouse a woman with sexual foreplay.

He guessed he should be grateful. After all, the information the books had imparted had allowed him to seduce a virgin without her realizing he'd been a virgin, too.

Big deal. What the authors had left out was advice about what a guy should say or avoid saying to keep his lover satisfied. The emotional stuff. Now Craig was miserable, and a whole lot hornier than he'd been before he knew what he'd been missing.

He took off his jacket and loosened his tie, then stared inside his almost empty refrigerator. He grabbed a beer, then put it back. No beer for him tonight.

Tomorrow he had to compete. And his leg ached. Tonight he'd pushed too hard with the weights.

Somehow his timetable for success didn't seem as important now as it had B.C. Before Casey.

He glanced at his watch. Eight thirty. She ought to be home by now unless one of the other horny bastards at the gym had hit on her and she'd said yes. He dialed her number but got the

damn answering machine again. As he was about to hang up, a human voice came on the line.

"Craig?"

"Casey?" It didn't sound like her.

"No, it's Lisa."

She sounded surprisingly friendly, considering that he'd most likely made it to the top of her roommate's shit list.

"Is Casey there?"

According to Lisa, she was, but she wasn't talking. She was, however, thinking about talking. "You stuck your foot in it, didn't you?" she asked.

That sounded like a question, but Craig took it as a statement of fact. After all, he'd told himself the same thing moments earlier. "Do you have any suggestions as to how I might get it out? Shoe leather doesn't taste too great."

"Grovel," Lisa said.

"I already did that. It just made her madder." Hell, he'd shared his deepest secret, and still Casey hadn't forgiven him. What else could he do? "She's punishing me for being honest. Damn it, she asked me why I asked her out. What was wrong with me telling her I thought she was one hot babe?"

"Nothing. If that's the way you said it."

"It was."

"And that made her mad?"

Craig tried to sort out the chronology. "Not exactly. She got mad after she asked me why I'd waited so long to ask her out."

"That's when you told her you thought she'd be an easy lay?"

"I never said that." But he remembered Casey putting those words into his mouth. "Hey, give me a break. How could I not have thought she wanted to get it on? She came on to me like gangbusters."

Lisa ought to know that. After all, she was the one who gave Casey the lessons with the cucumber.

"There's nothing wrong with you thinking it, but it wasn't smart for you to say. No woman wants to hear she was asked out because her lover guessed she'd be a fast, easy piece of ass.

"Even if she is one. I ought to know." Her voice dropped to just above a whisper, as though that admission hadn't come easy.

"How was I supposed to know she was a goddamn virgin?"

"Should she have hung a sign around her neck?"

"Of course not. But—"

"She didn't know *you* were. She wouldn't know now if you hadn't told her."

"That's different."

Damn it, Casey had confided in Lisa. Craig's ears burned. Good thing the woman couldn't see him turning red.

"She loves you."

That made no sense to him at all. "Then why won't she talk to me?"

"You hurt her."

From Lisa's tone, he guessed she assessed his cognitive ability as about equal to that of a three-year-old. "Damn it, I didn't mean to hurt her. I love her, too."

Suddenly it didn't matter that on his mental master plan he'd penciled in falling in love a few years down the road. He loved Casey now, and it felt good. It would, that is, if Lisa was right and Casey loved him, too. "I love her," he repeated, just to hear the words again.

Lisa chuckled. "You need to tell Casey, not me."

"I would if she'd talk to me."

"She went to bed early tonight. Maybe if you come over tomorrow—"

"Tomorrow I've got the damn charity games."

"I saw something about the swimming events starting early in the morning at the gym. What time will the games wrap up?"

Not soon enough. "I don't know. Why don't you and Casey come watch? Hell, bring along another friend or two. I left a bunch of tickets for the field events at the gym with Russ."

"I'll see what I can do."

"Thanks."

Lisa stared at the phone after Craig hung up. He seemed like a hell of a decent guy.

A good boy for her good-girl roommate who couldn't become a bad girl no matter how hard she tried.

Damn it, there was no need for Craig and Casey both to be depressed. He loved her and she loved him.

Unlike Lisa, Casey hadn't sworn off love.

Maybe if she asked Mike to take them...yes, that would work. Her dewy-eyed roommate would jump at the chance to play Cupid.

Telling herself that she was only doing this to help Casey and Craig out, Lisa dialed a familiar cell phone number.

"What changed your mind?" Mike asked a few minutes later when Lisa met him at the door.

"I missed you." It soothed her conscience when she realized that was the truth—just not the whole truth, so help her God.

"Good. I missed you, too."

The gentle kiss he brushed across her lips promised a lot. More than the hot and heavy, sometimes kinky sex they'd been sharing since their first date more than a month ago.

It promised more than Lisa was ready for.

She stroked down the length of his muscular body. When his cock swelled against his jeans, she gave him a playful squeeze. Hell, she could handle lust. And wallow in the erotic pleasure she found when they got it on together. It was the

tenderness she saw in his dark eyes and felt in the gentle brush of his callused fingers along her bare arms that scared her half to death.

She had to keep this carnal. "Come to bed?"

"Not so fast, love. We're gonna back up and take a few of the steps we skipped. Maybe then you'll believe me when I say—"

"Don't say it, Mike. Those are three words I don't ever want to hear."

"Why?"

"Because they're words. Just words."

"You didn't believe me, did you?" he asked.

"No."

No matter what he thought now, the time would come when he'd let her down. He was a man, and men did that. Lisa was a quick study. She hadn't needed another lesson in getting hurt since Jake ran out on her years ago.

"Come on, darlin'. We'll do it your way, but I'll make a believer out of you yet." He scooped her in his arms and carried her to her bedroom.

She let him do it because, after all, mindless pleasure was what she'd wanted from him all along. Even more than she wanted his help to get her roommate back on the road to romance.

Still, Lisa let him in on her plan for Casey first, before she let him take her to a place where there was no pain, no conflict. Only two steaming, straining bodies caught up in an erotic swirl of sexual sensation.

Chapter Fifteen

Funny.

The sounds of Lisa and Mike making love in the room next door had never bothered Casey before. Now that she knew from experience what they were doing, her body heated with embarrassment. And need.

She sat up, suddenly confused. Her mind must have been playing tricks on her because she was certain Lisa had gone to her room alone last night. Like Tom last month and Carlos the month before, Mike was history.

Wasn't he?

No, that definitely was Mike's deep, rumbling voice echoing through the thin wall.

"Open up for me, darlin.'"

And Lisa's high-pitched cry, "Oh, yesss. Fuck me, harder. I'll fuckin' kill you if you stop. Oh, Mikeee."

At least her roommate wasn't pouting now.

If only Casey could nudge time back a week. Her nipples tingled. Her muscles tightened, as though they remembered everything. As though they wanted Craig to fill the aching void he'd created inside her.

Why had she made such a big deal of his motives? If she hadn't, she wouldn't be aching now.

More erotic whimpers assailed her through the walls. They were driving her insane.

Casey got up, put on shorts and a top, and went to the kitchen to escape from the sounds. Hot black coffee scalded her throat a few minutes later. A week ago she'd wakened to the aroma of a fragrant coconut and coffee blend Craig had brought

to her in bed. She'd tasted it afterward on his lips and tongue. A hot breeze had kissed their naked bodies as he licked her pussy on that big, round bed.

She ached now. Not for anybody. Only him. Some bad girl she'd turned out to be.

Well, maybe she was a little bad, because she ached to touch his big, delicious cock, open her pussy for him to pleasure. Taste him on her tongue and have him fill the empty spot inside her and make her come.

She'd been a fool to walk out. To let pride get the better of her desires. Maybe in time he'd love her. Or maybe he wouldn't. Maybe it didn't matter that he'd asked her out because he was looking for some quick sex.

Casey had never been lonelier.

A few minutes later Lisa and Mike joined her at the kitchen table, both looking disgustingly satisfied.

"Come on, Casey," Lisa told her. "We're taking you out for the day. Time to quit crying over your lawyer and have some fun."

Casey didn't want to go. But Lisa wouldn't take no for an answer.

"Come on," she said when she followed Casey into her room. "You've got to help me keep this thing with Mike from getting out of hand."

"He's getting into your head?" Mike had obviously gotten to Lisa's pussy, Casey thought uncharitably.

"I'm afraid he may have. Come on, girlfriend, you don't want me to go do something I'll regret."

"Okay. Do I need to change?"

"You're fine. Brush your hair and let's get going."

* * * * *

Casey didn't want to watch the games Craig had trained so hard for. The games he'd said were one more rung on his ladder to success.

How could Lisa have dragged her here to the gym?

Chlorine stung her eyes. Or was it unshed tears? She didn't know.

Sunlight streamed through the fiberglass ceiling panels. Swimmers and spectators milled around on the deck. She liked the pool better in moonlight, when no one had been around to distract her from watching Craig.

Had it really been only eleven days since they'd swum here in the moonlight, since she'd admired his powerful stroke and his long, lean body while he did his workout? Eleven days? It seemed like years since she'd touched and tasted him, even though in her head she knew it hadn't been quite a week.

Trying to make herself as inconspicuous as possible, Casey hugged the damp concrete wall outside the women's dressing room and eyed the competitors.

"Wow. Testosterone city," Lisa said, her gaze drifting over the nearly naked competitors huddled near the edge of the pool.

Mike pulled Lisa close and wrapped his muscular arms around her. "My money's on the cops."

The detectives in their blue Speedos outnumbered the lawyers in their red suits. For the most part, Casey thought, they looked younger and in a lot better shape. Except for Craig. His washboard abs didn't hang out the way some of his teammates' beer guts did. Half a head taller than most of the others on his team, he had a body honed for maximum efficiency. Casey admired his hard, well-developed muscles, cut but not bulging.

Familiar muscles that made her drool. And made her wet with need. She watched the slow, easy rise and fall of his lightly furred chest and remembered how his flat coppery nipples hardened when she'd teased them with her tongue.

Apparently nothing fazed him. His jaw was set, his gaze focused. Totally focused, she imagined, on the races ahead. Last

weekend he'd been that focused on her. But he hadn't been that calm and collected.

Her nipples hardened. Moisture welled up between her legs. Damn him. He'd planted his cock in her brain as well as her body. She was a fool to have walked out. Twice a fool because she still wanted him to want her for more than sex.

When he climbed onto a starting block, his thigh muscles contracted visibly. The scar on his thigh looked more pronounced now than it had when she first noticed it. She wanted to feel those hard, well-defined muscles quiver again when he was buried deep inside her pussy.

A gun went off, and four guys hit the water.

Craig was good. Half a pool length better than the young detective who came in second, whose buddies were now hauling his oxygen-starved body out of the water. Craig's biceps bulged as he levered himself out of the pool unaided. Casey wanted to feel those muscles again, up close and personal.

"Your man's a hell of a swimmer," Mike said while the next race was going on.

"He went to college on a swimming scholarship."

Lisa rubbed the back of her head against Mike's chest. "You played baseball, didn't you?"

"Until I screwed up my elbow."

Casey half-listened to Lisa and Mike while she watched the next two events.

"Casey?" Craig's deep voice poured over her like honey.

How had he managed to sneak up on her?

She tried to back up, but the wall was in the way. She was neatly trapped. "Congratulations. You won."

"Did I?"

What did he mean? "Of course. You smoked the other guys."

"It would have been a shocker if I hadn't. Not to mention that my boss probably would have fired me. The best of my competition was an also-ran high school swimmer."

"Why are you asking me if you won, then?"

He looked into her eyes. "I'm asking about us. You're here. Does that mean you're willing to give me another chance?"

"I don't know." Could she risk shattering an already fractured heart to fulfill the fierce demands of her body?

"Hey, Craig, you're up again," one of his teammates yelled.

He cradled her cheek in his hand. "Please."

"They need you over there." She tried not to let his touch erode her resolve.

"Okay. Will you at least be at the finish line this afternoon when I get done with the triathlon?"

She couldn't resist the plea in his voice–not that she imagined Lisa and Mike would let her escape even if she tried. "I'll be there."

As she followed him with her gaze as he hurried across the pool deck, she made her decision. More accurately she remembered the decision she'd made after Buck had ditched her for a woman who fulfilled his fantasies.

Craig was the man of her dreams, and she intended to act out every fantasy she'd ever had with him.

So what if she wasn't the woman who fit perfectly into his well-defined life plan? What did it matter if he had an agenda that didn't include a serious relationship in the foreseeable future? Casey had no desire to be Craig's best buddy, no need for him to see her as the good girl who lived next door and no need to punish herself by playing the outraged former virgin she didn't want to be.

If he came to love her, fine. If not, she'd live with that, too. At least she would have lived. And loved. And experienced more of the incredible erotic sensations Craig had given her a first taste of last weekend. She closed her eyes, imagined his

wonderful blue eyes glowing with desire as he fit himself inside her and began an erotic dance.

Suddenly Casey couldn't wait until the games were over.

* * * * *

The marker ribbon blew in the breeze, a welcome reminder that this triathlon was almost finished. As was Craig.

One more kilometer to go. His lungs burned. Every damaged muscle, tendon, and ligament in his left leg screamed its protest every time his foot made contact with the blacktop pavement.

Damn, his three hundred dollar running shoes were supposed to have cushioned the impact, but they were doing a lousy job.

Spectators cheered. The fierce sun beat down on him. Sweat poured out from under the soaked band around his head and dripped into his eyes. And the sound of pounding feet behind him let him know someone was getting close.

Too close. He drew into his reserves, increased the pace. His leg protested. His best wasn't going to be good enough, he thought when a runner drew up beside him.

Maybe it was Dwayne. But it wasn't. From the corner of his eye Craig noticed a blur of dark blue. He had to cross the line first.

Gasping for air, he made himself move faster. Ignoring the pain, he matched the pace set by the cop who was trying to get past him.

Running had never been his forte. Bicycling, either. Even before the accident. When he'd climbed out of the water from the swim, no one had been close. This guy had been nowhere in sight, but he sure as hell had caught up now.

Suddenly Craig was staring at his back. And more pounding feet reverberated on the pavement not far behind him. *You've got to win. First and fourth will do it. Can't count on Dwayne*

to come in third. The boss's shouted admonition still rang in Craig's ears.

The team was counting on him.

He held the grueling pace, waited for an adrenaline rush that didn't come.

Then he remembered Casey. She'd said she'd see him at the finish line. He wanted her to see him as a winner. Not a loser. He didn't want to be a loser in her eyes.

He summoned the last of his strength and willed one last burst of speed his body couldn't deliver on its own. He saw red. Green. Bright flashes of yellow. A kaleidoscope of colors bathed in agony. And a finish line up ahead.

It was almost over. Five more steps. Four. Three. Two. Had he won? It didn't matter now. He'd crossed the line and collapsed at Casey's feet.

"Get him some water," a woman called out.

Someone else yelled, "Move back."

The shouts echoed in Craig's ears as though they came from another time, another place. He gasped for breath and cushioned his cheek on Casey's smooth, warm thigh. She wiped the sweat off his face, first with her palm, then with something that felt cool and damp.

"Try to drink this." The bottle she held to his parched lips was ice-cold and mercifully wet.

When he managed to control his breathing he gulped, then sputtered.

"Careful. Not too much at one time," she cautioned.

"Let's move him over in the shade, away from the finish line." Dwayne grabbed both his arms and heaved him out of Casey's lap.

Craig couldn't let her get away.

But he couldn't gather enough breath to talk, so he got a hold on the belt loop of her shorts and dragged her along.

"Are you okay?" she asked a few minutes later.

Craig's sweat-soaked hair cooled Casey's thigh when he turned his head. "I think so. Did I win?"

"Yes."

Bright sunlight filtered through the fat leaves of the tree where Craig's coworkers had brought him to recuperate, imprinting a pattern on his golden-tanned flesh.

"I had to do it, you know."

No, Casey didn't know. These games, though hard-fought, weren't about winning or losing as far as she could tell. They were about helping fund a children's shelter.

"Why?"

"Part of the plan. Keep the boss happy."

There it was, Craig's plan. The plan that had him picking out a wife a few years down the road and settling down, among other milestones that he'd mentioned the other night.

The plan that had kept him a virgin until an obstacle popped up in his well-orchestrated career path and made him hit on her to end that state.

"Hey Craig. Get over here. We need you in this picture," someone bellowed over the noise from the crowd.

"Help me up?"

He should stay here and rest until his pulse slowed down, but Casey knew he wouldn't, so she helped him to his feet and stepped away.

"Come with me."

"I'll wait here." This was his win, and he deserved to enjoy it.

"No."

With surprising strength for someone who had passed out moments earlier, he took her hand and pulled her up against his sweaty body. When they reached the crowd of celebrating lawyers, though, Casey hung back with Lisa and Mike.

"Traitors," she whispered.

Lisa smiled. "Give the guy a chance. Mike and I are heading out now. We'll be at his place if you need us."

So Mike was back in Lisa's life, at least for now. That was good. Casey glanced at Craig.

"He hasn't asked me to go with him."

"He will," Lisa told her. "He's the one who begged me to get you here."

With that, Lisa tugged at Mike's hand, and they left Casey standing there alone.

* * * * *

Craig wanted Casey with him. Not hanging back as though she didn't belong.

He responded automatically to his boss's congratulations and his co-workers' wisecracks. He laughed at jokes about the competition's ineptness—though as a matter of fact the detectives had been worthy opponents, even for him and the others Wells said he'd recruited for the main purpose of kicking Chief Delgado's butt.

Beating that weekend triathlete had damn near killed him. His lungs were still burning now, thirty minutes after having finished the race. And he could barely put any weight on his bum leg.

"Hey, Craig. Are you bringing your girl to dinner?" Dwayne looked like Craig felt– drained.

"I don't think so." The idea of eating food made his stomach queasy. Besides, even though Casey had stayed and nursed him after he collapsed at the finish line, he was none too certain she'd agree to go with him on anything resembling a date.

"Congratulations on finishing third," he told Dwayne. "That guy was good."

"Damn good. We're lucky you blew him away on the swimming leg. Hey, you ought to come celebrate. After all, we wouldn't have won without you."

Craig wanted to celebrate with Casey. Alone. Not that he was in shape to do much more than cuddle with her on his bed if she was willing, which was a big "if."

But maybe she'd like to socialize. "Casey?"

Noticing that Lisa and her boyfriend apparently had deserted her, he motioned for her to join him. He loved the way she smiled. And the bare expanse of satiny skin between her red shorts and the tropical-print sleeveless shirt she had on gave his cock ideas his body was in no shape at the moment to follow up on. "Would you like to go celebrate with these clowns?"

She looked down at herself and grinned. "I'm not exactly dressed to kill." Her gaze shifted to his torso. "Come to think of it, neither are you."

"We'll go change, first."

Suddenly his soaked-through biking shorts and tank top itched. The stench of his own sweat filled his nostrils. "I don't know about you, but I need a shower—bad."

Her nose was cute when she wrinkled it up. "You are a little ripe."

"We'll clean up, then celebrate. Okay?"

"Okay."

No argument. She had mellowed since Monday night. Craig made a mental note to do something nice for that hot little roommate of hers whose powers of persuasion must have done his own skills one better. Finally remembering the manners his mom had drilled into his head, he introduced Casey to Dwayne and other coworkers in the immediate vicinity.

"We'll meet you at Bennie's Place," he told Dwayne. "Seven thirty, right?"

"Right. Earlier if you want to down a few before we order. Aren't you planning to stick around for the trophy presentation?

Wells is expecting you to accept it for the team and say a few words."

"Let him accept the trophy. He's been waiting long enough to get the damn thing. I'm out of here."

Getting Casey back in his life meant a hell of a lot more to Craig than collecting a stupid trophy. She meant more than his timetable, more even than his carefully laid plans for success.

Chapter Sixteen

"Mr. Wells gave me the creeps," she said late that night when she crawled into his bed after the celebration.

"If he weren't the state attorney, I'd have decked him. I should have, anyway." The obnoxious bastard had barely been able to keep his paws off Casey. Of course, most of his male colleagues had kept shooting admiring glances her way, too. That hadn't surprised Craig. What had surprised him was that the women at the party seemed to like her, too.

Of course they hadn't seen her in those neon outfits she wore at the gym or the fuck-me please black minidress that had his tongue hanging out when she'd worn it last weekend. His balls tightened when he recalled that see-through nightie he'd peeled off her. No one but him had ever seen her in that. He wanted to keep it that way.

Tonight she'd stepped out of her room wearing a simple long sheath dress that veiled her most obvious assets, and he was damn grateful. The black mini might have made Wells' eyes pop out of his head.

"I liked your dress," he told her.

She looked damn sexy now as she sat up and slithered out of his T-shirt that she'd commandeered to use as a robe. Gloriously naked, she snuggled up beside him and propped her head up on one hand.

"You looked nice, too. But I like you best like this." She ran her hand down his bare torso, stopping to trace the jagged scar on his thigh.

Her warmth contrasted pleasantly with cool air that made its way from the air conditioner vent, and the faint fragrance of

his soap-on-a-rope lingered on her body. It smelled a lot better on her than it did on him.

"How's your leg?" she asked.

"In agonizing pain at the moment, but I'll live." He met her worried gaze. "Don't say it. I've got nobody but me to blame."

Every muscle in his body ached. He didn't want to move, but that didn't keep his balls from aching or his cock from standing at attention when she wriggled around and caught it between her small hands.

"Part of you apparently has made a quick recovery," she whispered, then nibbled at his ear.

"The key word is 'part.' If you want to fuck tonight, you'll have to do most of the work. I think I may die." As if to dispute him, his cock twitched in her hands.

Her hands warmed his back where she stroked him. Gentle pressure on his backside urged him closer. Her hard little nipples dug into his chest.

Damn it, he wished he had the energy to move enough so he could bathe them with his tongue. He stroked her satiny bottom, then moved his hand between her legs and stroked her wet, warm slit. She was just as silky there. Only hotter. And deliciously wet. He slipped one finger inside her cunt.

"That feels good."

Somehow lying here like this felt more intimate than being buried deep inside her. More personal than tasting her sweet, musky secrets or having her take him in her mouth and drive him crazy.

Craig felt her innocence and his own.

Was he losing his mind? Neither of them was innocent any more. They were lying in bed, naked, so close they might as well be fucking. Hell, if he hadn't nearly killed himself with that triathlon, he'd be pummeling her with his cock right now.

Then it came to him. Innocence was a state of the mind, not the body. Some professor in an ethics class he'd taken had said that, if he recalled correctly.

Today he'd gone for the image he wanted the world to see: success at any cost. He'd laid another cornerstone on his journey to success.

He was a goddamned fool. He'd ignored doctors' warnings about stressing his damaged leg and followed up the mile swim he'd enjoyed and a grueling bike ride he'd merely endured with a killer ten-K run, for no better reason than to win points with the pompous ass he worked for.

Now he'd be lucky if he could do more than hobble around for the next week or so. He'd paid a pretty stiff price for this cornerstone.

Worse, he'd exacted a high price from Casey. First he'd dismissed her as not the kind of woman he wanted for a wife. Then he'd hit on her deliberately, to get it on with her and round out his carnal knowledge before trying the Ranger case.

She deserved so much more. "I love you," he said, lifting his head off the pillow and meeting her gaze.

Her dark eyes widened. Unshed tears made them glisten in the dim light from a bedside lamp. "Do you really?"

"Yeah. I do. A lot."

"I love you, too."

Lisa had told him she did, but Craig hadn't believed it until now, when he heard it from Casey's own lips. He leaned over and gave her a gentle kiss.

As recently as this morning he'd been thinking timetables. He'd gloated over his string of successes in the courtroom, certain they would bag him a partnership in a major firm sooner than he'd first calculated. He'd revised his timetable downward, estimated that he could achieve in two years what he'd originally thought would take three or four.

Two years wasn't too long for an engagement, he'd decided. Not at all. The idea had actually fit pretty well into his

revised plan. He'd visualized a fancy wedding and an impressive house with an impressive address. Two kids later on–the son he'd always assumed he'd have someday, then a little girl who somehow had made her way into his well-laid plan.

That distant goal had seemed more real once he'd given a face and body to his intended partner, but he'd forgotten something vital.

It hadn't taken him too long to determine the problem. Two years was way too long to wait for the right to wake up with Casey every morning. And it was much too long to string her along when he knew some idiot had had hurt her when he'd left her practically at the altar. Craig almost felt sorry for the idiot, because he'd missed out on making love with Casey.

Hell, two weeks was too long to delay his future, now that he realized Casey meant everything to him. "Let's get married," he said, cupping her face between his hands and looking into her soft, dark eyes. "I want to make love to you every way I've ever read about and some I haven't. And to sleep next to you every night and see your pretty face every morning when I wake up."

Her smile lit up the room. "Every night?"

"Well, maybe not every night until my leg forgives me for entering that triathlon," he said, though at the moment he felt as though he could take on the world. "What about it, baby?"

"When do you want to do it?"

Craig wanted to tie her to him now, but he doubted he could drag his body out of bed, much less to the nearest justice of the peace. "How about next weekend?" He should be able to walk normally by then. Besides, that would give him time to find the perfect wedding present for his perfect lover.

"I'd like that. Now roll over on your back."

"Why?" he asked.

Casey gave him a playful shove. "I want to taste one of those cherry condoms we didn't try out last weekend."

He wasn't about to tell her no. "They're in the night stand."

While she rolled the triple-x confection onto his throbbing cock, he tried to memorize her features. "Love me, baby," he murmured when she met his gaze.

"I do. Now let's fuck."

* * * * *

They'd done it.

Gotten married. Five days after Craig's proposal, in Las Vegas, with no muss, no fuss, and no getting left at the altar.

Casey's brand-new wedding band winked up at her from its place on her finger beside the two-carat solitaire Craig had put there five days earlier. She set her heart-shaped bouquet of roses and carnations on a massive heart-shaped bed.

"Too bad Lisa didn't want to catch this," she told her brand-new husband who was busy baring his gorgeous body for her pleasure.

"Mike didn't argue about catching the garter." Craig looped his tie around her neck and dragged her to him for a long, hungry kiss.

"I know."

Neon lights from the strip flashed red and green and purple outside the bridal suite of the resort center's newest luxury hotel and casino.

The colors played against Craig's bare chest, drawing Casey's gaze there and lower when he pushed his dark-gray suit pants down and off.

He was gorgeous standing there, wearing nothing but his socks, his wedding band, and dark silk boxers. Casey had a hard time believing he was hers. If she pinched herself again, though, she'd be black and blue.

She shot him a sultry smile and shed the simple off-white sheath dress she'd worn for their wedding. "Do you think they'll stay over?"

"What? Lisa and Mike? Yeah. He booked them a room before we went to the chapel."

From the heated look in Craig's eyes and his ragged breathing, Casey guessed he liked the lacy half-bra, cream-colored stockings and matching lace garter belt that were all she'd worn underneath her dress. She knew for sure he liked what he saw when he shed his boxers and bared an enthusiastic erection.

"Come here, wife." He set her bouquet on the nightstand and pulled her down beside him.

With one hand, he urged her legs apart and opened her to his gaze. With the other he stroked her. First her satiny bare pussy framed by garters and pale silk stockings, then the little heart-shaped tuft of curls that seemed to fascinate him so.

He bent and ran his tongue along her glistening slit.

Watching in the ceiling mirror, seeing her pussy open and vulnerable and him paying homage to it with his mouth, had to be the ultimate turn-on. It certainly was the ultimate reflection of mutual trust.

He blew gently on her clit, then nuzzled her mound. "I'm partial to hearts. And to this velvety soft skin I love to touch and kiss."

"It's not natural."

"I guessed as much. But I like it. A lot."

Casey tried not to dwell on how often she'd have to visit Luisa to keep her Brazilian bikini wax job neat for Craig's pleasure.

He dipped his dark head down and used his fingers to spread her labia. His slick, hot tongue did its magic before he caught her clit again. It throbbed, as though anticipating his attention, and he sucked it in while tickling it with fast, hard flicks of his tongue.

His hands were warm and arousing on her breasts when he slid the half-cups down and plucked the exposed nipples until they throbbed.

The erotic sensations spread like wildfire through her body. When she looked in the ceiling mirror, she gasped at the sensual picture they made.

Slick red sheets. Vanilla lace and silk. Craig's dark head caught between her stocking-clad thighs as he drank the wet, pulsing juices that flowed from her pussy. Her breasts lifted by the half-bra, held in his big hands to bring them both pleasure.

Her face looked flushed, her hair spread around it like a veil. Her mouth was slack and her breathing labored, evidence of her desire. It was the most erotic picture she'd ever seen.

So erotic it spread incredible sensations to every nerve in her body, from her clit…her nipples…even from her eyes as they took in the ultimate intimacy between a man and a woman. Intimacy that transcended anything she'd dreamed of when she set out in search of pleasure.

Intimacy so deep, so complete that when her climax came, it seemed almost like a benediction…her body sealing the promises she'd made.

A few minutes later Craig set her on his lap and joined their bodies in one smooth thrust. His sapphire gaze enthralled her, as it had the first time they met.

"I love you." Finally. Her fear was gone. She could tell him what was in her heart, knowing he loved her too.

When he kissed her, she tasted herself on his lips. Their hearts beat in unison as they rocked back and forth, no longer separate but linked not only by the irresistible sexual attraction that brought them together, but also by something so much stronger.

The bonds of love.

Epilogue
Bone Gap, Texas, three months later

"Looks like ol' Buck was dead wrong about Casey."

"Her new husband's brought out the spice in our girl, that's for sure. They can hardly take their hands off each other."

The two elderly cowboys had staked out their usual spot at the Bone Gap Grange, near the water trough where they'd iced down the beer kegs.

It was party time, all right. Bob Thompson didn't barbecue one of his prime steers for just any old occasion. The aroma had the old men's mouths watering.

"Boss put on a fittin' welcome for Casey and her lawyer," one said.

The other nodded. "Casey's brother told me they eloped to Las Vegas two weeks after he asked her out. Guess he couldn't wait to stake his claim. Fast movers, them city boys."

"No, I couldn't wait." His arm around Casey, Craig joined the cowboys and held out his plastic cup for a refill.

"Zach, Rocky, this is my husband." She looked lovingly up at Craig. "These two old wranglers have been working at the Bar T since before I was born."

A lot had happened in the five and a half months since Casey had left Bone Gap. Good things, and she had Craig to thank for most of them.

Heat suffused her cheeks when she recalled last night–and the erotic games they'd played in the hayloft of her parents' barn.

They might have been curious teens risking getting caught, except that they had the added aphrodisiac of mutual, committed love.

She and Craig had learned a lot about each other in the three months since they'd exchanged vows in Vegas.

He liked his coffee hot and black, for instance. And he showered and shaved every morning even if he'd done it the night before. He wanted light starch in the collars and cuffs of his dress shirts, which thankfully he didn't expect her to wash and iron.

He didn't like to talk about his weaknesses, especially the leg she'd only realized was seriously damaged after he competed in that charity triathlon.

And she'd found he was possessive. He expected her to wear her rings all the time, especially when she was working with clients at the gym.

She didn't mind, even though she told him every chance she got that not even Todd, who'd lost thirty pounds and was starting to look almost human, could hold a candle to him. Besides, Craig wore the plain gold band she'd given him like a badge of honor. Turn about was fair play.

Casey got wet when she thought about some very personal secrets she'd learned, such as the way Craig's cock got hard when she blew on his ear but not when she played with his nipples. And that he blushed when she whispered outrageous, erotic suggestions in his ear.

He'd discovered things about her, too, such as the fact she liked the feel of the vibrator on her clit better than inside her pussy. And that she had a thing for watching them fucking in the mirror he'd glued to the ceiling above their bed.

Together they'd experimented with positions and techniques outlined in the books he'd bought. They'd found places on each other's bodies that turned them on, places neither of them had ever thought of as erogenous.

They'd also discovered supposedly erotic acts that sent them both into gales of uncontrollable laughter.

Casey wanted them to keep on learning together for years to come.

Now, though, they needed to socialize.

It looked as if nobody for miles around had turned down her parents' invitation to meet her almost brand-new husband.

She should have expected a crowd. After all, the harvest was in, and the cattle had gone to the big feed lots in Lubbock. Thanksgiving was just around the corner. Not to mention that folks were curious about what sort of guy she'd managed to rope and hogtie.

Everybody was ready to show Craig a good old-fashioned Texas hoedown.

There were her parents, chatting with Craig's mom. Casey had liked her the moment they met, and was glad she'd joined Craig's brother, sister-in-law, and their three daughters for the trip to Bone Gap.

"Our families seem to be getting along," Craig observed as they made their way across the wide-plank dance floor.

"I'm glad."

"Look. There are Mike and Lisa."

Her former roommate waved from across the room. The diamond on her finger sparkled in the light from one of the multicolored revolving spheres that hung from the ceiling.

"We'll have to find them something nice for their wedding next month."

"Yeah. If it hadn't been for them dragging you to that triathlon, we might not have made it this far," Craig said as he looked around the room.

Apparently he didn't find what or who he was looking for, because he shot her an expectant grin.

"Want to go check the barbecue pit? I've got something I want to give you."

A kiss, Casey imagined, or an erotic invitation she'd have to wait awhile to collect on.

"Let's do it," she said, always ready for whatever new sensual adventure he suggested.

The late autumn moon was full and high in the sky. The cool, dry air smelled of late-fall chrysanthemums and her dad's secret barbecue sauce.

Craig stopped outside the grange door, stilling her by caressing her shoulders through the clingy winter-white sweater dress he'd picked out for her to wear over the bra and garter belt she first wore to their wedding.

His breath was warm against her neck. Whatever he draped around it made her shiver.

She looked down and saw it. A perfect, heart-shaped ruby on a thin, gold chain. "Oh, Craig. It's beautiful."

"So are you."

He kissed her neck, at the same time drawing her close enough to feel the pulsing of his cock against her bottom.

God, but he knew how to make her crazy for him.

With one big hand, he cupped her smooth pussy through the soft knit material of her dress.

"I think I told you I'm partial to hearts," he said, and then he gave her neck a gentle nip.

"I am, too." And she was, in spite of the discomfort involved in taking care of that heart he liked so well. In the past three months she'd made three return visits to Luisa. She guessed she'd be making many more.

After all, what was a little pain compared to the erotic pleasures that heart symbolized?

Like she'd said she would, Casey had come a long way from being the plain vanilla PE teacher, perennial good pal and all-around good girl. She'd set herself free. And she'd caught the hunkiest man of all, not just for a moment but for always.

Craig turned her around, smiled down at her.

He still had a smile that could melt Antarctica.

And he'd made her hottest fantasies come alive.

"Later, baby," he whispered before they headed back inside.

"Yes. Later."

Casey was over being a good girl. Now she liked being a bad, bad girl—but only for her very own virgin hunk.

EYE OF THE STORM

Prologue

Marcy Kramer had to get out. After the day she'd had in court and the hour-long bitch session she'd endured afterward with Harper Wells, her asshole boss, she could have downed a pitcher of strawberry margaritas, so it wasn't Bennie's Place or the bustle of the crowd that had her making her excuses after one quick drink.

No. It was listening to her former colleagues crowing about their respective offspring's marvelous achievements that sent her running.

Somehow the furtive fucking she'd enjoyed last night with one of Harper's newest fair-haired law school grads seemed meaningless compared with babies' first words...first steps...first solid foods. Her lover's "Jeez, lady, you sure can fuck" paled in comparison with the loving way her friends' husbands greeted them.

Shit! Marcy, get hold of yourself. You decided eons ago that love wasn't worth the pain that being married to Sam had caused. You told yourself you didn't need support, and you didn't need love as long as you could find a hard body and a harder cock.

When she opened the door to her big, empty house, a welcome burst of cool air greeted her. Apparently no one had told the weatherman it was almost October...already fall, even in sultry Tampa, because it had to be close to ninety degrees outside. After she set her briefcase on the marble-topped table in the foyer, Marcy shed her suit jacket and pulled the tortoise-shell comb from her shoulder-length hair and stashed it in her purse so it would be handy the next time she had a court appearance.

Comfy now that she'd kicked off her high-heeled pumps, she picked up the mail her housekeeper had left for her and

padded into her office. Bills. Always bills. She didn't know whether she got more bills or junk mail. A large, cream-colored envelope addressed with calligraphy instead of plain scrawled handwriting sat on top of the stack.

Who the hell was getting married now? Curious in spite of her annoyance with slight acquaintances that trolled for gifts with wholesale invitations to their weddings, she ripped open the outer envelope, then fumbled with the inner one. The office gossip mill must have gotten clogged, because she hadn't heard of any of her colleagues who were planning a blowout wedding.

"Great. Just fucking great!" Ileana, her former next door neighbor, who she hadn't seen in ten years. She and Sam had offered Ileana comfort when she'd lost her husband in a drive-by shooting. Afterward, they'd lost touch when Ileana had transferred to medical school in Gainesville, unable to stand seeing places and old friends that reminded her of Ben. Now it was Ileana who'd apparently found a new lifetime mate, while she was the one alone except for a string of meaningless fucking partners.

Marcy wasn't going to cry. She wasn't. And she wasn't about to miss out on celebrating her old friend's good luck. Maybe she'd take Cam Willis. No, not him. If she showed up with that baby-faced boy-toy, it would look as though she were robbing the cradle. Hell, maybe she was. She considered several other potential escorts, discarding each when she figured spending an entire weekend with any of them on an island just might make her retch. For a minute she hesitated, then marked decisively that she'd be attending Ileana's wedding alone.

Determined to shake off the blue funk that threatened, she picked up the phone and arranged to meet her wet-behind-the-ears lover later. She might not have love, but she could always manage to scare up a bedmate.

* * * * *

So Ileana was finally getting married again. Good for her.

Sam Kramer stared down at the heavy invitation with its raised lettering, idly watching the tissue liner slide off the paper and float down onto the cluttered surface of his desk. Why the hell did they put tissue paper inside wedding invitations anyhow? Setting the invitation down, he made a mental note to send a present along with his regrets. Marcy would probably be there hanging onto one of her current lovers.

Fuck. Why should he stay away? He'd been Ileana's friend, too. He'd hurt for her as much as Marcy had after Ben's untimely death. The four of them had been practically inseparable whenever they had a few spare moments, since he and Ben had been lab partners in med school and Ileana and Marcy had been finishing their last year of undergraduate studies together at University of Miami. Ben and Ileana had been as much in love as Sam and Marcy.

Hell, they'd probably have broken up years ago if Ben had lived. Marriages rarely lasted long these days. His own marriage—even the coldly civilized divorce that had ended it— was ancient history.

If he didn't go to this wedding, Marcy would think he stayed away because of her. And no way would Sam do anything because of, or in spite of, his ex-wife. He didn't give a shit if she'd fucked damn near every lawyer in town and half the docs since their divorce. Picking up the invitation again, he noticed the ceremony was to be held on Cabbage Key. He knew the place, a rustic resort on a small island off Port Charlotte, accessible only by boat. Great place to kick back and enjoy the water and sand, get a little R&R. It had a restaurant that served the best stone crab claws he'd ever eaten.

He hadn't taken the *Lucky Lady* out as much lately as he'd have liked to. Maybe he'd motor down the Intracoastal Waterway from Tampa, fish a little, enjoy a few days' vacation— and witness an old friend taking the plunge into married bliss. Anyway, he hoped Ileana and—he glanced down at the invitation—Joshua Klosinski would be more successful at marriage than he and Marcy had been.

"You need anything before I head home, Sam?"

Sam looked up at Joanne, his capable office manager and sometimes-lover when they both got the itch at the same time. "Yeah. Can you clear my schedule for a day or two before and after this wedding?"

She glanced at the dates on the invitation he'd handed her. "Sure."

"Then let's do it. I need a few days off." He picked up the RSVP card and checked off that he'd be attending, hesitating only a moment before indicating that he wouldn't be bringing a guest. Then he handed it to her along with the envelope that came with it. "Mail this if you don't mind."

"Okay. Anything else?"

"Not right now."

Joanne smiled. "Don't forget, you're meeting Gray Syzmanski at the gym at six. I have a hard time understanding where you find the energy to work out after spending all day in surgery."

Sam groaned. Exercise was his albatross. He hated taking the time but if he didn't, he'd soon revert to flab, probably develop a paunch like his dad's. As he shrugged off his lab coat and grabbed his keys, he gave credit where it was due: Marcy. For all she'd done to hurt him, she'd managed to coax the skinny, nerdy kid he'd been to hone his body into some semblance of "hunkdom" as she'd called it. She'd also taught him how to dress for success and persuaded him, after a lot of badgering, that a good hairstylist beat a barber all to hell for taming his unruly thatch of curls.

Yeah, his marriage hadn't been a total bust. Even if it did hurt like hell every time he heard yet another cock was pleasuring the pussy that used to be his own.

Chapter One

Marcy heard the storm warnings but shrugged them off. For years now, the National Hurricane Service had been posting dire predictions about this storm or that one, but none in her memory had actually created much havoc on Florida's Gulf Coast. Likely as not, Tropical Storm Katrina would fizzle or blow on out toward the Yucatan Peninsula, providing them with no more than a brisk wind, higher than usual tides, and maybe a little rain.

Nothing in the warnings had been dire enough to make her miss Ileana's wedding, even if more than half the guests had already taken off on the ferry that stopped twice a day at Cabbage Key to pick up and deliver guests and diners. If the weather deteriorated, they could always set out for the mainland in the morning, as soon as the vows were said.

A cool, salty breeze filtered through screened windows in the thatched-roof restaurant at the top of a gentle rise. According to the resort owners who'd greeted her earlier, the flimsy building had been leveled several times over the years by storms, only to be rebuilt exactly as it had been before. Marcy had to admit, the place had a rustic sort of charm. The breeze ruffled Ileana's short dark curls and made her fiancé's tropical print shirt billow out around his slim, almost skinny frame. Josh Klosinski, a nephrologist at the teaching hospital in Gainesville where Ileana had recently been named chief of anesthesia, had apparently swept Ileana off her feet. In any case, they'd been seeing each other just a few months before deciding to make the relationship permanent.

Marcy envied her friend the emotional connection but not the man. And not the life they'd certainly lead with both of them being at the beck and call of patients twenty-four, seven. "How

will you ever find time for each other?" she asked, realizing they'd both been waiting for her to say something.

Josh lifted Ileana's hand to his lips, smiled. "Where there's a will, there's a way, I think the saying goes. Fortunately, neither of us is a resident, so we do have some control over our time."

Sam hadn't exercised that control once he'd finished his residency and taken over his dad's OB-GYN practice. If anything, they'd had less time together while he'd studied for specialty boards and worked to build a reputation as a fertility specialist. Damn it, she'd promised herself she wouldn't think about him—about the abject failure they'd made of a marriage all their friends used to say had been made in heaven. Besides, Sam's devotion to his patients had been just a small part of why they'd split up. Marcy forced a smile. "Good for you."

The ferry she'd taken over from Port Charlotte this afternoon had brought only a handful of guests who were staying for tomorrow's ceremony, and most of them had finished dinner and taken off to watch the sunset or stroll along the sandy Gulf side of the tiny barrier island. Couples. All couples. Not a single unattached guy who might help her keep her mind off ancient history. Marcy glanced down toward the dock and noticed a small, sleek cabin cruiser being secured beside a couple of larger boats.

"Sam's coming, Marcy."

Oh God. Pain cut through her as though it had been weeks, not years since she'd tossed him out. "When?" With any kind of luck at all, he'd blow in for the ceremony tomorrow morning and hightail it right back to Tampa and his precious patients.

"I'm not sure. He told me he was coming down by boat."

It took only a glance toward the dock and a brief perusal of the buff, chestnut-haired guy in faded cutoff jeans for her brain to process that Sam was already here...and that Ileana must have meant he was literally walking toward them, not that he was coming in the morning for the wedding. Marcy swallowed the alarm that had her wanting to run away, avoid facing the

painful memories. Damn it, why did he affect her like this now? She clamped down on wayward emotions and tried hard to ignore the sudden gush of moisture from her pussy that made her want to launch herself into his muscular embrace.

So he could shove her away again? Not in this lifetime. "I think that's Sam now," she commented, turning back to Ileana and Josh. "From the looks of that boat of his, I'd say the fertility business must be pretty good."

"I always wondered what went wrong between you two," Ileana said. "You seemed so perfect for each other."

"What went right?" Marcy wasn't about to air old, dirty linen period, much less to the prospective bride and groom. "Anyway, it's ancient history. We've been divorced five years now."

"Sorry. It's just that I liked both of you. Felt bad when I heard you'd split."

"Ileana, sweetheart, it's obvious Marcy doesn't want to talk about this."

Score one for Josh. Marcy's feelings for her friend's fiancé just moved up another notch. The guy obviously knew how to read between the lines.

Marcy drew in a breath of damp sea air tinged with a light aroma of stone crabs and the seasonings that made them taste so good but tickled her nose. Damn, what was it about this place, these people, that had her stomach doing somersaults as though she were sixteen and head over heels in love again? Why the hell was her pussy clenching at the sight of a man she'd hardly thought about since their divorce? The man who now was headed straight for Ileana...and, however coincidentally, her.

It wasn't as though she didn't run into Sam once in a while, for God's sake. She'd even exchanged a few words with him, introduced him to her man-of-the-moment and smiled at whatever woman had been clinging to his arm at some social or civic function. So why was she creaming her panties now? Why were memories of good times flooding her mind, keeping the

bitter ones at bay? Marcy tried to look away, but it seemed her eyes had other ideas because they remained glued on Sam. He'd filled out more since they'd split, developed impressive lats and biceps she hadn't noticed when he wore a suit or tux. They were mouthwateringly evident now, when he was naked except for snug cutoffs that emphasized his narrow waist and powerful thighs.

Shit. His bad luck that Marcy was sitting at the same table with the bride. Looked as though she'd left her latest squeeze back home, too. Sam willed his cock to relax when he felt it stirring. No way was he volunteering to fill the void. She'd probably already made plans to scratch her famous itch sometime during the wedding festivities.

He squared his shoulders and approached the table. "Ileana. And Josh, I assume." He held out a hand, smiling at the man's firm grip. Then he turned to his former wife. "Hello, Marcy."

"Sam." She met his gaze, her deep green eyes full of challenge—and something else. Desire? Not likely. Not that he was interested anyway.

"Mind if I join you?"

Marcy shrugged. "It's a public restaurant."

She didn't used to be so brittle. Her smiles used to light up her pretty face and make her eyes soften to a tone not unlike the smoky gray-green of the Gulf. For a moment Sam mourned the loss of love. Of friendship and trust. Not just hers but his. They'd once been kids in love. Kids who'd grown older and busier and left the magic behind.

Fuck if he didn't still wonder from time to time what specific thing he'd done that had caused her to have his belongings packed up and set on the porch of the home they'd bought together—the house where she still lived. Since he'd asked her a hundred times and she'd closed him out, he chose not to give a damn anymore. Determined to ignore Marcy as

fully as she seemed to be ignoring him, Sam turned to Josh and began making idle conversation.

* * * * *

By the next morning the clouds started rolling in. Waves broke noisily against the sides of the *Lucky Lady*, waking Sam and sending him on deck to survey the situation. Nothing too alarming, only a little more wind than he'd have liked to see. With any kind of luck, the rain would hold off until after Ileana and Josh had said their vows. The fact that the only transmissions he got over the ship-to-shore radio were spits and crackles didn't particularly concern him. Reception was always lousy in protected coves like this one on the eastern side of Cabbage Key.

Sam glanced at his watch. Five a.m. Too early for breakfast, or to socialize with the couples he'd met last night. Habit, he supposed, had caused him to awaken when he could as easily have slept. Dipping his head to avoid the doorframe, he headed back into the cabin. His bunk beckoned more insistently than the fish that might be biting in the deep channel that led into the cove.

Then he saw her through a porthole. Marcy, strolling along the narrow stretch of sand. Gusts of wind tossed her pale blond hair and molded something silky-sheer and hot pink to her gentle feminine curves. Curves he found as arousing now as they'd been twenty years ago when she'd flaunted them in a JV cheerleader outfit. There was something sad, something singular about the picture she made, staring out across the Intracoastal Waterway toward Port Charlotte as though looking for something...someone?

Wasn't he looking a little sad himself, staring out a porthole at the woman he'd written off five years ago? Yeah. He didn't often acknowledge it, but he was lonely.

Damn it, why did he still want Marcy? He fought off a compulsion to go to her, enfold her in his arms, drag her back here and assuage the loneliness. His as well as her own. He'd

hold her, take her, make her admit that what they'd shared had been better than her hundreds of casual fucks, a hell of a lot more meaningful than the few scratches of a mutual itch he'd shared with someone he called friend.

Still a little sleepy, Sam's mind wandered. The present began to mesh with old memories and latent dreams.

He strode quickly, quietly, behind her on that stretch of beach backed on one side by white-capped waves, on the other by deep-green sea grapes and gently swaying palms. When a gust of wind brought her familiar scent to his nostrils, his breathing turned ragged. His heart pounded in his chest when he finally overtook her.

Settling his hands at her slender waist, his fingers molded to flesh as familiar now as if he'd caressed it each night for the last five lonely years. When she turned at his touch, she murmured, "Sam."

Gently, for she seemed weightless, he lifted her, took her mouth. God, but she tasted as sweet as she had every time before, in reality and in his restless dreams. "I'm going to take you, fuck you, wipe out your memories of every man but me," he whispered against her slack lips when he broke the kiss.

She tunneled her fingers through his hair and sighed, then wrapped her arms tighter around his neck and shoulders. "Like old times."

"Not quite." No, this time he'd put his mark on her soul as he'd once put it on her body years ago, when he'd realized she needed to give over control in this if not any other aspect of her life. "This time I'm not asking. I'm telling you what I want."

Her nipples tightened visibly beneath her skimpy bikini top and the silky cover-up, telling him more clearly than anything she might say that the thought excited her. By the time he'd carried her back on board the Lucky Lady, they'd hardened and elongated and were pushing insistently against the fabric that contained them. His nostrils flared at the musk of her desire that surrounded her when he set her down inside the compact cabin.

Hands on her shoulders, he slid away the gossamer wrap. He'd never felt skin so satiny smooth as that in the hollow between Marcy's richly rounded breasts. And in the soft indentation around her navel.

She stirred his senses as much now as she ever had. "Take off the swimsuit."

She shot him a challenging look born, he supposed, of the vast experience she'd gained since their split. Apparently none of her affairs had lasted long enough for a lover to establish control over her. Her hands went to her back, though, and the stretchy fabric went slack over her beautiful breasts. He inhaled sharply at the sight of them, plump and white and tipped with brownish-pink, puckered nipples that tempted his lips. "Like what you see so far?"

Reaching out, he stroked first one tempting globe and then the other. "Yeah. Now strip out of the rest. I want you naked." His balls tightened painfully, reminding him how long it had been since he'd found release. When he released the zipper on his jeans, his cock sprang free, hard as stone and throbbing with anticipation while she slithered out of the tiny thong, revealing a sleekly shaven pussy.

Shaved for some other man or men. For a moment his cock began to shrivel, before animal instinct overrode the surge of possessiveness, the momentary stab of betrayal. White-hot lust flooded every cell of his body, made him struggle for control.

Control. He wanted to control her as he had so long ago. Impose his will on her and make her love it, beg him for more. "Get on your knees and suck my cock."

She'd hated giving him head when they were married, but now she knelt and caressed his swollen flesh with soft, knowing hands, taking his cockhead between moist, velvety lips and swirling her tongue around. He tried not to think of how many cocks she'd sucked to get so good at it…whether they'd tasted better or worse or if they'd stretched her lips as much when their owners forced them down her throat. Tunneling his fingers in the pale strands of her silky hair, he made her take him deeper, and she swallowed convulsively around him.

Her little whimpers told him she liked sucking cock now. A lot. Her moist hot breath heated the skin beneath his pubic hair. "Stop now, baby. When I come I want to be buried in your cunt as deep as I can go. Just like old times."

She let go his cock, stared up at him with tears glistening in her eyes. "Are you sure you want it the way it used to be?"

"Yeah." *Except now she shaved her pussy and had let God only knew how many cocks inside it.*

He lifted her to her feet and dragged her down onto the narrow bunk. "Hands behind your head, and spread those pretty legs." *Kneeling between them when she complied, he first donned a condom, then stroked the satiny folds of her labia, her plump mons.* "Be still," *he ordered when she began to squirm.*

"I can't."

"Don't talk. Just feel." *Deliberately, he stroked the wet, slick inner lips of her pussy, avoiding her hard little clit.* "Feel my fingers slide over your silky mons. Your labia. They're swollen. Wet. Slick with your honey. No. Don't move. I'll give your pretty clit some attention soon enough." *He'd often wondered when he examined women who shaved or waxed their pubic hair, but of course it would have been highly unprofessional to ask. He felt no compunction about asking Marcy, about whom he'd never felt the slightest bit professional.* "Tell me, what does my touch do to you? Does shaving make you feel hot? Sexy?"

"It makes me feel good. Clean and satiny smooth and ready for whatever you have in mind. Haven't you ever wondered how it would feel to have a woman suck your cock and balls without all that tangle of hair getting in the way?"

"Would you like it better?" *He took his cock in one hand and rubbed its head along her hot, slick slit, pausing when he reached her anus.* "Would you like it if I fucked you here?" *He'd been first to breech her cunt, but he had no illusions that her ass still remained untouched. She'd been too hot, too adventurous with him to have saved that hole for five long years, even though she'd been too scared after they'd tried it once and it had hurt her...until near the end, when they'd bought anal probes in graduated sizes to stretch her for his cock...ones they'd never used because neither of them had wanted to once she'd found out she was pregnant.*

"I love fucking with you. Always have. Guess I always will." *Against his command, she lifted her hands, framed his cheeks between them, traced the seam of his lips and the lobes of his ears.* "Have you missed me, Sam?"

He had, but he wasn't about to say so. Wasn't going to give in to the urge to gather her in his arms, take her with love the way he had so long ago. "I told you to keep your hands above your head. Now do it. I want to concentrate on making you come for me." Bracing himself on his hands and knees, he plunged his cock into her cunt, tried not to feel as though he'd just come home.

Being inside her felt like heaven and hell, her inner muscles squeezing and taunting him as he sank inside her to his balls. Shit, he was going to come, and he desperately didn't want it to be over. "How many cocks have you had here?" he asked as he retreated then slammed back into her welcoming heat.

"It doesn't matter."

"But it does. This pussy was mine. All mine. The idea of sharing it doesn't work for me." It worked in one way, all right. Thinking about the other lovers cooled his jets, kept him from flooding her immediately with his come.

Sinking onto her, he took his upper body weight on his elbows, rubbed his chest against her hardened nipples, fed the jealousy that let him maintain control. "Do you like all those other cocks? Do they make you come the way I used to?" He lifted his hips, changed the angle of penetration so his pelvis ground into her swollen clit with every hard, punishing stroke. "Do you get as wet for them as you do for me?"

Something like rebellion flashed in her eyes, but she licked her lips and shot him a saccharine smile. "Sometimes." When he fucked her harder and faster, she gasped, "If I tell you all about my lovers will that get you hot?"

"No, baby. Your cunt has my cock about to burst. Come for me. Let go and come the way you used to. Claw and scratch and scream for me until you forget all the others. Until there's only room for me." Increasing the pace, he pounded into her, the friction driving away his resentment, banishing everything but the primal need to come. To fill her with his worthless semen.

"Oh God, Sam. Oh yesss. Fuck me harder, faster. Damn you, you've always made me melt inside." Her cunt clenched around his cock, milked him, constricted flesh already about to burst. As her shouts turned to whimpers and the contractions of her pussy slowed, he shuddered above her. His entire being concentrated in his cock, his

balls, and he came in long, staccato bursts born of long denial. Coaxed out by the one woman who'd fed his adolescent dreams. And joined him on a trip to ecstasy…pain…and betrayal.

What the fuck was he thinking about, getting rock hard over ancient history? Imagining taking her, plowing ground a hundred other men had visited? Disgusted with himself, Sam stalked to the bunk where he'd pictured himself fucking her. He had to do something about this raging hard-on.

Dropping his pants and stepping out of them, he lay down, took his aching cock in hand and pumped away. Nothing. Nothing but a dull ache in his balls and an erection that was going nowhere. Damn. Maybe… Closing his eyes, he tried to picture Joanne, but all he saw was Marcy.

Marcy's pale hair, her full, sensual lips…her cunt sucking, squeezing, milking him… Oh God, why had she suddenly invaded his head again after all this time? Sam's balls tightened painfully. Then he came, the scalding hot semen spurting on his belly for what seemed like hours.

Yeah, he still wanted her, for what that might be worth.

Chapter Two

The last person on earth she'd wanted to see this morning was Sam, standing in the cockpit of the *Lucky Lady*, watching her with his intense hazel eyes until he disappeared into the cabin. Marcy strolled along the shoreline, enjoying the abrasive feeling when she dragged her toes through white, powdery sand. Sam reminded her of an ancient god, standing shirtless at the helm of a golden prow, the dawn light catching the wavy chestnut curls she used to love tunneling through with her fingers. Rippling muscles of a mature man who took pride in his body had replaced the lanky lines she remembered from long ago.

Why did Sam have to have gotten better, not just older? It would have been easier to ignore him if he'd developed a paunch or his hairline had started to recede. A lot easier. Her belly tightened, and the thong bottom of her bikini chafed her swelling pussy. She should have asked Cam Willis...or Todd...anybody...to come with her to this wedding. If she had she'd be in bed now, welcoming the morning with a lover, not staring into the rising wind and salivating over the last man on Earth she should be wanting to fuck.

Bringing anybody but Sam had seemed somehow obscene, though, for all her memories of Ileana centered around him and the dreams they'd once shared with such optimism...such love. To have brought another lover, particularly one for whom she felt nothing but quickly sated desire, would have somehow sullied memories of happy times she'd always cherish.

The wind whipped at her hair, and the eastern sky had an ominous tone. Gray mottled with the orange of dawn in fast-moving clouds that foretold danger. Not the storm the news had predicted, but a mirror of her own jumbled emotions. Warm,

damp air swirled around her, but the tempest lay within her as much as in the increasingly forbidding sky.

Still Sam's image stayed with her as she circled to the Gulf side and stared at strong waves breaking over the barrier reefs. Damn it, she had to banish it. And she knew just how.

She had to dredge up painful memories, remind herself what an asshole he'd been and why she'd thrown him out. Remind herself how he'd pampered every one of his patients but muttered a halfhearted, "Sorry, babe," when she'd lost their baby that she'd wanted so much. Recall his chilling accusation that the baby hadn't been his.

Arrogant bastard. He'd been that then and he still was, now. Holier-than-thou, certain he had every answer, every right to dictate to her as he did to his adoring patients and their desperate spouses. Certain he couldn't have fathered the flawed fetus she'd miscarried, and unwilling to believe her when she'd sworn no one but him had ever stuck his hard cock into her pussy.

The salt spray stung her eyes. It couldn't be tears. She'd cried buckets of them years ago, until there were no more to come and she'd still held the anger, the hurt, the resentment...and the deep-down love that wouldn't die. It hadn't died in the arms of what seemed like a hundred faceless lovers and probably never would.

Marcy squared her shoulders. For Ileana's sake, she'd get through this wedding celebration. She'd make it a point never again to put herself through this—to avoid her former husband like the plague and do whatever it took to sweep away the pain...the love...the desire that held her in its grip despite all that had gone down before.

* * * * *

By eleven o'clock, the wind had whipped the sheltered waters of the cove into a gray-white froth. Palm trees swayed drunkenly along the long expanse of beach. Sam glanced toward

the grotto where the wedding would be held in half an hour, noting with satisfaction that the lush vegetation there seemed not to be affected by the rising wind.

Concerned when the waves rocked the *Lucky Lady* against the dock, he checked the lines again. An oppressive damp heat permeated the lightweight linen of his slacks, settling uncomfortably in his gut. Katrina hadn't veered south across Cuba and into the Gulf as everyone had expected. She was headed straight across Florida toward them. Fighting the fierce wind, he made his way to the grotto where the wedding was to be held.

"You'd better be ready to get everybody out the minute this wedding's over," he said to the resort manager, who stared through the canopy of dark-green leaves and orchids at the darkening sky.

"I will. Katrina's still a Category Two, and it seems she's headed straight for us. I'll take the guests on the launch. Think you and the others who brought boats can make it to the mainland?"

Sam followed the man's gaze, then looked back at the churning water. "The *Lucky Lady*'s a deep-draft cruiser, and she's got two Volvo V6 inboards. She can make it. You'd better talk to the others, though, especially the guy with the sailboat. Wind's going to go against him, and his motor doesn't look any too powerful."

"Will do. Hate to put a damper on the festivities, but we'd better hurry if we're going to get everybody off this island."

Doing his best to put the storm out of mind for the moment, Sam glanced around the heavily shaded grotto. It reminded him of a *chuppah*, covered by Nature instead of with the draped cloth and roses he remembered from his and Marcy's wedding. Ileana stood, looking every bit the bride in something creamy white and filmy, next to Josh, whose gaze focused on his bride-to-be.

The manager, who apparently was also a justice of the peace, stepped up to them and said a few quiet words. Then he invited Ileana and Josh to say their vows.

Sam couldn't help looking at Marcy, who hung back with the other guests on the opposite side of the clearing and resolutely refused to meet his gaze. Sam remembered how she'd looked the day they'd married with the reluctant blessings of families who'd thought they should have waited. Their parents had said marriage and attending universities didn't mix. They'd been wrong. As students, they'd been blissfully happy. It had been after she graduated from law school and he finished his residency that the troubles had begun.

He'd never forget how beautiful she'd looked in her mother's gown of white satin and lace. Her tiara had sparkled with crystal beads, and her veil had kissed the floor. Remembering that veil made him think of tropical islands like this and netted beds like the one they'd shared on their honeymoon in the Bahamas. Oh, yeah, he remembered, and it hurt—but somehow reminiscing felt good, too. Today she wore something green and clingy. Silk, probably. The colors should have blended into the setting, but then Marcy didn't blend. With her pale hair and flashing eyes, she stood out against any background, this grotto included.

The vows he heard Ileana and Josh make now came from the heart. Personal, sincere, different yet inherently the same as age-old promises he'd made to Marcy and she'd made to him, promises set forth in the contract they'd signed before the rabbi and their parents and repeated in the presence of several hundred guests.

Vows not meant to be broken, intended to cement a man and woman's lives into one. Vows that, though severed, lay deeply buried in his heart, keeping him from seeking another love.

When he looked at Marcy again, she was staring at him, the look in her eyes as sad as any he'd ever seen. As if she were

regretting their split as much as he was. As soon as the celebrant declared Josh and Ileana man and wife, she tore her gaze away.

* * * * *

No way could Marcy stand any more of this celebration. Not when it meant seeing Sam and longing for what could never be again. She had to take a few minutes to collect herself before she could put on a happy face again. Drifting away from a crowd that headed for the docks and the reception Ileana and Josh had relocated to a restaurant on the mainland, she moved back into the grotto. It was as though something compelled her to stand where Josh and Ileana had stood, experience vicariously some of the joy that had radiated from them when they joined their hands and their lives.

The wind caught the full skirt of her short silk dress, whipped it up around her hips and plastered the fabric hard against the hills and valleys of her breasts and belly. A tempest not unlike the whirling dervish that had her heart beating faster, her whole body aching, seeking... God, she didn't know.

It had taken Ileana ten years to love again after she lost Ben. Ten years without seeing him or hearing him or feeling the weight of his flesh pressing into hers. Ten years, and Ben had been dead, beyond any hope that somehow fences might be mended, new bridges built to span chasms too deep and too wide to be conquered by words or deeds alone.

It might take Marcy forever, seeing Sam occasionally the way she did. Comparing other lovers to him in her mind and having them fall short every goddamn time. She didn't want to grow old, always seeking yet never finding the kind of emotional commitment she once had with him.

Shit, she wanted the impossible. Hot, committed sex, mastery by her beloved, as well as a love with whom to share a life, not lovers sharing only a moment's passion. No matter what he thought of her, she wanted Sam. She'd been innocent of the accusation that had driven them apart, but she'd made up for that these past five years.

Caught up in her daydream, she barely noticed the warm rain that began to fall, caressing her softly through the dense canopy of trees and vines. Soon, the soft drips became a deluge, and the wind tore at the natural protection overhead, breaking limbs like twigs and sending them flying about like whirling dervishes. As though Nature were giving her a warning too fierce to be ignored.

A boat whistle pierced the air. Damn, she had to hurry or they'd leave her.

The air grew heavier, the dampness more oppressive. Lightning crackled in the darkening sky, thunder clapping as furiously as Marcy had ever heard it. The soaked silk of her dress clung to her like a shroud. Who knew? Maybe it was. Perhaps it was her destiny to die here, victim of Hurricane Katrina. But she wasn't about to go down without a fight.

Struggling against the fierce winds, Marcy tried to make her way to the docks as the brackish waters rose among the sea grapes and mangroves, soaking the sandy ground and catching the stiletto heels of her Manolo Blahnik sandals, driving her to her knees. She stumbled, losing precious time trying to extricate herself from the muck that held onto her shoes as if it were glue. Finally she pried her feet out of them and started moving again.

"Damn it. Wouldn't you know I'd pick five hundred dollar shoes to wear during a fucking storm." Sand caught in the folds of her dress, on her bare legs, even in her hair. And there wasn't a fucking boat in sight by the time she'd fought her way to the dock. They'd left her as surely as she'd abandoned the ruined shoes. Trying hard to stay calm, she forced herself to move away from the water, toward high ground—the restaurant and cabins at the top of the rise.

Debris swirled in the air, bounced off her body, caught up in the snarls of her sopping hair. When she covered her face with both hands to protect it from the onslaught, she stumbled into a downed Australian pine sapling and sprawled into the dirt.

The temptation to stay there and accept that she was doomed was strong. But she wanted desperately to survive. She

dragged herself to her knees and crawled the last few yards to the top of the rise, stoically overlooking the pain of a twisted ankle, the stinging of a thousand tiny scratches over what seemed like every exposed inch of her body.

Oh God. The wind had ripped off a large chunk of the restaurant's thatched roof. No refuge there. Marcy's chest tightened. Branches cracked and fell, tossed like matchsticks in the wind. She had to get inside somewhere if she were to have any chance to weather the storm. Stumbling over debris on the pathway, she made her way to the rustic cabin she'd rented a day earlier.

Once inside the quaking walls, it hit her. She was alone. Seriously alone. Caught without another human soul in the leading edge of what promised to be one hell of a storm.

As sand swirled and sturdy palm trees groaned and cracked in the fierce wind, Marcy huddled in a corner against an interior wall, trembling and watching the rain come down in what looked like horizontal sheets that pounded the windowpanes as if determined to break them down and invade her flimsy sanctuary.

Teeth chattering, she stripped off her soaked clothes and wrapped up in a cotton blanket from the bed.

When driving rain shattered the window, Marcy dived under the bed, crying out in terror. For a long time she stayed burrowed in a blanket there and prayed for deliverance from this hell. For someone, anyone to share it with her. Another window shattered, on the other side of the room that seemed to grow smaller with every crashing piece of debris that attacked. She dragged her blanket to the farthest corner from the creaking windows, closed her eyes against Nature's onslaught, and prayed for Sam.

* * * * *

Raindrops driving into his flesh like tiny needles, Sam lashed down the *Lucky Lady* and made for the relative safety of

the Flying Fisherman Marina. Once inside, he shook off the worst of the water, blinked, and searched the crowd of soaked, disheveled wedding guests.

No Marcy. He'd have sworn he saw her leaving the grotto with the others. He assumed she'd taken the resort's motor launch or one of the other guests' boats. But she was nowhere to be found. Ileana stood trembling in Josh's arms near an inside wall of the sturdy cement block building.

"Where's Marcy?" he asked, his teeth chattering as he joined them.

Ileana's dark eyes widened. "Didn't she come with you?"

"No." He'd have been the last guy on earth Marcy would have willingly hitched a ride with.. Sam's gut clenched. Surely she hadn't waited for the ferry that wouldn't be making its twice-daily trip today. "You haven't seen her?"

"She gave us her best wishes, then said she was going back to the grotto. I assumed she was looking for you." She paused, her full lips curling in a nervous little smile. "That she'd wait until we'd left, then take that as an excuse to ride in with you."

"Hardly. I'd be the last guy she'd want to hitch a ride with." Then it struck him. Marcy was out on Cabbage Key, alone, with Hurricane Katrina bearing down. "I'll go back and get her."

Ileana reached out and clasped his hand. "My God, we should have evacuated yesterday. If I hadn't insisted on having the wedding go on as scheduled, Marcy wouldn't—"

"Don't worry, I'll get her." Sam squeezed Ileana's hand, hoping to reassure her.

"Don't, Sam. Let the resort manager go. It's his job."

"No time. And the launch might capsize. My boat's built for heavy seas." Not that he'd ever taken her out before during a hurricane. But never before had he had such a compelling reason.

Hanging onto posts along the weathered pier when the wind threatened to blow him into the water, Sam made it back

to the *Lucky Lady*, fired up both motors, and cast off. Five-foot waves broke against the sturdy fiberglass hull, soaking the deck and making the boat lurch slowly ahead.

He could use help. Not able to work the marine radio and hold the boat on course in the heavy waves—no Coast Guard ship could make its way through the narrow, shallow corridor anyhow—he pulled out his cell phone. He barely managed to dial 911 before the boat rode a wave then slammed down, wrenching the phone from his hand and slamming it into the deck.

Shit, he wouldn't be calling anyone now. The phone popped apart on impact, its pieces scattering across the deck and bouncing crazily every time the boat rode a wave, then careened back into the murky water.

The noon sky was black with clouds, backlit by a struggling sun and lightning bolts that cast an eerie orange on the eastern horizon. Thunder clapped, its noise deafening. Sam clutched the wheel, his knuckles white as he struggled to hold the boat on course for Cabbage Key.

Stubborn, willful Marcy. Leave it to her to ignore Nature's warnings, get herself marooned on a barrier key while a hurricane raged around her. When he got his hands on her, he'd shake her until her teeth rattled. Spank her until she begged for mercy. Then he'd drag her foolish ass back to the mainland and wash his hands of her for good.

Who the fuck was he kidding? If he found her in one piece, he'd wrap her in the love that had never died. He'd humble himself if he had to, do whatever it took to make her listen. He'd bare his soul. Hell, he'd sell it to the devil if that meant he could have her back.

A wave crashed over the bow, making him struggle to hold the boat in the channel that led into the cove where he'd docked the night before. A fierce tailwind practically sent him airborne into the calmer waters of the cove, propelling him toward the shore.

Working frantically once he reached the dock, Sam tied the boat down, trying to gauge how much higher the tides would go and leaving slack that might keep the *Lucky Lady* from snapping the lines—but which might also, probably would, cause her to break up when the storm surge tossed her into the main pier or up on land. He wouldn't be leaving Cabbage Key anytime soon, in any case, not with the way the winds were building and the storm tide rising.

It didn't matter. Nothing mattered but finding Marcy, protecting her as he'd vowed to do so long ago. Keeping her from harm. Wading along the half-submerged pier, Sam made it to shore and spied Marcy's silly high-heeled sandals mired along the pathway to the restaurant. Bending to avoid flying branches and debris, he fought a wind that seemed intent on lifting his two-hundred-pound body and propelling it like an insignificant twig.

The roar of the wind shut everything out. A fork bounced off his temple, and a square of plywood screamed past him like a lethal boomerang. He plunged forward as if he were in a raging river. In a manner of speaking, he was. A river of air boiling and surging around him like whitewater rapids. Tearing away everything in its path.

Where the restaurant had been, an empty concrete slab bore testimony to the violence of the storm. Cutlery and shards of broken dinnerware blew around on each fierce gust of wind, potentially lethal darts if they found a human dartboard.

Sam's breath caught in his throat. Where to look next? A couple of guest cabins remained mostly intact, the ones that lay along the pathway toward the raging Gulf. Lowering his head to protect his eyes from flying missiles, he made his way to the first one. All right, it seemed, but for a hunk missing off the roof and shattered window glass. A carved wooden plaque with the number seven hung drunkenly from the door that flapped open and shut in the rain and wind.

The porch floor creaked under Sam's feet, as if protesting his weight as too much an insult in light of the onslaught it had already endured. "Marcy?"

Nothing. He caught the door, pulled mightily against the wind. Inside the cabin clothes blew about, silent testimony to the storm's power. The clothes didn't look like Marcy's. And Marcy wasn't inside. Sam stepped back outside, pushing the door shut as though that might hold back the storm and protect belongings left by guests in their haste to run for safety.

Thunder clapped, and lightning crackled. A palm tree near the beach snapped and crashed to the ground as Sam made his way along the decimated path. "Marcy!" he yelled as he approached another cabin. Pray God she had the sense to get inside and stay there. That she hadn't fallen victim to flying silverware or dishes, and wasn't lying somewhere among the storm's inanimate victims, hurt or dead.

No. She couldn't be dead. He'd feel it if she were, just as he'd sensed the moment when his mom had slipped away from them...as he'd known before his partner had told him that Marcy had lost the baby he hadn't been able to convince himself was his. He stumbled, righted himself, hurried to the only other remaining shelter on Cabbage Key.

He forced the door open, then fought the wind to close it. Thank God. There she was, shivering against the bathroom wall. Her pale hair lay plastered to her skull, and her skin looked pasty beneath the golden tan she maintained with such pride. She stared, her pupils dilated, eyes unfocused at first, then registering recognition. For a moment she just stared. Then she dropped the blanket and held out her arms to him. "Sam. You came. I prayed you would."

Desire punched him in the gut, banished his initial relief and made him gasp for breath. He took one step forward, then another, until he lifted her to her feet and dragged her naked, trembling body against him. For a long time he held her. Shivered with her while the wind pummeled their shelter, reminding him of the danger. Not only that which threatened

them, but that which promised to consume him if he gave his raging emotions free rein. If he took her, claimed her now the way he'd been too young and green to take her at first. The way he'd quickly learned she wanted to be taken, possessed.

"T-take off your clothes, Sam." Marcy tugged his shirt from his pants, her teeth chattering all the time.

"What?" Though his cock twitched with anticipation, he hesitated. Then he realized he was sopping wet, chilling her as well as himself as they stood there in a tiny cabin that shuddered in the wind. Cold air burst through shattered windowpanes, brought goose bumps up on his skin as she exposed it. "Here, let me."

Sam loosened his belt and dropped it with his rain-soaked pants and boxers to his feet. Toeing off sodden deck shoes, he stepped out of the puddle as she tossed his shirt onto it. "Come here, I'll warm you."

The loopy pile of the towel she rubbed over him brought circulation back. She'd often dried him off like this when they were kids at the beach, after they'd swum back from a favorite haunt. Closing his eyes, he visualized her on the sandbar they'd claimed as their own. They'd loved making sandcastles and exploring crystalline tide pools full of sand dollars and teeming with fascinating sea life. *Then* he wouldn't have hesitated. He'd have lowered her to the bed in his parents' condo on Tierra Verde and fucked her the way he had every chance he got since that first time under the school bleachers, after a pre-game pep rally.

But too much had gone down between them. Too many harsh words had been said. Sam stood there shivering as the storm raged outside the little cabin, trying to think of her as just another woman with a problem—just another woman who'd asked him for his help.

It didn't work. This was Marcy, and the only help she'd ever needed from him, he'd failed to give. A tree crashed down outside, the clattering noise sending her into his arms, the towel apparently forgotten. "Take care of me, Sam," she whispered,

clutching his shoulders as she pressed her breasts hard against his chest. Belly to belly, thigh to thigh, her softness to his rougher, harder planes. The way it should be, male protecting female, giving her safety and strength.

His balls tightened, and his cock swelled against her silky mons. Years fell away, resentment forgotten as the thunder roared and the wind sluiced noisily among the trees and vines outside. As the walls of the cabin shook with the strength of Katrina, Sam trembled in unison with Marcy. It was as though the thin veneer of civilized behavior shattered like the windowpanes, leaving only male and female and unquenched need.

Animal lust. The compulsion to sink his cock into her hot wet cunt and pump her until his semen flooded her womb. To feel her heat and see her face flush when she came. To hear her scream his name, smell the scent of sex flowing between them. To suck her clit and her breasts and taste her honey on his tongue just one more time.

Out of control, Sam lifted Marcy, bracing her back against the quaking wall. "Put your legs around my waist," he ordered, his tone urgent, terse to his own ears as he flexed his hips and mated their bodies.

No one else had ever made her feel so full, so taken. The storm that raged outside was nothing compared with the one that erupted in her heart when Sam thrust home. Naked flesh to naked flesh, sensation she'd denied herself for five long years of lovers wearing condoms for her protection and their own. His thick cockhead stretched her, sliding sensuously within her well-lubricated pussy, nudging her womb. Long, impossibly hard yet smooth as velvet, his cock claimed her, driving her harder into the rough wooden wall with every pistoning of his narrow hips.

Her nipples throbbed, wanting his attention there, too. His hands were busy, kneading her ass cheeks, lifting her. Opening her for his next forceful thrust, his thumbs caressing her anus, as though he intended to fuck her there, too.

As though he read her mind, knew her need, he dipped his head, took one distended nipple between his teeth and nipped it sharply before drawing it into the moist heat of his mouth and suckling.

Her pussy clenched around his cock, the sensation one of rightness. She felt possessed as she hadn't for five long years. Overwhelmed, she let her head loll back against the wall, closing her eyes and ears against the storm that raged around them. All that mattered was here. Now. Sam. The white-hot fire that spread from her pussy to her ass to her breasts. Even her brain tingled when the bubble of desire burst and she shattered into a quivering heap, held upright in Sam's strong arms.

Mastered. Satisfied as none of the meaningless string of lovers ever had...as she now knew no one else could. Sam had claimed her once. Now he claimed her again. Whether because of lust or nostalgia or animal need to mate in the face of death, she had no idea. It didn't matter. Marcy could fuck a thousand men, but she was certain no one but Sam could ever make her feel like this.

"Oh, baby. Yeah. Squeeze me. Like that. God, you're wringing me dry." His scalding semen bathed her cervix, her womb in powerful bursts that seemed to go on forever. Clasping her tightly, he laid her on the bed and lay down beside her, still breathing hard.

It was after they'd lain there a long time that she noticed the wind no longer moaned all around them, and the driving rain had become a gentle shower. "I think the storm has passed."

"No, baby. We're in the eye of the storm."

Chapter Three

Calm. Cool, damp air rich with the smells of Earth surrounded them as they sprawled on the tangled sheets. Marcy laid her head on Sam's chest, the way she always used to after they'd made love. He stroked the silky skin of her back, remembering.

Late nights when he'd come to her grainy-eyed from studying and she'd rolled over, warm and giving, welcoming him into her bed and her body. Lazy days they'd spent in bed and learned more about what made their bodies feel good than anything he'd studied in medical texts. Fun days when she'd dragged him out of his shell and taught him there was much more to life than studying and work and taking care of the basic human requirements for survival.

Yeah. The memories surrounded him, wrapped them in a special cocoon much like the one with which Hurricane Katrina had temporarily surrounded Cabbage Key. A cocoon through which Sam saw everything with rose-colored glasses, but one he knew would soon give way to the tempest of love and hate that had gripped him since that fateful day five years ago.

Unless…unless they could use these moments of suspended time to open old wounds and lance them so the venom would flow out and they might heal. Sam stilled his hand in the hollow of her spine. Thunder clapped in the distance, and bolts of lightning crackled. When she shuddered, he drew her closer.

He felt ambivalent, loving her as he did, yet hating the brittle, hedonistic woman she'd become since they'd split up. Blaming her—and himself—for severing a connection that had begun with childish innocence and withered with suspicion and

accusations. His suspicion. His accusations. His refusal to believe her, not the scientific near-certainty that told him the baby she'd lost in the first trimester couldn't have been his. Her turning a deaf ear each time he'd tried to apologize. To explain and beg for absolution.

His cock stirred again when she cradled his balls in her palm. A sweet gesture, one she'd made a thousand times when they'd lain like this in the aftermath of sex. Had she done the same with the faceless men she'd fucked in the past five years?

Damn it, he didn't give a shit about the divorce. Marcy was his. She might have fucked half of Tampa, but she belonged to him. Would always belong to him.

"Sam?" When she turned her head, damp strands of her hair tickled his chest.

He lifted his head, looked down at her. Her eyes had turned the soft gray-green of a calm sea, the way they always did after they made love. It would be so easy to sweep the past away, start again as though this were a new relationship. No old hurts, no issues, no resentment.

The hell it would. If he wanted his wife back — and he did — he'd have to bare his soul, make her listen now to what she'd refused to hear back then. Make her understand and forgive him. Right. Make her forgive the unforgivable. He stroked her cheek, then brushed an uncharacteristically tousled strand of her hair off her forehead. "What is it?"

"I'm glad you came back. Glad we made love. Damn it, I've hated you for what seems like forever, but part of me still loves you, too."

"Me, too. You snatched my heart when you were fifteen years old and never let it go. Will you listen to me now, let me try…"

"The baby was yours, Sam."

"I know." He should have known it from the start. It shouldn't have taken DNA testing to make him believe. "I should have trusted you. I'm sorry. You've never let me tell you

how sorry I was—how sorry I still am. Will you now?" He stroked her cheek, soothed an angry welt caused, he guessed, by the same sort of flying debris that had pelted him while he'd clawed his way to her.

The wind began to howl again, and rain sluiced through the shattered window, enlarging the puddle already on the rough wooden floor. Marcy shuddered. "I guess so. I don't want to die not knowing what I did to make you believe I was unfaithful."

"We're not going to die. We're going to live." Recalling the rising tide and the devastation that he'd seen from the leading edge of the hurricane, Sam hoped to hell he wasn't lying. "You didn't do anything. It was me."

"I don't understand."

"I'm sterile, or so damn near it that the chances of me fathering a child naturally are something like one in a million. I thought—"

"How long did you know that?" She sat up, riddled him with the kind of gaze he imagined she usually reserved for hostile witnesses in the courtroom. "And why didn't you tell me?"

He had the decency to look abashed. "Since about six months after we quit using birth control. Don't know why, but I decided to run tests on myself while I was sending in some samples from a patient's husband. I didn't tell you right away because I was fucking ashamed. Ashamed I couldn't give you one thing every goddamn man should be able to give the woman he loves. Yeah, I know there are a lot of men who've got my problem—I see a good many of them in my office—but I've never run into a one who wasn't devastated, hearing that kind of news."

So that was why Sam had turned surly. Why he'd closeted himself in his study every night with his goddamn medical journals and acted as though he didn't give a damn when she told him she was pregnant. Finally she knew why he'd

stammered around like a defendant caught on the stand in a lie whenever she'd tried to talk with him about the baby.

Marcy might understand his behavior now, but that didn't mean she'd forgive him. "The one thing you owed me—besides your trust—was the truth. And you didn't come through with it."

"I know, but damn it, I tried to tell you. You weren't willing to listen. Understandably," he added before she could lay into him the way she wanted to. "You never gave me reason to think you were anything but faithful. You deserved my trust."

The look in his eyes said it all. Sadness, regret, apology…and something else. Unresolved grief? "Sam, did you ever let yourself mourn for our baby?"

"Yes. What I've never let myself regret much until now was losing you. Knowing you were giving what belonged to me to half the guys in Tampa."

She wanted to lay the blame for that back on him. Badly. Before she could form the words, the flimsy walls began to shake again. Her anger forgotten, she dived into Sam's arms when an entire palmetto frond, torn by the storm from one of the tough plants, flew through the shattered window and landed not six inches from her side of the bed. She stared out the ruined window, transfixed, as a whole small tree the storm apparently had ripped by its roots from the sand flew by. Vegetation, chunks of roof and walls, even swirling sand all tossed about like seedpods in the wind. Would anything be left after the storm passed? An ominous roar rang in her ears. Water slapped against wood and shot under the door, undulating over the rough boards like a deadly serpent.

"Marcy. We'll get through this. Just like we've managed to survive everything else. Right now we need to find something and block off that window. Sorry, baby, I should have thought about this before the wind started blowing again." He hugged her hard, then rolled to the edge of the bed, waded through the rising puddle of water on the floor, and started taking the bathroom door off its hinges.

Funny how being close to Sam seemed to calm her fear. Firmly refusing to think about what might come through that window next, Marcy slid out of the bed to help. "How are you going to keep the wind from sending that door flying?"

"We'll prop it with that dresser. It ought to be heavy enough."

Marcy gave the knotty-pine armoire a tentative shove. "It's heavy enough that I can't move it."

"Together, I think we can manage." Setting the door flat on the floor, he added his strength to hers. Droplets of water glowed on his tanned, muscular body, slithering over his bulging muscles each time he leaned into the heavy chest. By the time they got the window blocked, they both were panting and soaked. "Now we can be fairly well assured that nothing's going to fly in here and skewer us. Grab some towels out of the bathroom and let's dry off as best we can. Much as I like looking at you naked, I don't want to get the blankets soaked."

"What about the water? It's rising awfully fast."

"That's the storm surge. I don't expect it will come much higher, and it'll recede soon enough as the storm blows out to sea." Sam's voice lacked its usual authority and assurance.

Maybe...but maybe not. Perhaps they'd be swept away on the wind, never to be heard from again. Damn it, she didn't want to die, but if this was going to end up being their watery grave, she wasn't about to leave so much unresolved. So much resentment where there used to be so much love. Lying back on the bed, she forced a smile. "Let's make this time for us...now. No yesterdays and no tomorrows. Please, for God's sake, love me now." The roar outside subsided, replaced by an even more ominous quiet. Another lull as Katrina gathered her destructive strength to strike again.

He sat beside her, regarding her sternly as though she were an errant child begging for absolution of her sins. For some reason, that look got her juices flowing even thicker, as did his

next words. "If you want me, babe, it's got to be just me. You've got to take me for better or worse, the way I am."

Was he talking about his sterility or her other lovers? It didn't matter, because she wanted him now, whatever the terms. "I do." Reaching out, she laid a hand on his thigh, thrilled at the reflexive tightening she saw in his balls, the stiffening of his big, thick cock. "I always have. You just didn't believe me."

He took the towel he'd been drying with and pressed it to a damp spot in the hollow around her belly button. "I didn't care about you obeying me when I was a wet-behind-the-ears kid, but I do now. Show me now you want a guy who can't give you a baby and didn't have the balls to tell you when he first found out, the way you proved to everyone when we were kids that the ultimate princess could actually get hot for the bookworm nerd I used to be. Do it if you really want me now. Get me hot, baby. We both know you know how."

Yes, Marcy knew how. "Like this?" she asked, sitting up and raking her nails gently up the inside of his thigh, then stopping to rub the pad of her thumb gently over the soft curly hair that cushioned his sex.

"Oh, yeah." His cock lengthened and thickened, rising up against a belly whose muscular ridges were more defined than she remembered.

God, he was gorgeous. His chest muscles rippled when he moved, and the light sheen of sweat made his body glow golden in the dim light. He might have started out an ugly duckling, but he'd turned into the sort of guy women would fall all over. "How many lovers have you had, darling?" She encircled his erection with one hand, caressed his heavy scrotum with the other.

"None that matter now. Damn. I've missed you. Missed this." When he cupped her breasts, with his large warm hands, her nipples began to tingle.

His big hands on her hips, he urged her to lie back down, following her and continuing the sensual massage. "I want to

feel your mouth on me. Your hands. Oh, yeah, you make me so hot..." His words faded into a rumbling sort of purr, made her glad she was a woman—his woman.

She trailed hot, wet kisses along his jaw, loving the feel of his late-afternoon stubble abrading her lips before moving lower, along his throat. His coppery nipples hardened when she bathed them with her tongue, and when she flicked his navel, he shuddered.

"You know, I always liked the taste of this," she murmured when she licked away a glistening drop of fluid from the tip of his big beautiful cock.

"But you didn't like doing anything more than tasting."

"I know. But I know you like it. And it's something I've never done for any other man." Taking a deep breath, she took him in her mouth, hoping she'd do it well enough to please him.

It felt right, doing for him what she'd never done for any other lover. Tangling her fingers in his soft pubic curls, she cupped his balls, rolling them gently between her palms while she used her tongue to map the velvety surface of his cock, each vein and ridge and pulsating inch of the shaft. Every inch around the ridge of the corona. She sucked the plum-like head of him, eagerly tasting his essence. When she backed off and lapped at the dimpled slit at its tip, he grasped her head and lifted it, forcing her to meet his glittering gaze.

"I wanted you to get me hot. Well, whether it was what you said or the feel of you giving me what you've never given anybody else, or a little bit of both, I'm on fire. My balls are ready to burst. Come here. My turn now." He drew her up the length of his body. "Sit on my face. I'm hungry."

He'd never let her grow hair here again. Her wet, swollen labia felt satiny to his tongue, gave him easy access he'd never considered as a benefit when examining a woman who was shaved. Of course he never examined *them* with his tongue. He licked the slick folds now, loving the taste of her honey, loving more the knowledge that her cunt still wanted him. Her rigid

little clit, always sensitive, seemed to swell more when he took it between his teeth.

When he reached up and found her breasts she whimpered, sinking down on him. He opened his lips and sampled more of her glistening flesh, flailing her swollen clit with his tongue as he tugged on her nipples. He loved the sound of her breathy scream that carried even over the booms of thunder in the distance.

She squirmed on him, as though wanting more, then rose on her knees. "Fuck me, Sam. Fuck me now. Put your big, beautiful cock in me and make love to me until I can't hear the roar of the wind. Fuck me until there's nothing on my mind but you."

He wanted her on her knees, helpless, her naked pussy gleaming, her cunt and anus open and inviting his rock-hard cock. Submissive, offering whatever he chose to take. But despite her raw plea, he sensed she needed more. To see his face, feel his touch and return it. Taste herself on his lips and drown out the noise of the storm with the wet, primal sounds of mating.

He slid her down his body until her wet slit caressed his eager flesh. "Ride me. Ride me hard, the way you used to do. I'll chase away the demons."

When she took him in her hand and rubbed his cockhead against her clit, he almost came. He clenched his fists, closed his eyes against the incredibly erotic picture of Marcy straddling him, rubbing his near-to-bursting flesh along the wet satin of her slit. Seating the head of his cock in her cunt, she sank on him until it came to rest at the mouth of her womb.

Hot. Wet. Tight. Her inner muscles hugged his turgid flesh as she rose, then loosened to let him in when she sank back down and sucked him deep into her cunt. Sam grasped her hips, took control of the rhythm. Flexed his hips and drove deeper, harder with each downward motion she made. God, how he'd missed this. Missed her.

"Come for me, baby."

"Together." The word came out on a whimper as he slid his hands to her breasts, tugged her tight, hardened nipples between his thumbs and forefingers. He'd give her the taste of pain she'd always liked with her pleasure, making her feel him. Only him. He'd drive out the memories of her other lovers. From his own mind as well as hers.

"Oh, yesss."

Her cunt clamped down on him, milked him. Her wild orgasmic contractions triggered the surge from his balls to his cock. He shuddered, trying to hold on, prolong every sensation, savor how she screamed out his name.

"God, Sam, I'm coming. Hold me." Her nails dug into his shoulders, stinging just enough to let him regain a measure of command. When she bit his earlobe as though she wanted to devour him, he withdrew until just the tip of his cock felt her scalding heat. Arching his hips upward and grasping her ass cheeks, he buried his cock to the balls. The pressure built, then gave way to the incredible pleasure of impending release. Of claiming her with his seed, useless though it might be.

With each hot burst of come, he made her his. Only his. Her whimpers and moans punctuated his sense of possession, let him know she wanted this. Wanted him. As his climax receded, she collapsed on his chest, holding onto him as though she'd never let him go.

"I'll never let you go now." As the storm raged outside Sam held Marcy and prayed. Prayed he'd have the chance to make things right...to make a new start with the only woman he'd ever loved. The woman who might have had sex with dozens of other men. The fact she'd held back, saved a lot of herself for him, spurred his resolve to win her back.

Chapter Four

Through the night the storm raged on, its intensity lessening as dawn began to break. Black skies gave way to gray by midmorning, prompting Sam to believe they would survive. He'd have the chance to get Marcy back. To make things right between them once again.

"Shall we go see if we've got transportation home?"

Marcy rolled over, stretched, making him painfully aware they'd only scratched the surface, satisfying needs he'd bottled up for five long years. Longer. "Mmmm. I'd rather stay here and escape reality."

So would he. But he doubted there was much left on Cabbage Key to support life for any amount of time. "Come on, sleepyhead. Get up. We've got no electricity or running water and nothing to eat here. There's no reason we can't continue the fantasy in the comfort of home. If the *Lucky Lady*'s still out in the cove, and still in one piece, that is. If we're really lucky, the marine radio will still be working." He imagined the devastation at the docks would be as bad if not worse than it was here, but he didn't want to alarm Marcy. After all, the boat could have survived the storm. If it hadn't, he was a strong swimmer. He could always swim across the waterway to the mainland for help if worse came to worst.

"Okay." She rolled out of bed, bent, and picked up the sodden green mess that apparently was the dress she'd worn to the wedding. "Damn. I itch all over. I'd give a month's pay for a shower."

"Come on, then. There's one aboard the boat, along with some clean clothes. You don't need to dress. I'm not."

"But—"

"Marcy, there's not another soul on Cabbage Key. Everybody else evacuated right after the wedding." He grinned. "It's not as though we haven't seen each other naked before."

She dropped the dress. "Okay."

Putting his shoulder to the cabin door, he shoved it open. "Better put on some shoes. The porch is full of broken glass." Kicking away his wet clothes, he found his wet deck shoes and shoved his feet into them.

"No shoes. My weekender was on the launch when it took off. The ones I was wearing at the wedding got caught up in the muck by the docks."

"Right. I saw them. It's okay. I'll carry you."

When he lifted her, he found Marcy lighter then he remembered, or maybe it was that he'd grown stronger. Sam loved the feel of her arms around his neck, the naked skin of her thighs and shoulders beneath his hands. The soft whoosh of her breath against his ear. "Hold on. Baby, it feels so good to have you in my arms again."

A strong breeze tossed raindrops around them. Downed Australian pines, uprooted shrubs, and pieces of decimated buildings along the path gave silent evidence of Katrina's power. They were damned lucky. Sam looked toward where the dock had been, hoping to see the *Lucky Lady* moored where he'd left her yesterday.

No such luck. The storm surge had ripped her from her mooring, sent her drifting, and apparently tossed the port side of her stern up onto a sandbar.

"Sam?"

"Yeah, baby?"

She cast a dubious look at the boat, then looked at him, her expression full of worry. "Can we get the boat back in the water?"

"I think so, if we wait for high tide. The question is whether we'll want to once we assess the damage. Keep your fingers

crossed that the radio works, and that I can scare somebody up on it."

"Where's your cell phone?"

"Overboard, I imagine. I broke it on the trip back here from the mainland." Sam's feet sank into muck dragged in by the storm surge. "Hang on. It's going to be a rocky ride from here on, until we get onto the boat."

"All right." Her trust touched him—but then she'd always trusted him to keep her out of danger. The Gulf had been their playground—and the only venue where he'd been superior to her as a kid—at swimming, sailing, and snorkeling along the barrier islands off Fort DeSoto Park. "Just think of this as another Sunday adventure," he said once he was up to his knees in the murky, debris-filled water and her feet were dangling into it, catching muddy seaweed.

The *Lucky Lady* faced the mainland, its mooring ropes dragging off the bow and stern and tangled in remnants of the dock. Other than sitting at an odd angle, she looked intact. He bent, setting Marcy in the water by the stern ladder. "Let go. Climb aboard and move over toward the starboard side. I'm going to dive underneath her and inspect for obvious damage."

"Be careful, Sam."

He dived once, spitting silt out of his mouth when he came up for air. "Looks okay on this side as far as I can tell." Then he went under again, wishing to God he could see better in the murky water. Feeling his way around, he finally determined after several more dives that even if they couldn't move, they probably wouldn't sink. The salesman apparently hadn't lied when he'd said this boat's hull would stand up to a hurricane.

Marcy huddled against the starboard side of the *Lucky Lady*, hugging both arms across her naked breasts. "Well?" she asked when he climbed aboard and joined her.

"She's safe enough. I doubt we can dislodge her before high tide, though. Go on below, you look like you're about to freeze. I'll be down as soon as I see if the radio's working."

"I-I'll wait for you."

"I said for you to go below. Do it. And put on one of my shirts. Drawer below the bunk." He watched her until her blond head disappeared through the cabin door.

Treading lightly, Sam made his way to the cockpit and turned on the radio. The crackling noises sounded promising, and soon he made contact with a Coast Guard cutter searching for survivors from a wrecked fishing boat somewhere off Sarasota. "I'll try to break us loose," he said before setting down the microphone and firing up the starboard engine.

"Sam?" Marcy poked her head through the cabin door, a worried frown on her face.

"Stay down there. I'm going to try to rock us free. If I can, we'll soon be on our way."

"But you got hold of help?"

"No boat as big as a cutter will be able to get into this cove, and nobody's likely to be manning Coast Guard auxiliary boats in this weather. We may or may not be able to get out of here, depending on whether the channel's full of silt. But I'm going to try. We've got at least one good engine."

The *Lucky Lady* shuddered but didn't move. Sam let out a curse, then shut down the engine and went below. "We might as well clean up. We might even find something to eat unless it got destroyed during the storm. We're going to be here until high tide. At least."

"When's that?"

"Late this afternoon. If I can break her loose, I'll take her over to what's left of the dock and tie her up for the night. You're going to be stuck with me at least another twenty-four hours. I'm not trying to navigate the Waterway at night, not with the debris that's bound to be floating around."

Her expression softened, and she shot him a smile that reminded him of the old Marcy he'd loved so much. "I don't mind. After all, you did come back for me."

"Yeah. I did at that."

* * * * *

Fresh, cool water sluiced over her body and his in the tiny shower. Marcy didn't mind, though usually tight places made her nervous. Sam's presence drove away her fear, made her feel young and whole and...

He lathered her breasts and pussy, following up by taking the showerhead and directing the soft spray on her most sensitive spots. "Hey, turn about's fair play," she said, taking the hose and spraying his crotch. He was hard, lusciously so.

It took real effort for her to remember why she'd thrown him out...the loneliness when he'd held himself aloof, the humiliation of being accused of unfaithfulness while heartbroken over the loss of their baby. At least now she knew why, though she wasn't at all sure the explanation should excuse him for having broken her heart.

Decisions could wait. Now she had Sam, and she intended to enjoy every stolen moment until they returned to the real world, their separate lives. Handing him the shower head to put away, she stepped out of the head and began to dry her body.

"Let me." Dripping wet, he took the towel from her and blotted away the water, his hands gentle—arousing. Warming her where she was cold, ever so gently, the way he used to when they'd bathed together in the small Miami apartment where they'd loved so deeply.

In the past twenty-four hours they'd faced death and survived. Together. It seemed only right that they celebrate life together, too. Marcy sighed, wishing for more than these stolen moments yet afraid to forgive and ask forgiveness. Then she reached up, caressed Sam's stubbled cheeks, drew his face down to meet her eager lips.

His long surgeon's fingers entwined with hers, dragging them away. "First I want to feed you. Come here, let's see what we can find in the galley."

Out of the chaos the storm had wreaked on his food supply, they salvaged a bunch of grapes...a slightly battered banana.

Crackers, though they were reduced to nothing but crumbs from the beating they'd taken. A wedge of cheddar cheese. Some olives. Bending, Sam salvaged a slightly bruised cucumber from the floor and set it on the sink. "I think I'd rather play with this than eat it," he said, the twinkle in his eye reminding Marcy of the old days, when they'd whiled away a lazy day in bed, feeding each other and playing—with makeshift sex toys neither of them had the spare change or the balls to go and buy from the adult store around the corner from their first apartment.

Plate in hand, he led the way to the cabin—and the narrow bunk in its corner. "Feed me," he ordered once he stretched out atop the taut, crisp sheet. "Let me feed you, too." His voice softened, and she heard a catch, as though he were as overcome by memories—emotions—as she.

Almost as though he were afraid of rejection. When Marcy sat on the edge of the bunk beside him she saw not the handsome, supremely confident physician Sam had become, but the gawky redheaded boy he'd been when he very hesitantly asked her for their first date. She recalled his shyness, his sweetness...the endearing hesitation when he'd dared to steal a kiss. And the crackling, miraculous connection she'd felt from the moment their lips had touched.

There was still something of the wonder in his face as he smiled up at her, and it touched her heart as his bold direction did her body. A connection bitter words hadn't quite been able to sever still made her heart beat faster in his presence. His, too, if she could believe the words he'd said in the heat of passion as they lay in the eye of the storm, not certain they'd survive its wrath.

"You know, there's something about a first love...something that's so damn hard to let go of." She fed him a grape, and then a sliver of cheese, wishing her voice held the ring of confidence for which she was known in court. But no. She sounded much like the pretty sophomore cheerleader who'd fallen deeply and inexplicably for the gawky nerd of the senior class. "Come on, you big lug. Do something to make me

remember why I packed up your stuff and had it laid out on the front porch for you. Don't make me fall in love with you all over again."

He turned his head and nibbled gently at her finger. "I'll never do that again. Baby, I don't have the words to tell you how sorry I am. What will it take to get you to forgive me? Give us another chance?"

She wanted to. God how she wanted to. But...Sam had a possessive streak a mile wide. He couldn't help but know about her years-long search for satisfaction...the string of lovers who hadn't been able to take his place in her heart, or pay him back for the one he'd wrongly accused her of having. "For now, let's just say that like this boat, we're on an island. An island where reality dares not to intrude. Let go my hand, and I'll feed you. You're going to need all your strength for what I have in mind."

"I'll drink to that. Here, you're going to need some energy yourself." With that, he held the peeled banana to her lips. "Eat up."

She closed her lips around the soft, sweet fruit, licking its smooth surface the way she wanted to devour Sam's big, throbbing cock. Funny. She'd never cared much for giving him head before, but now she could barely wait to take him in her mouth and love him. She chewed and swallowed, her gaze on his growing erection as she imagined doing with him the few acts she'd never shared with anyone else. Acts that to her seemed more personal, more intimate than taking a cock into her pussy and fucking it to a mutual release.

She met his amused gaze. "I want to suck your cock."

"I won't complain. Later. We've got hours before the tide rises. A whole night before we've got to head for Tampa. There's nothing I don't want from you...with you. I intend to have it all."

"All right." Just as it had seemed right last night to put her safety—her life—into his hands, now it seemed right to submit. To follow his lead, enjoy his body while he sated himself on her.

"Another grape?" She caught one between her teeth, then joined their open lips.

His tongue darted out, caught the small globe and bit into it, sending sweet, tart juice into her mouth and his. Sending shards of sexual excitement to her brain, and from there throughout her body.

A day out of time, for feeling and loving and living in the present. No past and no future. Tomorrow would be time enough for recriminations. Now Marcy would let go, bask in desire, affection, and—she'd admit it to herself if not to him— love for the man Sam was today that had nothing to do with nostalgia or survival or anything but what lay buried in her heart.

Intent on arousing him fully, Marcy picked up the cucumber and sucked it into her mouth, her gaze never wavering from his smiling face.

Soft, full lips, pink and inviting, closed around the dark-green flesh of the cucumber he'd brought along for a salad. Sam's cock swelled at the thought of her taking him that way. His pulse accelerated at the memory of her tonguing him last night as they'd lain in the eye of the storm not knowing if their next moments might be their last. The urgency was gone now, yet the passion remained. With every lazy motion of her mouth on the lucky vegetable, he grew harder.

Wanted her more. For a moment he imagined dragging her home, locking her away for no one's eyes but his. No one's cock but his. His heart pounded in his chest. Damn it, no one but Marcy had ever engendered such fierce possessiveness in him, such an animal urge to claim her, hold her as his own.

"You're wasting it on that cuke. Come down here and suck on me. Let me feel your hot, wet mouth. Swallow my cock. Make me come if you can."

Pouting prettily, she withdrew the cucumber and bent over him, her lips brushing his chest, each ridge of his tensed abs. Then she sucked him into her mouth the way she'd sucked him

into her life from their first date. Sexily, sweetly, with warmth and infinite care, as though this was a new and wondrous experience.

His balls tightened when she tightened her lips on his shaft, took more of him. When he spread his legs she caressed them briefly, then stroked the insides of his thighs. She remembered. He liked being stroked there, and on the backs of his knees. Something no other lover had discovered.

But then with other lovers he'd been scratching an itch. With her having sex had always been making love. Still was, in spite of everything. Sam shoved away the regrets that bubbled up inside him, concentrating instead on the heat of her mouth on his cock, the soft yet incredibly arousing touch of her soft fingers, the rake of her nails. The moist heat of her breath on his belly and the brush of pale damp strands of her hair along his hipbones.

He sank his fingers in her hair, drew her off him. "I've got to touch you, too. And when I come, I want to be buried so deep inside you, you won't be able to push me out."

"I won't want you out. I love what you do to me, how you make me feel."

Carefully, as he might have handled a precious, fragile artifact, he laid her back against the dark-blue coverlet and looked at her with wonder, the way he had so many times before. Marcy's beauty awed him. Aroused him. Made him feel like twice the man he was, just because she'd once loved him. Still loved him if her declaration in the face of death were true.

Satiny tanned skin, with pale triangles that gave away the shape of the bikini she must wear beside the pool...triangles Sam now traced the way a kindergartner might follow the lines on a drawing, not straying from the lines. Just enjoying. Taking in the firm flesh, the silky skin, feeling her heartbeat accelerate under his fingertips.

Bending, he took one turgid nipple between his teeth, sucked it in. Urged on by her whimpers and breathy little

moans, he laved it with his tongue. When she threaded her fingers through his hair, holding him there, he nipped her gently.

"Harder," she murmured. "I won't break. Please." She never wanted him to go slow, not when she was hot. As she always had from the beginning, Marcy wanted immediate gratification.

He liked to play, though, and though she'd whine and beg him to fuck her hard and fast, she always came harder and longer when he'd tortured her into a frenzy of need before giving her his cock. "Be still. If you come for me this way, I'll reward you with a good, hard fucking." Not stopping to explore the soft curves and flat planes of her belly, he cupped her baby-soft mound, spreading the hot, wet core of her with his fingers.

Then he remembered the cucumber. Grabbing it, he slid it along her slit, rubbing its blunt end in a circular motion around her anus. Her little whimper told him she liked it, wanted more. Good thing he'd bought the smooth, burpless variety at the store. Very carefully he pressed it against her until she relaxed enough to take an inch, then two.

"Feel good?"

"God yes. Sam, make love to me now."

He slid the cucumber in another inch, imagining it was his cock invading that tight, tight hole. Every minute he got harder and hotter, watching her anus throbbing against the dark-green vegetable. Lubrication gushed from her cunt and gathered along her slit, wetting his fingers and the swollen, stretched tissue around her anus. "You want my cock here?" Did he have a condom anywhere aboard the *Lucky Lady*? He didn't think so.

"Not there. My pussy. Oh God, yesss. Sam, I'm coming." The way she whimpered and squirmed had his balls ready to burst. "Please. Don't make me wait any longer," she gasped.

He wouldn't. Withdrawing the cucumber and setting it aside, he knelt between her legs and sank into her hot, wet cunt. "Like this?"

"God yes. Fuck me hard. Make me come. Damn it, make me forget there's ever been anyone but you. Oh, God, Sam. Nobody can fuck me the way you do."

Nobody else ever had brought out the need in him to conquer, to master. Nobody else had made him bubble over like this on contact, ready to explode. His balls tightened more painfully with every plunge of his cock into her heat, each retreat against the sucking motion of her cunt.

Determined to fuck her hard enough, well enough to make her forget every other man she'd ever had sex with, he clamped down on the urge to come, to claim. Not yet! Not until he made her scream with pleasure.

Maybe if he thought of something else…shit. Trying to recite the periodic table in his head reminded him of the powerful chemistry that flowed between them. Concentrating on human anatomy got no farther than his cock, her cunt, the explosive reaction when the two merged.

Sam gritted his teeth, increased the motion. Marcy's whimpers spurred him to go faster, fuck her harder. She liked it rough. Always had. She wanted him on the brink of meltdown, herself caught up in the storm of sex.

He'd give it to her. Hard. Fast. His cock slammed against her cervix with every punishing stroke. The bed shook as he pressed her body into the bed and she threw her cunt at him. He had to taste her, mark her *his*.

"God yesss," she hissed when he sank his teeth into the tender spot where her shoulder met her throat. "Ohhhhh."

He tasted blood, soothed her damaged flesh with his tongue. "Sorry."

"Don't stop. Fuck me hard. Make me come. Please."

"Whose cock's inside you?" He had to hear his name on her lips. "Tell me, damn you."

"You. Only you, Sam."

"Only me. Now fuck me." Over and over flesh met flesh, the slapping sounds of his balls connecting with her sopping

pussy, his hard breathing punctuating her whimpers and moans. He couldn't think, only fuck. "Damn it, I can't be gentle. I don't want to hurt you but—"

"Be rough. I like it that way. Make me forget...oh, yess."

At the first convulsion of her flesh around his, he bent and caught her scream in his mouth.

And let her take him the rest of the way, shooting his load inside her in staccato bursts of searing heat as she shuddered with the force of her own orgasm.

Chapter Five

"How'd you get down to Port Charlotte?" Sam asked the next morning, once they cleared the treacherous shallows in the channel to the cove and he set a course for the Flying Fisherman Marina.

She shot him a shamefaced grin. "I flew to Fort Myers and took a cab to the ferry dock."

So Marcy still didn't like to drive long distances. Good. "Want a ride home?"

"Sure. Think you can scare up somebody on that radio who can get word to my office that I'm still alive?"

Just then the port engine stalled, making the *Lucky Lady* try to go into a spin. Swearing, Sam wrestled the wheel and slowed the starboard engine to a crawl. "You can call in from the marina. I've got to have them see what's going on with this engine. Hopefully it will be nothing but seaweed caught up in the exhausts."

The marina owner ran down the dock, grabbing the line Sam tossed out. "Thank God you made it. I was about to send one of the ferrymen over to Cabbage Key."

"We're okay. The *Lucky Lady* has an exhaust fouled, though, I think." Climbing onto the dock, Sam held a hand down for Marcy. "Can you take a look?"

"Sure thing. Joe, bring the forklift around and haul this boat." He turned back to Sam. "Can't tell much about what's wrong with her in the water. Incidentally, your friends have been worried sick. They got evacuated, but they've been calling here nearly every hour asking whether you two got off the island. You might want to let them know you're okay."

Marcy smiled. "I'll go do that in just a minute."

Sam and Marcy watched the *Lucky Lady* teetering on the forklift as it came out of the water. It was immediately evident that the storm had done more damage than Sam had been able to see with a few quick dives into the murky water of the cove. Damn. What would have been a relaxing all-day trip on water would take only a couple of hours on the Interstate. He'd been looking forward to some heart-to-heart conversation, maybe even another session of lovemaking. Neither was likely to happen along the busy concrete corridor.

He turned to Marcy. "While you're calling Ileana, you might as well arrange for us to rent a car. The *Lucky Lady* won't be going anywhere today." Sam couldn't help grinning at the sassy picture Marcy made in his shirt and a pair of his running shorts. When she came back from the payphone, he put an arm around her. "So what's happening with our friends?"

"Ileana was frantic. Thought we were both swept out into the Gulf or something. I assured her we'd made it, that we were both okay, but she just kept crying. When she finally calmed down, all she could do was tease me about what had gone on between us." Marcy shrugged. "I insisted it was nothing."

"It was a lot more than nothing to me."

She squeezed his arm. "To me, too. What happened meant too much to talk about with anyone, even a good, old friend who's enough of a romantic to want to see us back together."

"Doctor Kramer?"

Sam turned to the marina owner. "What's the verdict?"

"I can have the *Lucky Lady* running by the weekend so you can get her home. She's gonna need some major repairs, though. Things I don't have the equipment to do. If you want, I can get one of the ferrymen to bring her up to Tampa for you. Won't be much tourist trade around here for a while, 'til the mess from Katrina gets cleaned up."

At first Sam hesitated, mentally visualizing him and Marcy taking a lazy trip back up the Waterway next weekend, the way he'd planned for them to do today. Then he came to his senses.

He had to work, and she did, too. Not to mention there was no guarantee she'd want to spend another weekend on the water, with or without him. "That's a good idea. See if you can arrange it."

"Sure thing. Make sure you leave a number where we can get hold of you if I run into any problems I don't see now." The mechanic disappeared under the stern of the *Lucky Lady*, apparently anxious to start the makeshift repairs.

"Sam?" Marcy turned to him from the pay phone. "The rental agency will bring the car around in a few minutes. Do you need to call your office?"

"No. I'm signed out to my partners until tomorrow. What about you? Will they be able to get along without you for another day?"

She smiled when he put his arm around her and laid his hand lightly along her hipbone. "I think so. Only pressing thing I had going today was a meeting with Gray Syzmanski. It can wait until tomorrow. It's not as though his client's locked up in jail. It took all of five minutes after the judge had set bail last week for the kid's parents to bond him out."

"Gray's a good guy. We work out together twice a week."

"So I heard from Andi. I've gotten to know him pretty well since he's been with Winston Roe. Of course I've known Andi for years." Marcy's smile faded, but she recovered quickly and shot him a grin. "Leave it to you to exercise with a guy who's crippled and can't push you."

"Gray pushes plenty hard. Just about as hard as any guy I've seen. Wants to keep as fit as he can for Andi and those two kids of theirs."

"I guess. Look, I think that's our car coming now."

There it was. That brittleness he hated. At first Sam couldn't figure out what brought it on—then it came to him. Gray and Andi's kids. He should have kept his mouth shut, realized Marcy wouldn't like reminders about the babies she'd wanted but didn't have.

Though he should have dropped his hand from her hip, let her get on with her life, he couldn't. The connection was still there, still too strong. If five years' bitterness hadn't severed it, Sam figured nothing would. "Come on, baby, let's go home." He opened the car door for her, then strode around to the driver's side.

After dropping the rental company attendant off, they rolled onto northbound I-75. For a long time they rode along past evidence of Katrina's decimation, the only noise being the hum of the economy sedan's tires over stress seams in the road. After turning off the highway and heading through downtown Tampa toward the house they'd once shared in Old Hyde Park where she still lived, Sam glanced at Marcy. From the way she stared out the window at passing cars and wrung her hands together, he guessed she was upset. "What's wrong?"

"You said we were going home."

He reached over and laid his hand over hers. "Calm down. We are. We'll be there any minute now."

"Don't you understand? It's over. We're going home. Our separate homes, Sam. We're still divorced. There's still unsettled baggage between us. Too much for what happened on Cabbage Key to have been any more than a nostalgic interlude. Let's just say Katrina swept away our good sense, made us face the fact there's still a lot of feelings that probably won't ever go away." She reached up, brushed something off her cheek. "I'm glad we had the chance to be together for a little while. It makes me sad, but I know it's got to end."

"It doesn't." If Sam had anything to say about it, they'd move ahead, not back. He pulled into the driveway, the way he'd done so many times before. "If you think I'm walking away now, you're not thinking straight."

"You don't have a choice. What you did to me wasn't something that can be dismissed with an apology, even though at least now I halfway understand why you didn't trust me."

Hurrying around to her side of the car, he opened the door, blocking her with his body so she couldn't bolt. "Baby, I trust you now. It was only at first—"

"What would you say if I called you next week, told you I was pregnant and said you were the father?"

Sam's hand tightened on the open door. "I'd say I was thrilled." He would be, even though he'd be hard-pressed to believe the same miracle had happened twice. "And I'd get down on my knees and beg you to marry me again and let me come back home."

"But would you believe me?" she asked, her tone incisive.

Fuck, he couldn't lie. Chances were, if she were to learn she was pregnant, one of her lovers' condoms had failed in the past few weeks. The odds against him impregnating her again were too goddamn high. "I'd try. But it wouldn't make any difference. I'd still want you. I'd believe you'd made your choice and wanted me to be the baby's father, whether or not it had my DNA. "

"That's what I thought." She got out of the car and stared him down the way he imagined she would the toughest crook in the courtroom. "Now let me go. We've got too much baggage ever to get back together and make it work."

She might have been right. But Sam wasn't convinced of anything except that around Marcy he felt complete, fulfilled in a way no other woman had managed to accomplish since their split. Yeah, they had baggage—resentment, distrust, probably a dozen other disquieting emotions. Still, Marcy had reached out to him when they faced mortal danger. She'd admitted she still harbored a few warm feelings toward him, too.

He had to touch her. Do something to reach her. Following her to the door, he set his hands on her shoulders and turned her to face him. "What we had back there was good. More than good. Do you really want to toss it away without—"

"It was sex, Sam. Incredibly hot sex and memories and fear, all jumbled together. Maybe, in a way, the storm forced us to

acknowledge the parts of our relationship that always had been good. Perhaps it forced you to talk and me to listen. If there's a God, maybe now He'll grant us closure."

Closure. The last thing Sam wanted. He knew, though, from the sound of Marcy's voice and the tight set of her chin that now wasn't the time to pit his limited debating skill against her innate talent for argument that she'd honed in courtrooms for over ten years now. "Maybe. Don't count on it being over, though. I don't give up easily."

"Go on, Sam. Thanks for saving me. And for the best time I've had in bed for longer than I can remember. Thanks, too, for explaining after all this time why you shoved me away when I needed you most. Maybe now I can let go of the hate." She stood on tiptoe, brushed a quick kiss across his lips.

Then, before he could stop her, she'd turned and stepped inside, leaving him staring at the dark-blue door with its bright brass knocker he remembered having installed there soon after they'd bought the place.

Sam had never felt so alone.

* * * * *

Inside, Marcy regarded the blinking light on the phone, wondering if she dared ignore it, crawl into bed, and forget about the outside world. Damn it, she'd wanted to ask Sam in, so much she ached inside. It had taken every bit of strength she'd been able to muster to stop with that brief touch of lips to lips, then close the door in his face.

No. She'd made a life apart from him. She had lovers, as he so painfully had reminded her with his hesitation, his carefully chosen answer to the hypothetical question she'd raised about how he'd react this time if she turned up pregnant. She had a job as important as his, and since it was only a little past noon, she might as well keep the appointments she'd made before leaving for Ileana's wedding. After listening to her messages, she called her office, then dressed and headed downtown. If she were

lucky, she'd have an hour or so to go over the case of *Florida v. Stephen Katz* before her meeting with Gray.

Would Gray leave her office after their meeting and go join Sam at the gym? Disgusted with herself for mooning over Sam when she should have been working, Marcy slid her briefcase under her desk and rifled through case folders until she found the one she wanted. Setting aside her vanity, she fished a pair of reading glasses out of the drawer and began reading.

Stephen Katz. Twenty-one years old, a senior at the University of Florida. Marcy had met his parents, although she didn't know them well. Prominent couple, always taking part in some charity or other. Neighbors of Sam's parents. In any case, they'd attended her wedding. Stephen would have been starting kindergarten about then. As she read the charge—aggravated assault that took place a week ago at a sleazy club on Nebraska Avenue—she felt for the boy's family. What the hell had the kid been thinking, venturing into an area of town known best for its pimps and whores and dealers?

Now he was in hot water up to his neck. Though he claimed he'd been robbed at knifepoint and that he'd fought back in self-defense, the arresting officers had looked at him and at the other guy and arrested Stephen. Apparently Manuel Soto, the would-be robber, was still hospitalized, while Stephen had escaped serious injury.

Harper Wells, her boss, apparently would take heat from the large Latino community if Stephen were allowed to walk. That had been one of the messages waiting for her when she got home. It made no difference that the so-called victim had a rap sheet that required a binder clip, not a staple, to hold it together. He'd been badly hurt, from the information in the file that mentioned a cut throat and serious blood loss.

Marcy closed the folder. Gray would be along any minute. While privately she considered the case in question one in which a variant of the old southern defense, "He needed killin'," might have merit, she dared not decline to prosecute the case. Not if she wanted to keep her job. Maybe…but Gray hadn't sounded

when he made the appointment as though he'd entertain the thought of letting his client plead to a reduced charge.

Stephen could have been her son. Hers and Sam's. Well, it wasn't likely, but it could have happened. If she'd gotten pregnant that first time they made love under the bleachers... There was no use thinking about that, or getting sympathetic toward an accused even before Gray presented the silver-tongued plea she knew was coming. Trying to be fair, she opened the file again and read the medical report on Stephen's supposed victim.

She shouldn't have bothered. The lab test results showed Soto had been high on coke and booze upon admission...and that pot apparently made up a significant portion of his diet. The injury Stephen supposedly had inflicted—some bruises and a shallow cut on the neck—was consistent with Stephen's claim that he'd defended himself with his fists and a box-cutting tool.

"Hey, hot stuff. Welcome back." Cam Willis stuck his head inside her door, a big grin on his face.

"Go away, Cam. Can't you see I'm busy?" Normally Marcy would have said something provocative and flashed a sexy smile at the tall, blond, and handsome assistant state attorney, but today he seemed so young—so trite. Hell, it wasn't his fault he couldn't hold a candle sex-wise to her ex, or that her memories of Sam had been refreshed, in spades, during the past seventy-two hours or so. Cam would probably be a great lover, too, in another ten years or so.

"Bennie's after work?"

Marcy forced a smile. "I don't think so. Thanks anyhow."

"Sure." Cam shrugged, as though her refusal was of no consequence to him. It probably wasn't. "Thought I'd let you know Gray Syzmanski's waiting to see you. Must be exciting, going up against him and Tony Landry."

"Yeah. Real exciting. If you're not busy, go tell him to come on back." Setting the file back on her desk, Marcy ran a brush through her hair and checked her lipstick. Habit, because she

might as well have been invisible for all the attention Gray had ever paid her as a woman. Must be nice for Andi to have a guy who had eyes just for her.

An eye, that is. Far from being off-putting, the guy's scars and the black patch that covered his ruined eye socket gave him a rugged look as well as reminding everybody he'd gone through hell and survived to tell the tale.

Marcy smiled and rose when Gray came through the door. "Sit down. I have the copy you asked for of the Katz file."

"Thanks." Propping his crutches against the side of her desk, Gray sat and set out some papers. "Here's some information our investigators have found. You might want to take a look."

"I'm not dropping charges. We may as well get that straight up front."

Gray nudged the stack of papers her way. "I've got witnesses to Soto's pulling a knife and demanding Stephen's money before Stephen ever laid a hand on him. Two of them. One's a hooker, but the other is a seventy-year-old lady who's been staying at that fleabag motel because it's the only place she can afford."

"Motel?" Marcy hadn't seen anything in the police report about a motel.

"The one next door to the club, the kind of joint where they rent by the hour or the week, customer's choice. Most apparently choose the hourly plan. There's a clear view out the old lady's window to the parking lot where the action went down. The hooker was in the parking lot, apparently trying to drum up more business."

"What was your client doing, hanging out in the parking lot of the Club Tetras? It seems hardly the spot for a clean-cut college boy to go." Drugs? A possibility, although if he'd been buying them, it apparently wasn't for himself. Stephen had tested squeaky-clean following his arrest.

"Trying to score with a lady of the evening." Gray shook his head. "Yeah, it was stupid, but you don't want to let it ruin the kid's life forever. Come on, cut him some slack. Forget filing charges. File 'em against Soto instead. Get a real criminal off the streets for a few years."

"Don't worry. We'll be filing charges against Mr. Soto, too. May I assume Winston Roe won't be representing *him*?"

"You can. Come on, Marcy, Tony picks and chooses the firm's criminal clients. Our scumbags have to have some redeeming qualities, or at least a defensible case. Soto doesn't have either."

Marcy sighed. "Okay. I sympathize with young Mr. Katz. Really I do. There aren't many of us who've never done something abysmally stupid." *Including me.* "Let me think this over. I'll get back to you by next Monday."

"Fair enough." Gray grabbed his crutches and heaved himself off the chair. "Andi said to tell you, we're having some friends over on Saturday. We'd love for you to join us. Mexican food, margaritas, and so on."

"I'll be there." Sex with anybody but Sam held no appeal, and Marcy figured by the weekend she'd need diversion or she'd be likely to chase him down and jump him. "Want me to bring something?"

"Just yourself, and a big appetite. Cocktails at seven, dinner at eight. Casual. If the weather's good, we'll do it outside by the pool."

"Okay. I'll try to come to a decision before then on your case. Give Andi and the kids my best."

For a long time after he'd left, Marcy sat at her desk, going over the file and the additional information Winston Roe's crack investigators had dug up. When she called chief of detectives Rocky Delgado, he verified that what Gray's investigator had turned up rang true. Stephen Katz no more belonged in prison than she did. Now she had her job cut out: persuading Harper that they should decline to prosecute.

Damn it. She had no trouble rationalizing dropping charges against a young stranger who'd foolishly gotten caught in the wrong place, the wrong time.

Why the hell can't I understand and accept that the man I love lashed out at me because of his own pain?

That night Marcy lay in bed, still pondering whether she could let go her hurt, her defensiveness. If Sam hurt her again, she doubted she could survive...but she wasn't sure she could survive without him.

Chapter Six

Damp, muggy air bathed her skin. The sheets clung to her body. The fragrance of crushed rose petals and the musk of sex surrounded her. Marcy woke up slowly, drenched with sweat. His body heat scorched her back, and his hot breath tickled her neck.

She never minded the heat, so long as they were generating it together. "Sam?"

"Huh?" His sleepy rumble reminded her he'd been out late, delivering somebody's baby.

He was home now. Home and hard, she realized, her pussy twitching in time with the insistent prodding of his big cock between her legs. God, how she loved him! "Boy or girl?"

"Girl. Shall we make one for ourselves?" He slid his hand along her damp skin, each long finger branding the pathway over her breasts, splaying possessively over her belly before he moved lower and cupped her mound.

"Let's." She wanted his baby, had wanted it ever since they were hardly more than kids themselves. Now that they'd finally settled down in their jobs and bought a home, it was time. "I'll toss out my pills first thing in the morning."

"Good." He rolled her onto her belly. Flexing his hips, he entered her from behind and began to move. The tension built up with every slow plunge, each tantalizing retreat. "Baby, I love how you're always wet for me. Come on, tell me how you want me."

"Harder. Faster. Oh God, Sam, give me a baby now."

"First you've gotta come for me. Oh, yeah. Squeeze me. Harder. You're so hot, so tight. So mine."

What she'd always wanted to be. His. Unequivocally, totally his. Her pussy clutched him tighter, harder, as if it never wanted to let him go. She had to hold onto all the sensations that had every nerve in her

body on edge, wanting release. The delicious feeling of fullness had her on the brink of coming. Slapping sounds of his hard, demanding cock invading her softer, swollen tissue…the pervasive musk of sex mingled with the clean, crisp smell of freshly changed bed linens…

Every time they made love he put her on sensual overload. She loved it. Loved him. Oh God, she couldn't hold back any longer when he changed the angle of penetration and slammed into her G-spot. "Yesss. Give me your come. Damn it, I want to feel you spurting hot and fast. Sam, I want your baby."

Marcy woke to sensations of spurting semen in her cunt and hard breathing against her neck. She reached out for Sam, but he wasn't there.

She'd had the dream before and fled into the arms of other lovers. Tonight she wanted only Sam. As though in a trance, she got up and went where she hadn't been for five long years.

Afraid of what she'd see and feel, she trembled when she cracked open the door of the bedroom they'd shared. The room so full of memories she hadn't been able to face it until now. Thanks to her housekeeper's conscientious cleaning, it looked the same. Same king-size canopy bed draped in sheer midnight blue, tied at each of the four posts with matching bows. Same armoire and chest and vanity table they'd picked out together on a trip to Amish country. Marcy remembered the toys in the drawers of the matching nightstands, smiled at the knowledge they still were there, as if waiting for their owners to return and play.

The last one Sam had brought home had been a set of pink gel anal stimulators in graduated sizes. A preliminary, he'd said, to introduce her to the joys of anal penetration—something they'd never tried since she'd discovered the next day that she was pregnant—and he'd withdrawn emotionally. Physically, too. Strange. She'd never had anal sex with anyone else, either. Never wanted to. The act seemed too personal, even more intimate than welcoming a lover's cock into her pussy. Something that needed doing with love, not just to satisfy curiosity or scratch a sexual itch.

Memories flooded her mind, the way she'd known they would the minute she opened that long-sealed door. They'd made so many here, in the thirteen months after buying the house and before splitting up.

The early morning sun still cast its shadow across the room, distorting the watered-silk pattern of cream-colored wallpaper they'd argued about buying. An argument she'd finally won, only to lose him. Nothing but an empty walk-in closet and a bathroom missing the accouterments of occupancy bore testimony to the beautiful room's disuse.

She ought to get rid of it all. Toss it away and consign Sam firmly to the past. Get on with her life. Damn it, she should redecorate and move back in here from the guest room.

Or she could risk it all and welcome him back into her life. Forgive him, hope he'd understand and excuse her for the frantic sexual explorations she'd been making since their divorce. Bank on him trusting her more now than he had back then. Marcy stepped further inside the room, sat on the edge of the bed she hadn't slept in for five long years, and debated opposing arguments in her head and heart.

Much like the hung jury that had capped off her last court battle against Tony Landry, the arguments she posed with herself ended in a stalemate.

Should she reach out, take a chance on suffering devastating pain? Or play it safe and satisfy herself with less than the kind of breathtaking joy she knew could happen when the chemistry was just right? Marcy still didn't know when she left that room full of memories and closed the door firmly behind her.

With any kind of luck, Andi and Gray's party would be lively enough to distract her from the blue funk she was in.

* * * * *

If she showed up with another guy, he'd feel like a fish out of water for sure, one lonesome, tongue-tied doc trying to keep

his head above water in a pool full of silver-tongued legal sharks. Never mind that he numbered some of them among his closest friends. Sam stared at the clothes in his closet. What the fuck had he been thinking a couple of days ago when he'd heard Marcy would be at Gray's party and wangled himself an invitation?

As he drove down Bayshore Boulevard, Sam watched waves slap against the shore. Joggers and inline skaters zipped along the sidewalk, the bay corralling them on one side while fast-moving traffic passed by on the other. Just part of living in old Hyde Park, Marcy used to tell him when he'd mentioned how unhealthy it was to exercise while inhaling gas fumes from the constant stream of cars.

Although he'd visited Gray at home several times and despite his own six-figure income, the stately mansion overlooking Old Tampa Bay still awed Sam. Built in the early nineteen hundreds by one of Gray's ancestors, it smacked of status and old money. He pulled onto a narrow side street lined with venerable oak trees, then made a sharp turn onto the driveway that circled in front of the house. A huge swing set on one side of the place reminded him this might be a historic landmark, but it was home to Gray and Andi and their two kids.

Kids. Suddenly it struck Sam that it wasn't the house that intimidated him, but the children who'd be running around in it, constantly reminding him of his own shortcomings. With any kind of luck, this would be an adult party, not a family affair. That had been the impression Gray had conveyed by mentioning margaritas by the pitcher and an assortment of blow-your-head-off spicy Tex-Mex food.

Okay. Tony Landry was here minus his eighteen-month-old son, if the presence of his sleek black Ferrari was an accurate indicator. Not long before the baby's arrival, Kristine had mentioned to Sam how carefully Tony had researched cars before bringing home a Volvo wagon for them to haul little Anthony around, quoting reports that said it was the safest

vehicle around. Sam pulled up behind the costly sports car and made his way toward the front door.

When he spotted Marcy's little silver Honda they'd bought for her when she'd passed the bar eight years ago, his gut clenched. Damn it, she had to listen. Had to give him another chance. His normally steady hand shook when he rang the doorbell. Hell, he hadn't been so scared and ill at ease for more than twenty years—since that day in second-year French class when he'd finally summoned the courage to ask her for a date.

Andi swung open the heavy door, a big smile on her face. "Hey, Sam. Come on in. Gray said you'd be joining us. Party's just warming up out on the patio."

"Where are the kids?" he asked as they moved through the house. "Don't think I've ever been here before when Brett didn't answer the door."

"Ours are with my brother for the weekend. Sandra and Rocky took theirs to his mom. Kristine and Tony left Anthony home with his nanny." She went up on tiptoe and whispered in Sam's ear. "Tonight's party time for us big kids. Marcy came alone, in case you wanted to know."

"Thanks." Pumpkins and Indian corn decorated each of the glass-topped wrought-iron tables, and amazingly lifelike looking blow-up Pilgrim and Indian figures sat under a palm tree next to the free-form pool. "Pretty impressive decorations."

"They're leftovers from the birthday party we had for Brett the other day." Andi stepped behind the bar and grabbed a salt-rimmed stem glass. "Here. Have a margarita. Your choice. The virgin ones are in the white pitchers, the high-octane stuff in the neon green ones."

Sam's breath caught when he spied Marcy laughing with Sandra and Rocky Delgado, and an attractive young couple he didn't recognize. Marcy looked good enough to eat in pale-yellow slacks and a halter top that showed enough cleavage to make him drool but covered her up enough so no one would doubt she had class. His fingers itched to dig in to that loose

twist of her hair and watch it settle like spun gold against her shoulders.

"Sam?" Andi had obviously caught him staring, and she appeared amused.

"Sorry. Better make it high octane. I'm not on call tonight. Where's Gray?"

"In the study going over a case with Tony and Hank Ehlers, one of the junior associates. They'll be out shortly. If they aren't, Kristine and I will go in and drag them away. God knows, they work long enough hours during the week. Their weekends belong to us. Come on, I'll introduce you to the folks you haven't already met. You know Sandra, don't you?"

"Sure. I know Rocky, too. He docks his boat at the same marina where I keep the *Lucky Lady*. I don't believe I've met the other couple with Marcy."

"That's Craig and Casey McDermott. He works with Marcy. I'm going to introduce you now to Hank's date."

Pru Gordon, a bland dark-haired debutante who apparently had set her marital sights on Hank Ehlers, paused in her conversation with Kristine Landry long enough to greet Sam with a murmur and a smile that distinctly lacked sincerity.

"She's upset that Hank's deserted her," Andi explained as they headed across the patio toward some of the other guests. "Don't sweat it if you don't meet with her approval. Kristine's probably the only one here—besides Hank and Gray, that is— whose blood is blue enough to impress that snooty little airhead."

Craig McDermott had an easy grin and a distinct Texan drawl. His wife Casey wasn't a stranger after all—Sam ran into the sexy personal trainer from time to time at the gym where he worked out with Gray. Except for the fact that Craig looked more like a young Arnold than a string-bean medical student, the two reminded Sam of himself and Marcy when they were kids, stealing kisses and caresses every time they thought no one was looking.

"They're cute, aren't they?" Marcy asked later after they'd finished dinner, looping an arm through Sam's and nodding toward the McDermotts as they circled the pool.

Encouraged by her friendly manner, Sam caught her hand and laced his fingers with hers. "They remind me of us."

"Yeah. They do, don't they? Sam, did you know I was going to be here?"

He bent, nibbled on her earlobe. "Uh-huh. I badgered Gray into inviting me. Do you mind?"

"No. It feels good, almost like old times. " She snagged his second leaded margarita and took a sip. "I take it you're not on call tonight."

The way she cleaned the salt off her lower lip with her tongue made him think of how fantastic it had felt when she'd licked his cock aboard the *Lucky Lady*. God, he wanted her to love him like that again. "No. Tonight belongs to me. To us, if you want. What was Gray looking so serious about when he was talking with you a few minutes ago?"

"A case. Aggravated assault. A kid was in the wrong place at the wrong time and defended himself a little too vigorously against a would-be robber. He just may have ruined his life. Gray's handling his defense, and he's pushing me not to file charges." A frown furrowed her forehead, and a worried look shadowed her beautiful face. "Harper stuck me with the prosecution, and when I tell him it's a lousy case that ought not to be pursued, he keeps reminding me how politically damaging it will be with the Latino community if we don't go to trial."

"What do you think is right?"

As he always had, Sam cut to the chase. No bullshit, no spin. Just the bottom line. Marcy wished the answer were so simple. "Right? For the accused, it would be right to let him walk. He's not a criminal, but his so-called victim is. For me? I've got to do what my boss says if I want to keep my job."

"Is this boss the same asshole who hired you ten years ago?"

"I'm afraid so. The voters keep re-electing him every four years. Harper's the consummate political animal. Pity he isn't more ambitious. If he were, he'd have moved onward and upward by now, and left us prosecutors in peace." Marcy found it somehow comforting that Sam still kept his head in the sand when it came to local politics. A constant among the many changes that had taken place in him—and her.

"Do what's right, baby. Let the bastard fire you. You've put up with Harper Wells too damn long. Go work for Winston Roe or one of the other big firms. They'd be stupid if they didn't hire you the minute you let them know you're available." He sat on one of the wrought-iron benches and drew her down beside him. "Or become a lady of leisure. Stay home and let me support you, the way you said you wanted to do once I started making enough to keep us out of the poorhouse."

Damn it. Sam knew how to throw a curve. Marcy had to clamp her lips shut to keep from blurting out a fast "yes" to his offhand proposition. "Mmm. Sounds good. Except I'm so used to working, I'd go stir crazy staring at the four walls of home all day. As for the other, I just may do it one of these days. It would be fun, debating the other side for a change—although I can't say the idea of defending hardened criminals appeals all that much."

He glanced around the patio, as though he wanted to be sure they were alone. "Want to cut out of here and find someplace really private?"

Marcy's pussy twitched with anticipation, and her nipples poked against the soft fabric of her halter top. "That would depend on what you've got in mind, Doc."

"Talk. Serious talk. Then fun. Trust me. Go tell Gray you're letting his client off the hook, and say goodnight for us. I'll meet you at home. Your home. Unless you'd rather go down to the marina. I can always borrow the keys to Rocky's boat since the *Lucky Lady*'s stuck down in Port Charlotte for a few more days."

"*Neptune's Dungeon*? From the whispers I've heard around the office, I doubt we'd get much talking done on Rocky's

floating playpen. Let's save that for another time. Tonight, let's just go home." Home to the lonesome room she'd frozen in time, the house that hadn't been a home since she'd tossed him out and wouldn't be again until they resolved their differences. Suddenly all the arguments she'd mustered against risking another broken heart seemed meaningless. "I'll go make our excuses."

She found Gray and Andi laughing over something with Tony and Kristine. "Excuse me. Gray, you can tell your client he won't be facing prosecution after all."

Gray left the group, limped over to a quiet corner where they wouldn't be disturbed. "What changed your mind, Marcy?"

"Sam. He made me realize I'm not a slave to Harper, that I can always defect to the side of the defenders." Suddenly she wanted him to know. "And he told me to do what I think is right. To drop the charges and let the shit hit the fan. That's what I'm going to do, even if it means I'll be unemployed by the end of the week. "

"Knowing Harper's temper, I won't argue that. But for what it's worth, Stephen will thank you. I thank you." A grin lit Gray's face as he turned and yelled across the deck. "Tony, come here."

The tall, compellingly handsome lawyer she'd come on to not all that long ago—to no avail, though he'd been gracious and spared her undue embarrassment—jogged over to them. "What's up?"

"Marcy may not be working for the state attorney's office much longer. I thought you might like to know." Briefly, Gray explained the situation. "We owe Sam our thanks. He's the one who told her to fuck Harper and do what she knew was right."

"Another submissive female, huh? Strange I never noticed you rolling over and playing dead for me in court." Tony shot her that little-boy grin that had female jurors practically falling over themselves to heed his every word. "Seriously, come on

over to our side and see what it's like, working regular hours, getting paid a living wage, and coming to know and love some of Tampa's most notorious criminals. I've always got room for a trial lawyer as good as you."

"Thanks. I just may be looking for that job, even though I'm sure what you mean by regular hours means regularly working twelve or fourteen hours a day, six or seven days a week, the way Andi assures me that Gray does. Come to think of it, I may decide to take Sam up on his offer to support me while I laze around the house. We've got a lot of lost time to make up for. Speaking of which, I hate to leave a great party, but I'm supposed to meet Sam at home." She turned to Gray and held out her hand. "Thanks for inviting me. I'll be filing the paperwork to drop charges on Katz first thing Monday morning."

As she drove home, a kind of peace washed over Marcy. A lack of doubt or uncertainty. She wanted Sam. Not just in her bed but back in her life, no matter what emotional pain their reconciliation might bring.

* * * * *

A new moon shone brightly in the cloudless sky, illuminating the narrow brick driveway. Cool air blew through the car windows, leaving a pleasant, slightly salty scent after Sam closed them and shut off the engine. He got out and strode to the garage, saw the empty spot where he used to park. Felt a corresponding empty space in his heart.

A space only Marcy could fill.

She laid her hand in his, a gesture he found soft, warm and—he hoped—trusting. It felt right, walking hand in hand onto the polished hardwood foyer, up the staircase where they'd once pictured their children sliding down the gleaming banisters.

When they came to the closed door to the master bedroom, Marcy seemed to hesitate. "You said you wanted to talk. Maybe we should go downstairs first."

"Sure. Too many ghosts in there?" Damn it, he wouldn't let on that thinking about her with her other lovers tore him up inside.

"More like not enough. Just the ghosts of you and me." She flung open the door and practically dragged him inside.

Sure his mind was playing tricks on him, he blinked. Not a single one of the details etched permanently in his mind *had* changed. Their bedroom looked the same as he remembered it, right down to the dark-blue paisley shawl draped over the back of the recliner next to the window. He'd brought that back to her from a medical convention in New York City a month or so before their split. "What the—"

"Nobody but the housekeeper has been in here since you left. Not even me, until today."

She'd closed their private space off like some sort of macabre shrine? "Why?"

When she turned to face him, her eyes looked unnaturally bright. "I couldn't come in here. Couldn't stand the idea of disturbing the things we'd shared. Silly, isn't it?"

He looped both arms loosely around her slender waist. "Think it might be because you knew someday we'd get together again?"

"Maybe."

Nothing mattered. Not the lost years or the men she'd used to stave off loneliness. Not his guilt for having hurt her. Bending, Sam buried his face in the pale silk of Marcy's hair. "I want to come home. Be your best friend again. Your lover. I want to give you a couple of kids and watch them grow up as we grow old."

She tilted her head and looked into his eyes. "But you said—"

"I know. Lie down. I need to see you stretched out on our bed, your pretty hair draped over your pillow. I'll explain."

When she did, he sat beside her, stroking the strip of satiny bare skin around her navel. "We both know I'm not completely sterile. I'll help nature along the way I do for my patients who share my problem, by spinning down several semen samples and combining them to concentrate the sperm. Right here in our bed, when I know you're ovulating, I'll inject some of it directly into your uterus."

"You think it will work?"

"Oh, yeah. It will work." Especially if he combined his puny sample with a potent one from the sperm bank. Patiently, he told Marcy exactly how the process worked, the way he always told his patients—except that his hand never left her skin, and he never let his gaze wander from her beloved face. "The babies will be ours. It won't matter if they've got somebody else's DNA."

Five years ago he'd been too arrogant, too certain of his self-diagnosis to believe in the miracle they'd created and tragically lost. He'd been an idiot then. He wouldn't be one now. This time their marriage would be forever, and their children would belong to them both, no matter whose seed made them. "I love you, baby. So damn much it hurts."

"Then come here. Show me. " Her eyes softened to the deep-sea green he remembered so well, and her lips curved upward in the sassy smile that had stolen his heart.

Reaching behind her, she undid her halter top. It fell away, revealing her beautiful breasts...the pert nipples that begged for the touch of his hands, his mouth. Ravenous, Sam ripped off his shirt and toed off his loafers while she wriggled out of her slacks and panties, baring her satiny mound...the tempting little bud of her clit. Her gaze scorched him, made his cock swell painfully and his balls tighten.

Damn it, why wouldn't his belt come loose? Probably had a lot to do with his hard-on, and the fact he couldn't tear his gaze

off Marcy. There, finally. He shoved his pants and underwear down and kicked them away. Slowly, for he had trouble believing this was real and not an incredibly erotic dream, Sam stretched out above her on the bed, propping himself up on his elbows. "Baby, you don't know how much I've needed this. Needed you."

Marcy needed him just as much. She smiled up at him when he flexed his hips and thrust into her slick, wet cunt. "Welcome home, Sam. Stop talking and take me. Make love to me the way I've dreamed you would."

He loved her with slow, easy thrusts of his long, thick cock into her wet, willing pussy. Long hot kisses and light nips at the sensitive flesh of her throat, the upper curve of her breasts each spoke of Sam's love more eloquently than any words he might say. Any gift he might give her.

She was aroused, yet the frantic need to come that had driven her so long seemed to have disappeared and been replaced with a sense of quiet assurance. Sam would take care of her.

Last weekend she'd faced death, and he'd come to her as she'd never dreamed he might. They'd clung together in the eye of the storm when neither of them had known if their next moment might be their last. And they'd relearned — at least she had — that there was more to loving than fucking, so much more to fucking than a hard cock and a ready pussy.

"Ooh. Don't stop." Not that she didn't appreciate Sam's big shaft stretching and filling her. She did. It was just that the whole sex thing worked better when there was love driving the act. Love for his innate goodness and decency…for his need to master her in every way. Adoration for his hard, muscular body and pride that his looks made other women stare at her with envy.

God, she loved touching him, stroking his tanned, satiny skin and feeling rock-hard muscles twitch under her seeking fingers. The rasp of his beard stubble, the lightly callused pads of his fingers on her cheeks…even the faint scent of the cologne

he'd used since she blew two weeks' allowance to buy him some to wear for her senior prom worked to keep her body at a slow, delicious simmer.

He took his time, almost as though it were their first time — her first time. Conventional, loving sex — the way a bridegroom might take his virgin bride. With every stroke Sam claimed her, decisively but with love.

So much love. An aura surrounded them as the pressure built up in her body. He gritted his teeth, obviously hard-pressed to wait, determined to ensure her pleasure before taking his own. Marcy had never wanted to satisfy a man so much — not even Sam when they'd been kids. Digging her fingers into his shoulders and wrapping her legs hard around his narrow waist, she told him without words that she was close...that she needed him to take his pleasure. To take her, bring her along to the culmination of all her childish hopes and dreams.

Dreams that weren't dead after all.

Harder. Faster. The slapping sounds of flesh to flesh, body to body and soul to soul drove her higher. Her pussy clenched around his hot, driving shaft. Her orgasm started there, set off a chain reaction that had her whimpering and moaning and clinging to him while he buried his cock deep and let out a primal scream.

A scream she'd have heard even over the roar of the storm that had brought them home.

About the author:

Whether she's writing as Ann Jacobs, Shana Nichols, Sara Jarrod, or herself, Ann Josephson loves creating sexy Alpha heroes and stories packed with hot sex as well as sweeping emotions that carry lovers to "happily ever after". Six of Ann's 2003 Ellora's Cave romances have gathered major honors this year. She won the Golden Quill for best hot, sexy and sensuous romance (*A Mutual Favor*), the More Than Magic erotic division (for *Bittersweet Homecoming*), two EPPIES finalist placements (best erotic, "Mastered" and best anthology, *Mystic Visions*) — and placements in From The Heart Romance Writers' LORIES contest for *Gettin' It On* (third place erotic/steamy romance) and "Eye of the Storm" (second place novella).

Married with children (a lot of them!), Ann has lived for all her adult life in west central Florida. She belongs to the TARA chapter of Romance Writers of America, Authors Guild, and Novelists, Inc. A regular speaker at local and regional writer events, she most recently joined Cheyenne McCray and members of the Ellora's Cave staff to present a panel on erotic romance at RWA's 2004 national conference.

Ann welcomes mail from readers. You can write to her by e-mail (ann@annjacobs.us) or PO Box 151596, Tampa FL 33684.

Also by Ann Jacobs:

Why an electronic book?

We live in the Information Age—an exciting time in the history of human civilization in which technology rules supreme and continues to progress in leaps and bounds every minute of every hour of every day. For a multitude of reasons, more and more avid literary fans are opting to purchase e-books instead of paperbacks. The question to those not yet initiated to the world of electronic reading is simply: *why?*

1. *Price.* An electronic title at Ellora's Cave Publishing runs anywhere from 40-75% less than the cover price of the <u>exact same title</u> in paperback format. Why? Cold mathematics. It is less expensive to publish an e-book than it is to publish a paperback, so the savings are passed along to the consumer.

2. *Space.* Running out of room to house your paperback books? That is one worry you will never have with electronic novels. For a low one-time cost, you can purchase a handheld computer designed specifically for e-reading purposes. Many e-readers are larger than the average handheld, giving you plenty of screen room. Better yet, hundreds of titles can be stored within your new library—a single microchip. (Please note that Ellora's Cave does not endorse any specific brands. You can check our website at www.ellorascave.com for customer recommendations we make available to new consumers.)

3. *Mobility*. Because your new library now consists of only a microchip, your entire cache of books can be taken with you wherever you go.

4. *Personal preferences are accounted for.* Are the words you are currently reading too small? Too large? Too...**ANNOYING**? Paperback books cannot be modified according to personal preferences, but e-books can.

5. *Innovation*. The way you read a book is not the only advancement the Information Age has gifted the literary community with. There is also the factor of what you can read. Ellora's Cave Publishing will be introducing a new line of interactive titles that are available in e-book format only.

6. *Instant gratification*. Is it the middle of the night and all the bookstores are closed? Are you tired of waiting days—sometimes weeks—for online and offline bookstores to ship the novels you bought? Ellora's Cave Publishing sells instantaneous downloads 24 hours a day, 7 days a week, 365 days a year. Our e-book delivery system is 100% automated, meaning your order is filled as soon as you pay for it.

Those are a few of the top reasons why electronic novels are displacing paperbacks for many an avid reader. As always, Ellora's Cave Publishing welcomes your questions and comments. We invite you to email us at service@ellorascave.com or write to us directly at: 1337 Commerce Drive, Suite 13, Stow OH 44224.

"...emotionally charged...sizzling love scenes... This novella proves to be a satisfying read and it will certainly appeal, not only to Ms. Jacobs' fans, but also to all lovers of contemporary romance." - *Mireya Orsini, Just Erotic Romance Reviews Newsletter*

IN HIS OWN DEFENSE:

5 STARS: "LAWYERS IN LOVE 1: IN HIS OWN DEFENSE is another great contribution by Ann Jacobs. This is the type of story you'll not want to put down. It's compelling, interesting, and a pleasure to read, with well-rounded characters that you can easily identify with and a hot plot that will have you breaking out in a sweat. The city of Tampa, Florida, comes alive under the deft writing skills of Ms. Jacobs. I highly recommend this story and look forward to re-reading this great series." -- *Aggie Tsirikas, Just Erotic Romance Reviews*

"...I highly recommend this passionate story, and am looking forward to reading the sequel." - *Jennifer Bishop, Romance Reviews Today*

BITTERSWEET HOMECOMING:

4 ½ Stars: "...beautiful story, about acceptance and growth, with a strong and loving sexual relationship between Gray and Andi. Definitely not to be missed." - *Sara Sawyer, The Romance Studio*

4 ½ Roses: "Author Ann Jacobs has done a wonderful job of showing us that physical limitation doesn't have to stand in the way of love. Her handling of Gray's disabilities was honest, open and refreshing. She didn't attempt to gloss over his difficulties and his limitations. She showed that with help and determination you could still live a full happy life. It also helps that the sex was hot, Gray was sexy and Andi was a wonderful example of what a strong woman can bring to a relationship." - *A Romance Review*

What the critics are saying about...

GETTIN' IT ON

FOUR STARS: "...a romantic romp in the style of Doris Day and Rock Hudson, only this time we get to see what happens after they close the bedroom door--and it's steamy! Readers will laugh out loud as Casey and Craig explore everything from sex toys to how-to books--and in the end discover the one thing that makes sex perfect: love. " - *Pamela Cohen, Romantic Times*

"Ms. Jacobs writes with such verve and appeal. ...refreshing and entertaining... I enjoyed this story about two virgins and I look forward to future stories of Lawyers in Love." - *Gabby Royce, Just Erotic Romance Reviews Newsletter*

"...a sweetly funny love story... Ms. Jacobs has continued her successful Lawyers in Love series with another winner." - *Denise Powers, SensualRomance*

"For a fun, sensual read, be sure not to miss GETTIN' IT ON." - *Jennifer Bishop, Romance Reviews Today*

EYE OF THE STORM:

Five Flames: "Ms. Jacobs has a real winner with Eye of the Storm... A must read for those who like a contemporary story filled with hot desire and unforgettable love scenes." - *Miriam, Sizzling Romances*

"...exciting, stimulating, hot...this book just keeps you hooked. Excellent reading." - *Jaymi, Fallen Angel Reviews*

"Eye of the Storm is a tumultuous ride, but love will prevail in the end. Another great tale from the talented Ms. Jacobs." *Denise Powers, SensualRomance*